Red Rose
RISING

True Marks Series
Book 1

A.J. MANNEY

Edited: Caryn Pine
Cover Design: Germancreative
Interior Design: Manney Resource Solutions
Printed by Kindle Direct Publishing

THE PROPHECY

A Dawn will arise,
When four Marked befit allies.
The Dark will dispel
With the four who will tell
A tale only courage could bring.

The four will restore
The Realm once more
Through gifts uniquely she.
Healer,
Seer,
Telepath,
and Abjurer
They will be.

Chapter One

Zalia rolled over for what seemed like the millionth time before finally giving up and sitting up in bed. Sighing quietly, she slipped out from under the silk sheets and onto the hardwood floor. Shivering in only her chemise, she walked over to her wardrobe and quickly slipped a dress over her head. She threw her cloak around her shoulders, grabbed her warm leather shoes and slipped them on. In the dark, she felt around for her sketchbook and pencils. She found them and headed for the door. The floor made no sound as she quietly stepped across it. She slowly opened the massive bedroom door and peered out into the hall. The castle guard assigned to her hall remained stationary at the end of the long hallway. Without a sound, she slipped into the darkness, being sure to close the door silently behind her. She crept further into the darkness down the hall, away from the guard on duty.

"I see you, Your Highness," an amused voice quietly called out.

Zalia stopped and smiled, turning slightly. "You always do, Silas." Silas had been assigned to protect her hall for as long as she could remember. Silas was older than her father. For as long as she could remember, she had always sneaked out and he had always caught her. Never once had she actually made it without being seen, but she supposed that's why he made such a good guard. She paused for a moment and called out to him, "I can't seem to sleep. I'm heading for the tower."

"All right, my lady. Shall I accompany you?" Silas asked politely, even though he knew what she would say.

Zalia grinned. "Not this time, Silas. Maybe next time." It was her standard answer. The one she had given for years. Zalia always had trouble sleeping. She had grown accustomed to it. Many a night, she would wake in the early hours before dawn and go to her tower to sketch. Today was no different.

Zalia bid a good night to Silas and headed down the dark hall to the door at the end that would take her to her destination. When she opened the door, she stepped up onto the first step and reaching down, she felt for the lantern she always kept there. With the lantern lit, she was able to start her ascent up the well-worn steps.

At the top, she opened the door and walked into a guest room. A beautiful bed sat in the corner next to an elaborate writing desk, similar to the one in Zalia's room. This room was always unoccupied; most of the servants and staff believed it was for visiting royalty. Zalia made her way across the large room and walked over to the huge desk. Sliding the chair out of the way, she knelt under the desk and felt under a panel for a small compartment. Upon opening it, she pulled out a large key. She took the key, stood up, and pushed the chair in. Then she walked over to the intricate tapestry adorning one large wall of the bedroom. Pushing aside the tapestry, she slid the key into the hidden door behind it. The door squeaked open, and Zalia slipped inside, pocketing the key and bringing her lantern with her.

Slipping the door closed behind her, she began to ascend the stairs. At the top, she opened yet another door and stepped into the smaller dark room. This was a safe room built into the castle, deeply set inside the castle walls. Few knew of its existence. They had never had to use it, but Zalia knew the door was equipped with all sorts of special security features to keep anything or anybody from coming in, should they ever need to use it. Whenever Zalia came into this room, she shut the door behind her but never engaged the powerful set of locks that would secure it behind her. Once inside, she knew you could hear nothing outside the walls of the room—another security feature. You couldn't hear anything from outside, and no one could hear anything from inside the room. Zalia wasn't really sure how it worked, but the royal family knew of its existence and the King and Queen could operate the room and its door in case of attack. Zalia used it instead when she couldn't sleep at night, which was many a night.

Closing the door behind her, Zalia walked over to a small table and set her sketchbook down. She walked over to the window seat and sat down gazing out the tiny window. The window was hidden in such a way that it was invisible to all those on the ground as it was hidden between two castle towers. The window was small, but if she sat up, Zalia could gaze out and catch a small glimpse of the sea. It was dark, but the moon shone bright. Zalia could see the waves rolling in and out, the foam staying behind on the rocks.

Zalia could sit for hours looking out at the water. It mesmerized her and calmed her spirit. After a few minutes, she walked over and picked up the book containing her drawings. She spent many a night in this room, drawing people and places, most of which she made up in her head.

Her parents told her she had been born weak and sickly. Because of that, they protected her, keeping her sheltered and safe from the outside world. Her father, King War-rick, ruled over Arrosa, Kingdom of the Red Rose. Arrosa was mostly closed off from other kingdoms and her father seemed to prefer it that way. He had no patience for Zalia's requests for independence. Her mother, Queen Evelyn, was more sympathetic to her frustrations but still didn't allow Zalia any freedom. "Someday, you will understand, my sweet Zalia," she often said.

Now at seventeen, nothing had really changed. Zalia sighed. She was still protected and sheltered. Zalia plead-ed with her parents on many occasions to be able to leave the castle grounds, to visit other kingdoms, to experience life outside the castle walls, but they never allowed her to. Her older brother, Kael, lived a normal life. He was al-lowed to come and go as he pleased. She knew her parents meant well, but it was a suffocating life.

They always insisted it was for her protection. She begged to train like Kael did. As the first-born prince, he was trained in all the arts of war—sword fighting, knife throwing, hand to hand combat, fighting with a dagger, and archery. He was strong and fit, and Zalia longed to strengthen her body. But her parents' answer was always the same—no. They couldn't risk her health, she was too weak, she wasn't strong enough, and so on. Zalia sighed. She loved her parents, but some days they made her feel worthless.

Not Kael, though. He understood her better than her parents. He often would sit with her and tell her stories of his travels to the other kingdoms within the realm. He was so good to her. He was the only person who seemed to understand the need within her to get out and experience life. He often snuck her outside for training. Kael was an amazing archer, and he taught Zalia everything he knew. Over the years, Zalia had developed quite the skill of shooting a bow and arrow.

Sighing deeply, Zalia opened her book and began to draw. She often soothed herself by drawing. Tonight, she drew her mother's face. Her mother may not always understood her, but Zalia knew her mother loved her. Zalia spent the next few hours lost in her artwork. Finally taking a break, she looked up and saw the sun was just starting to rise over the sea. Zalia loved sunrise. It brought with it the hope of a new day. She closed her book and stared out at the water, lost in thought.

Sometime later, Zalia woke up and sat up. She hadn't even realized she had fallen asleep. Looking out at the water, she realized she had slept several hours. The sun was directly over the water now. It was probably after lunchtime. On cue, her stomach let out a rumble. She stood up and stretched, her neck kinked from sleeping in the window seat. Gathering her drawing book and pencils, she looked out one last time at the water and walked over to the door.

Grateful for a few hours of sleep, she smiled and opened the door to begin the descent down the stairs. Soon she was in the guest room again. After closing the door behind her and making sure the tapestry was in place, she walked over to the desk and replaced the key. She looked around the room one last time, making sure everything was back to normal.

Zalia straightened and pulled her cloak tightly around her. She walked slowly to the door of the guest room, opened the door, and began descending the second set of stairs. At the bottom of the steps, she turned down the lantern and took a deep breath. She was not looking forward to the next few minutes. She was certain she would receive condemnation from her father for not showing up to breakfast and her studies, and her mother would just look at her helplessly as she always did. She didn't know what to do to help Zalia.

"Well, time to face the music," Zalia muttered to herself as she took a deep breath and stepped out of the stairway and into the hall, the hallway that led to her room.

The moment Zalia stepped out into the hallway, she knew something was wrong. Something was amiss. She stood still for a moment to listen. Nothing. That was the problem. All she heard was silence. It was the middle of the day; there shouldn't have been silence. Where was everybody? Where were the servants? She looked up and froze. Where was the guard? There was always a guard posted in this hall every moment of every day and night. This hallway led to the safe room, and it was never left unguarded.

Zalia started breathing faster, and she could feel her heart banging in her chest as she walked quietly down the long hall. As she came to the end of the hall and rounded a corner, she stopped breathing. Throwing a hand over her mouth to stifle a scream, Zalia stared at the scene in horror. Her castle and home had come under attack while Zalia had been in the castle tower.

Unable to breathe, Zalia pinched her eyes shut and leaned against the wall. Her mind refused to take in what she had seen. Guards lay unmoving on the ground. Blood everywhere. With her heart pounding, Zalia knew she had to keep moving. She had to get to her father and mother's chambers, but her feet seemed unable to move. Her breath was coming fast and uneven.

As she started moving again, she heard voices and footsteps. Not knowing who it was and without time to hide, Zalia pushed herself up against the wall and into the shadows, hoping they would hide her. As the sounds got closer, Zalia took in what she saw. Soldiers dressed in all black wearing the crest of a crescent moon.

She stifled a gasp. They were soldiers from Astra, Kingdom of the Dark Moon. The dreaded King Mylan had sent his army to attack! Zalia had grown up hearing the stories of the deranged king who cared nothing for his people and only sought his own pleasure. His wife apparently died years ago, and it had pushed him over the edge.

Zalia waited until the soldiers passed her before trying to move. Desperation flowed through her. She had to find her parents and brother. She quietly crept towards the stairs, seeing downed servants and guards on the way.

Hearing voices and more soldiers, Zalia ran quickly back to her hall. She heard voices coming closer and then moving away again. She waited until the last of the footsteps faded away. Trying to be patient, she counted to ten before she started moving again. She took a few steps, rounded the corner, and slammed into a hard chest.

On instinct, Zalia turned to run, but she was snagged from behind. A hand slapped across her mouth, and an arm grabbed her hard around the waist, yanking her back into a rock-hard chest. Panicking now, Zalia fought her assailant. She tried to break free from the hold on her. The arm only tightened around her waist feeling like iron, and a low deep voice rumbled in her ear.

"Don't make a sound or you're dead." Zalia froze for a moment before her panic pushed her into action again. She struggled against the hold he had on her. "Stop fighting me," he said in a low growl as he shook her. "If you want to live, you do exactly what I say. Do you understand?" Zalia was frozen in shock and terror. He turned her around to face him and shook her hard. "Do you understand?" Zalia stared up at him silently. He was tall, taller than anyone she had ever seen before. She noticed his black clothing with the crescent of the moon on his tunic. But it wasn't his clothing that caught her attention. No, it was his eyes. They were a stormy gray, making him appear angry. Instinctively, she took a step back. He tightened his hold on her. She opened her mouth, but before she was able to get out her protest, he slapped his hand over her mouth again and dragged her into the shadows. He pulled her up against his chest and kept his hand over her mouth. A second later, she heard soldiers coming their way. "Not a sound," he growled in her ear. Zalia held herself absolutely still, afraid to even breathe as the soldiers came closer.

They were talking but stopped as another soldier approached them. She could tell by his tone and demeanor that he was a commanding officer. "Report," the man barked at them.

"We have successfully taken control of the kingdom. The servants have been captured and told of their new leadership. All is set for the King to come and take over," one of the soldiers answered.

"What of the royal family?" the officer asked. Zalia felt her blood turn to ice in her veins as she waited for the answer.

"All dead, Captain," the soldier reported.

"Are you sure?" the Captain asked.

"Yes. King Warrick, Queen Evelyn, and Prince Kael are all dead. I checked them myself," the soldier answered confidently.

Zalia's knees gave out on her, and she would have fallen if not for the strong arms holding her up. Her heart slammed in her chest and she wanted to cry out in grief and anger. As if sensing that, the hand over her mouth tightened painfully. Zalia felt her tears begin to fall and couldn't catch her breath at the overwhelming sorrow plaguing her soul.

She froze at the soldier's next words. "What about the rumors of a princess?"

The hold on her tightened, and she strained to hear the next few words. "There wasn't a princess with the royal family, but that doesn't mean she isn't here. King Mylan seems pretty confident she exists."

The other voice said, "Tear apart this castle and find her or at least find evidence of her existence. Did you check the bedchambers?"

"Not yet. We're headed there next."

She didn't hear the rest of the exchange over the beating of her heart. *What was going on? They didn't know she existed?* She didn't realize the soldiers had moved on until the hand loosened around her mouth. She heard the quiet words low in her ear.

"We have to keep moving. Follow my lead. Don't make a sound." Before Zalia could respond, she was lifted off the ground into strong arms. She lifted startled eyes to the soldier. He looked down at her for only a moment and said quietly, "Appear to be dead." He pulled the hood of her cloak up and over her hair and pulled it as low as it would go over her face. That was the only warning she got before he took off right out into the open where anyone could see them.

Chapter Two

Everything in Zalia screamed at her to fight the soldier carrying her and run, but she knew her only choice was to stay with him and see how this played out. She remained deathly still and felt the rhythm of him carrying her. She also tried to listen to what else was going on around her. Soldiers were barking out commands. From the shouting she heard, it sounded as if they had brought servants with them.

Cool air began to seep into Zalia's body. Instinctively, she knew they had left the castle and gone outside. She knew when they began to descend the stairs. She tried to take everything in to determine where he was taking her. It seemed like they walked for ages; in reality, it was probably only a few minutes. The sounds of soldiers and servants working got louder before they started to recede. As the sounds started to fade, she began to wonder where this stranger was taking her. She finally dared to open her eyes, just a crack to look up at her captor. Just then he looked down, and she caught her breath as stormy eyes glared down at her. She shut her eyes quickly. Just when she was going to open her eyes a little more, she heard a voice call out.

"Hey, where are you going? The wagons are over here."

The soldier carrying her didn't break stride, calling out over his shoulder, "I've got orders to take this body over to the other wagons."

Again, the voice called out, a little closer this time. "Whose orders? And what wagon? Let me see." Zalia could hear the suspicion in his voice.

The soldier carrying her pulled her slightly closer and barely whispered, "Don't move. Don't breathe, and don't make a sound." Then slowly he turned to meet the oncoming soldier. Zalia stopped breathing and tried to control the shaking in her body. Holding herself absolutely still and holding her breath, she waited to see what would happen.

"Oh, Your Highness, I didn't realize it was you. Here, let me take the body for you. I can deal with it for you," Zalia heard the soldier say.

She felt the man carrying her pull her closer to his chest. "I've got it. Thank you, soldier." He turned with her in his arms and started walking again.

After they had walked a little bit, he lifted her closer to his mouth. "It won't be long before someone figures out I'm here when I wasn't supposed to be, and chaos is going to ensue." Zalia was confused, but he continued talking in a low tone. "You have to escape into the woods. Run as far from here as fast as you can. I'll send help."

He quickly set her down. She looked up at him. "I don't understand, where..." she didn't get the words out before he whirled around. A soldier was walking their way but froze when he saw Zalia.

Turning to Zalia once more, her captor pushed her towards the woods and said, "Run." She watched as he drew his sword and stepped toward the other soldier. Zalia whirled around and started running towards the woods.

There were sounds of a scuffle behind her, and then someone cried out in pain. Too terrified to see who it was, she willed her legs to carry her faster, away from danger, away from everything she had ever known. She ran like her life depended on it. Because it did. She fled into the forest that lay to the east of her home. Crashing into the woods, she tripped and fell over a root. She didn't stop to assess the damage but jumped to her feet and kept running. She knew if she stopped, she would be caught. Branches scratched her face and thorns caught her arms and tore her cloak as she charged through the brush; she didn't feel any pain. On and on she ran until her side ached and she didn't feel as if she could go any further. Her lungs were bursting, needing oxygen. She knew she was fading and would need to stop soon. She paused for a second to look behind her. When she saw no one directly behind her, she continued to stand there a moment longer to catch her breath. Then fear took over, and she started running again. This time she slowed her pace a little, not used to running. Finally, when she was convinced nobody was following her, she began looking for a place to rest.

She had never been to this part of the forest before. Everything was so unfamiliar. She didn't know anything about surviving in the wild. Finally, she found what looked to be a small clearing. Exhausted, she let herself fall to the ground. Her heart was still slamming against her chest. She needed to rest a few moments if she was going to keep going.

The second she stopped, her thoughts jumped back to her family. Suddenly she couldn't breathe. A despair so deep it took her breath away settled inside of her. Before she could begin to process those thoughts, she closed her mind to it. She couldn't allow herself to think of her family. She had to survive. She had to get to safety; then she could properly grieve.

She turned her thoughts to the man who had rescued her. Why had he helped her? Was he still alive? He was obviously royalty by the way the soldier had greeted him. Her breath caught. Was he the son of King Mylan? Why had he helped her then? Zalia shook her head, trying to clear her thoughts and focus.

Her breathing finally started to slow as she began to take in her surroundings. She hadn't had time to really look at anything until now. She saw unusually tall trees, bushes with a kind of blue fruit she didn't recognize, mushrooms, and even a few wildflowers. She looked behind where she sat and saw more of the same. She lay back and tried to rest her weary body for a few minutes.

She wasn't sure how long she had laid there when she heard something. It was a rustling of leaves coming from the path. Whoever or whatever it was, was coming quickly and not bothering to be quiet. Zalia shot up and tried to think quickly. Could she outrun it? Or was she better off trying to hide? Her panicked mind couldn't think fast enough. She whirled around and crept behind one of the nearby bushes, hoping it would hide her.

Just then a head came into view. Zalia sat perfectly still. *Please don't look this way,* she silently pleaded. As if the person had heard her, the head turned to look in her direction. Zalia was startled to see a girl about her own age.

After a stunned second, Zalia jumped to her feet and started running again. The girl turned quickly to her and said, "Wait." But Zalia had already started running away from the clearing and deeper into the forest. She ran as fast as her shaky legs would carry her. She didn't look back but didn't hear anything behind her. Maybe she could make it away again. She had just started to slow her pace and catch her breath when out of nowhere a body slammed into her, taking her to the ground. In surprise, Zalia screamed. Immediately somebody rolled her body over and slapped a hand against her mouth. Now pinned down under her assailant, Zalia began trying to buck the offender off her. He reached down and grabbed both her hands, effectively pinning her to the ground. Just as she opened her mouth to scream again, he hissed at her.

"Shh," he said through clenched teeth. "Do you want the soldiers to find you?" Zalia shut her mouth and looked at him. He wore the same uniform as the soldiers who had invaded her kingdom, all black with a crescent moon insignia on it. He looked younger, though. He appeared to be maybe a year or two younger than her.

The girl came running up to them a second later, her eyes round as saucers when she saw Zalia pinned to the ground under the boy.

She looked at the soldier on top of Zalia and frowned.

"He said to help her, not hurt her." The soldier looked up at her and scowled.

Zalia glanced up at the girl. She appeared to be a servant girl. Her clothing signified that. She was beautiful, though, with dark-bronzed skin and long thick black hair.

The boy looked down at Zalia, "If I let go, are you going to scream or try to run away again?" he asked.

Zalia hesitated for a brief second, apparently a second too long because the girl jumped in. "Please, Princess, we're here to help you."

Zalia shook her head, and the boy rolled off her and stood up. He reached out a hand and pulled Zalia to her feet.

The girl came over and took Zalia's hand. "I'm Raven," she said kindly. "We're here to get you to safety."

The boy grabbed her arm and started pulling her forward. Zalia angrily shook off his arm, and said, "I'm not going anywhere with you."

"Yes, you are," he said. Zalia pulled her arm away from him in desperation, looking for an escape.

"Wait, please," Raven said. "We're trying to help you. We were sent to help you."

"Sent by whom?" Zalia asked. Raven looked quickly towards the boy.

He gave a tiny shake of his head. "All you need to know

is that I am here to get you to safety. You can find out everything else once we get there," he said.

Zalia stood uncertainly looking back and forth at the two of them trying to determine if they were telling the truth. "Was it the tall soldier who got me out of the castle? Are you friends with him?"

Raven looked again at the boy, and he just scowled.

"Well then, where are we going?" Zalia asked, trying to get some answers. Again, the girl looked at the boy. This time, Zalia didn't wait until he shook his head. "Let me guess," she said sarcastically. "You won't tell me."

The girl squirmed under Zalia's stern gaze. She looked to the boy for help. "Why do you keep looking to him for answers?" Zalia asked, harsher than she intended. She was way past her tipping point. Her life had just shattered around her, and she needed answers.

"I don't know where we are going, Your Highness," Raven replied.

Zalia stepped closer to her. "Who are you? Are you from Astra too?" she asked, indicating Reid's uniform.

Raven let out a surprised laugh, "Oh no, Your Highness. I am a servant girl from the kitchen," she responded.

Zalia couldn't keep the shock off her face. "Oh," Zalia said lamely.

Raven responded, "I was hiding in the kitchen during

the attack when the tall soldier from Astra came in. He grabbed me and asked me to follow him. He told me that he would spare my life and the lives of those hiding in the kitchen with me if I went with him. I agreed, and he sent me off with this guy," she said pointing at the boy. "The man told me I was saving the Princess."

Zalia looked at the boy who hadn't said anything during this exchange but was looking guardedly around like he was waiting for an attack.

"Listen," he snapped. "We have a long journey ahead of us. Once we get there safely, you can ask all your questions and become best friends. Right now, we need to get moving before the soldiers find us."

Zalia tried again, "What's your name, and where are you taking me?"

He sighed in frustration. "My name is Reid, and I'm taking you to Cascadia. That's all I can tell you. Now let's *move*," he said forcibly. With that, he turned and walked away.

Zalia looked at Raven questioningly, but she just shrugged her shoulders and waited for Zalia to make her decision. Zalia pondered her choices. She could go with these two, or she could send them away. Sadly, she knew she would never survive in these woods on her own. She needed to get away from the castle and she needed to get out of these woods. She might as well let somebody guide her. She wasn't sure what would happen when they got to Cascadia, but she would just deal with it then.

Resigned, she said to Raven, "Okay."

"Okay?" Raven questioned.

"I'll come with you," Zalia replied.

"Good," was all she said before smiling tentatively.

Zalia wasn't sure what she had gotten herself into. She had either just found the help she needed to survive, or she had just made a huge mistake. Only time would tell.

Chapter Three

Zalia glanced up wearily at the sun, trying to determine what time it was. It seemed like it was about dinner time. She was exhausted and so thirsty. They had been walking for hours. She glanced at her companions. They had said little during the hours they walked together. Zalia learned that Raven was named after her thick, dark hair. She had been taken from her home when she was twelve years old and brought to Arrosa to serve in the kitchen.

The thought that her father had done that made Zalia sick to her stomach. All she could manage was a quiet, "I'm sorry." Raven just nodded. After that, Zalia stayed mostly quiet. The longer she walked, the more her head hurt from her pain of loss and her endless questions.

Zalia tried to shut down her torturous thoughts. Right now, she needed to focus on the present. She was on the run with people she neither knew nor trusted, well at least Reid.

She took a moment to study her companions. Raven said she was seventeen, the same age as Zalia. While Zalia had dark, stubborn curls and smooth white skin, Raven had straight black long hair and dark bronzed skin. Zalia looked toward where Reid walked in front of them. She imagined he was probably about sixteen. He was solidly built, like a soldier. He seemed to not make any sound as he forged ahead of them through the forest. Zalia, on the other hand, felt as if she had the grace of an elephant; she made so much noise and tripped constantly.

She felt embarrassed by her lack of grace. Years of being trapped inside had made her weak, she realized. She tried to keep herself strong and fit inside the walls of the castle, but she was realizing now that she hadn't done a good enough job of it.

She was exhausted now and every bone in her body ached, but she was too prideful to ask Reid to stop. She tried to keep focusing on putting one foot in front of the other, but she knew she was slowing them down.

She pushed her tired thoughts away and focused on keeping herself upright on her feet. The more tired she got, the more sluggish she became. She found herself tripping more often.

After the fourth or fifth trip, Raven called out to Reid, "We need to stop. The Princess is not used to this kind of exertion. She needs to rest."

Reid didn't even look back as he called back over his shoulder, "Can't. We have to keep moving. She'll just have to deal with it."

Zalia didn't know what to say. She just stopped and stood there. Raven looked at her apologetically. Raven turned toward Reid and started walking again.

Zalia stood there a moment longer, determined to hold her ground; but when Reid didn't stop or even bother to turn back and look at her, she sighed and began walking again.

Pushing aside her weary thoughts, Zalia turned her focus to her surroundings. Being so preoccupied with following Reid, she hadn't bothered looking around. All around her were plants and trees she had never seen before. If Zalia wasn't so exhausted, she would have enjoyed taking in her surroundings. However, the weariness she felt took over her desire to notice anything. Darkness descended quickly in the forest. The sun seemed to drop in minutes and when it did, the darkness felt wet, heavy, and oppressive. The forest seemed to come alive with noises. It was all unfamiliar and ominous.

Just when Zalia thought she couldn't take another step,

Reid stopped suddenly in front of her and she plowed into his back. He didn't say anything, and Zalia was too exhausted to apologize.

Reid told them to wait there. He stepped away from the girls and deeper into the woods. Raven and Zalia stopped and quietly waited. After what seemed like an eternity, he appeared in front of them.

"Follow me," he said before turning back to return the way he had come. Raven stepped quickly after him, but Zalia followed much slower. By the time Zalia caught up to them, Reid had made a small clearing where they could sleep. Zalia was so exhausted, she couldn't talk. She walked over and sank to the ground. She thought she would just lay down for a moment and rest her weary body. That was the last thought she had before she fell asleep.

Zalia felt somebody shaking her shoulder, but she was so tired, she couldn't open her eyes. Mumbling something incoherently, she rolled over on her side to go back to sleep. As she did, she felt the hardness of the ground and awareness began to sink in. She popped open her eyes and looked around at her surroundings. The world around her was just beginning to lighten up; the sun would be coming up soon. She looked over her shoulder and saw Raven looking down at her.

"It's time to get up and get moving," Raven said apologetically. Zalia nodded but didn't say anything. She looked around the campsite and didn't see Reid anywhere. Good. Maybe he got fed up with me and left. Zalia smirked to herself. If only she could be so lucky.

She slowly sat up, groaning as she did. Every bone in her body ached, but her stomach hurt the most. She thought back and couldn't remember when she had eaten last. Her stomach chose that moment to complain loudly. She looked up at Raven, and Raven smiled.

"I found some berries we can eat for breakfast," she told Zalia as she held out a handful of berries to her.

Zalia looked down at them. They were different than any berries she had seen before. "Are they safe to eat?" she questioned Raven. Raven just smiled and ate her berries silently. After watching Raven and not seeing anything to worry about, Zalia put the berries into her mouth. They were surprisingly tart and tangy. They had a different texture but being as hungry as she was, she didn't really care. They did little to help the huge pit of hunger in her stomach. Her stomach growled again. She looked apologetically at Raven, but Raven simply smiled.

"Reid told me he's scouting the path. We have to get moving, but we will try to catch something we can eat for lunch," Raven sympathetically explained.

Zalia stood and stretched her aching muscles. She could

hardly move for the stiffness that was setting in. She wasn't used to sleeping on the ground, nor was she used to all the exercise. She didn't know if she could even move but watching Raven start walking in the direction they traveled, she realized she would have to make it work.

She quickly joined Raven, and they walked quietly for a few minutes. Without a sound, Reid stepped out of the woods and joined their small group. He stepped in front of Raven and Zalia and started leading them again. Zalia didn't greet him as he didn't seem to be in the mood to say anything. They began their trek forward just as they had the day before.

They walked for what seemed like hours before Zalia finally worked up enough courage to ask if they could stop for a break.

"Um, Reid, do you think…" Zalia hadn't even finished her question when he whirled on her, grabbing her hand and yanking her to the ground.

"Soldiers coming," he whispered urgently.

He motioned her to follow him and led her to a thick cropping of vines and trees. She was just about to ask where Raven was when Raven slipped in quietly next to them. She looked out to where they had stood only moments earlier and waited to see what would happen next.

Soon, soldiers from Astra marched loudly into the area.

Zalia sucked in a sharp breath. Those dreaded crescent moons would be in her nightmares. Reid glared at her in anger for making that tiny noise. Zalia did her best to hold absolutely still and not make another sound.

The soldiers kept up their pace and moved through the area quickly. Looking around them as they went but not seeming to notice anything suspicious, they kept moving. A few minutes later, all was quiet. Zalia dared not open her mouth. Her heart was still pounding in fear. She didn't think she could say anything if she wanted to. Finally, Reid quietly stood to his feet and slipped off in the direction the soldiers had taken. Raven shifted closer to Zalia and crouched next to her but didn't say anything.

She was getting the impression that Raven didn't know anything more than she did. They were both at Reid's mercy, but he had hidden them and protected them from the soldiers, soldiers that were surely hunting for Zalia. She suppressed a shudder and pulled her arms around her stomach as if to protect herself. It was a few minutes longer, then Reid was back. His expression was grim.

"That was close," he said quietly. "But we're good to go now."

Zalia blew out her frustration. She had had enough. "Look," she whispered earnestly. "I need some answers. Who was that tall soldier? Why did he save me and send you to help me? What's going to happen in Cascadia? Why..."

Reid whirled around, glared at her, and whispered back, "You are not a princess out here. Out here, you are a nothing. So, don't act like the spoiled brat that you are because it's not going to get you anything." With that, he whirled away and started walking again. Zalia stared at his retreating back with anger.

What is his problem! What did I do to him to have him treat me this way! Zalia huffed out a breath and turned to Raven, ready to give her a piece of her mind; but Raven simply held up a hand. That stopped Zalia and surprised her.

"Look," Raven said, not unkindly. "He's not going to tell us anything. Let's just keep moving."

Zalia looked closer at Raven. "Why are you just following him? Don't you want answers?"

Raven looked at Zalia and simply said, "I am a servant. I don't get to decide what I want to do." With that, she turned and began to walk in the direction Reid had gone. Zalia groaned in frustration.

"Fine," she groaned and began walking once again.

After another few hours of walking, Zalia's stomach was growling in protest so loudly she was sure neighboring kingdoms could hear it.

Reid turned back to look at her. "Not used to skipping any meals, are you, Princess?"

Zalia scowled at him in return. After a few more noises from her stomach, he finally decided to take a break. They found a place to sit in the high grasses, and Reid went off in search of food.

Raven and Zalia collapsed ungracefully to the ground and lay down.

"I'm so tired and sore," Zalia told Raven.

Raven looked back at her with a small smile on her face. "You're not used to being pushed like this, Princess."

"I don't think I'm going to make it," Zalia muttered.

Raven looked over at her from where she lay next to her. "You'll be okay, Princess."

"Just call me Zalia," Zalia said. Raven looked at her like she had grown two heads.

"But, Your Highness," Raven stuttered.

Zalia interrupted her, "Like Reid said, I'm not a princess out here. Out here, you're not a servant, and I'm not a princess. We're just two girls, friends."

A slow smile crossed Raven's face. "Friends," she said quietly. "I like that."

Zalia rolled back onto her back. "Me too." Their quiet rest was interrupted when Reid walked back to where they were laying. Too tired to sit up, Zalia watched as he began to start a fire with the kindling he had gathered. Her eyes grew heavy, so she closed them to rest for a little bit. A firm hand shaking her woke her from her drowsy slumber.

"Eat," was all Reid said. Zalia's senses started coming back to her and she smelled meat. Her stomach growled hungrily.

"That smells heavenly," she said. At this point, she didn't even care what it was. She was so hungry. Raven gave her a piece of meat and Zalia tore into it. "This is amazing, Reid. Thank you."

Reid seemed surprised by her gratitude. "It's just a rabbit," he said quietly.

"Well, I'm pretty sure it's the best rabbit I've ever had," Zalia said in between bites. Raven heartedly agreed. They finished their food in silence. All too soon, it was time to get moving again.

The hours blurred by, one day turned into another and another. Zalia began to lose track of days. Each day brought more pain and exhaustion. She was getting slower and slower, making them take more and more stops. By the end of the fifth or sixth day, Zalia no longer felt like eating. She was so tired, she felt like her body was shutting down. After multiple stops all day, and not making much distance, they finally stopped for the evening. Reid went to find wild game to eat for supper. Not able to stay awake,

Zalia passed out in oblivion. When she awoke hours later, Reid and Raven were sitting around the dying fire talking.

Raven spoke quietly. "Each day she gets worse. She's hardly even eating anymore."

Reid snapped, "Well that's what you get when you've lived your entire life waited on by everybody else. She's just not used to the exercise."

Raven sighed, "I don't think that's it. I think there's something wrong with her."

Reid was quiet for a few minutes. "Well, there's nothing we can do about it but get to Cascadia," he said softly.

Zalia lay silently, thinking. She didn't know much about Cascadia. Of course, she didn't know much about any of the other kingdoms either. She only knew little bits and pieces from what Kael would tell her. She'd only learned the history of her own kingdom growing up and basic geography of the other four kingdoms in their realm. If she remembered correctly, Cascadia was about a three-day ride from Arrosa. So, walking would probably be five days or longer, but with her slowing them down, maybe even longer. Zalia silently hoped they were getting close. She closed her eyes to rest her weary body.

Two more days passed agonizingly slow. Zalia went through the motions without thinking. Finally, on the seventh day, Reid stopped them.

"We are getting close. Soon we will start running into scouts or guards. When we do, let me do the talking," he said sternly. Both girls nodded, and they started walking again. It wasn't until several hours later that they were suddenly surrounded by soldiers. These soldiers were all wearing blue and the crest of Cascadia, two broken semi-circles overlapping each other. They all were fierce and tall and massively built. They looked like giants. Zalia and Raven instinctively took a step closer to each other.

Reid put down his sword and held his hands up in a sign of peace. "We need to meet with your king. I can't tell you our business, but we mean you no harm. We must speak with your king right away." The lead warrior stepped closer to Reid and looked at him closely.

He must have approved of what he saw because a second later he nodded, and said, "Follow me." He turned to one of the other soldiers and said something quietly to him. The other warrior nodded and began running in the direction the soldiers had come from. Raven turned her head to look at Zalia. Zalia grabbed her hand and together they started following the soldiers. After what seemed like an eternity, a castle began to take shape. As they got closer, Zalia could see that it was beautiful, but she was too tired to be able to appreciate it. A few minutes later, they saw the warrior who had run off come walking toward them. By his side was another warrior. This one was massive, even more massive than the soldiers surrounding them. He was wearing a blue cloak and dressed like royalty. Zalia watched him approach. He was obviously somebody important. When he got closer, Zalia couldn't get over the size of him. He had the broadest shoulders she had ever seen. He was huge! When he got closer, Reid bowed down on one knee. Zalia and Raven quickly followed suit.

"I am Prince Beckam, first-born prince of Cascadia, Kingdom of Waters. What can I do for you?" the broad warrior said.

"Your Highness," Reid began as he stood, "we need to see the king. We are here seeking sanctuary. We mean you no harm, but we must speak with the King privately." Raven hooked an arm through Zalia's and helped her to her feet. The huge warrior looked closely at Reid then at Raven and Zalia, pausing in surprise when he saw Zalia. Zalia wasn't sure what that meant, but a moment later he nodded.

"Follow me," the Prince spoke and turned to start walking towards the castle. Reid began to follow when he spoke again. "Leave your sword with the guard, young warrior," he spoke over his shoulder to Reid. Reid didn't look like he wanted to. "You will get it back in time," Prince Beckam said, now further away. Reluctantly, Reid handed his sword to the warrior standing next to him.

"Be careful with it," Reid grumbled to the man. The entourage started forward.

Zalia didn't know if it was the excitement of finally arriving at their location after a grueling week or if it was the stress on her body and everything she'd been through, but she started feeling herself get weak as she walked. She grabbed Raven's hand as she slipped and everything around her faded as she fell to the ground.

Chapter Four

Muffled voices sounded around her as Zalia tried to open her tired eyes. No matter how hard she tried to open them, she kept failing. She started moving around, trying to figure out what was going on.

"Easy," a soothing female voice said. "Drink this." A moment later a cup was held to her lips and somebody propped her head up with an arm behind her head. Zalia obediently opened her lips. A weird drink entered her mouth. While not entirely unpleasant, it wasn't the best thing Zalia had ever had to drink. She obediently drank until the cup was pulled away from her mouth. The person lay her back down gently. After a few moments, Zalia was able to open her eyes and look around. Five sets of eyes looked down on her. She quickly sat up, then regretted it when her stomach rolled. "It's okay, just take your time," the lady standing next to her kindly said.

Next to the lady stood Prince Beckam, whom they had met outside. Next to him stood Raven and Reid. Finally, her eyes met the last person standing there. He was a very distinguished-looking man with gray hair, looking perfectly regal in his blue robe. Zalia figured she had just laid eyes on the King.

The King looked down at her quietly with kindness and something else reflected in his eyes. Zalia wasn't sure what it was.

"How are you feeling, dear?" the kind lady standing next to her asked.

Zalia thought about it for a moment. "I actually feel better," Zalia said, kind of surprised. "My body doesn't ache as much, and I don't feel as exhausted."

"That's good," the lady responded. "I gave you my healer's tea. I brew it myself. My name is Henrietta." She smiled down at her.

"Oh, my name is Princess Zalia of Arrosa, Kingdom of…" Looking around quickly, she quickly amended, "My name is Zalia." She was so used to giving her full name. She looked around again and met the eyes of the older king. He was staring at her so intently it was beginning to get awkward. "So," she began, and died out, not knowing where to even start with the king.

The King shook his head. He looked around the room at everybody standing around. "Would everybody please excuse us? I need to speak to the Princess alone." At the King's command, everybody started moving out. "Prince Beckham, please stay with us. We have much to speak of." At the King's words, the Prince turned back from leaving and nodded. Everybody left the room, and everything got awkwardly quiet.

Zalia's pulse started quickening. She didn't know what was going on. She looked back and forth from the Prince to the King. She could see the resemblance between them. While they were both tall and had similar blue eyes, the Prince had bulk to his height and an intensity in his eyes. He was much more intimidating than the king.

"I confess, I don't know where to begin or what to say, and that is a first for me," the King began. "First of all, let me introduce myself. I am King Avery," he said kindly. He stared down at Zalia. Zalia didn't know what to say, so she kept her mouth shut. She did try to sit up though. She felt as if what the King was going to say would be important, and she didn't want to hear it lying down. The King leaned down to gently pull her up against the pillows into a more supported position. Then he sat down wearily into the chair next to her bed and let out an exhausted sigh. Zalia looked away from him and stole a quick glance at the

Prince. He stood rigidly near her bed watching the King. At her gaze, he looked down at her with a quick glance and then turned his attention back to the King.

The King looked at Zalia intently. "You have your mother's eyes," he said sadly. Zalia felt a wave of grief slide through her and her eyes began to water.

"You knew my mother?" she questioned in surprise. He looked at her with so much sorrow.

Then quietly he stated the words that rocked Zalia's world. "She was my daughter."

Zalia gasped quietly, her eyes shooting to his. She took in the grief in his eyes and knew he wasn't lying. "I-I don't understand... she never mentioned... how could..." her voice trailed off. She couldn't feel anything but shock. How did she not know she had other family, a grandfather, and he was the king of another kingdom! She glanced quickly at Prince Beckam and saw her shock mirrored on his face. He hadn't known either. Her head was starting to pound in confusion when she felt the King take one of her hands in both of his.

"Your mother, Evelyn," he began, "was our second child. She was a beautiful girl with chocolate eyes and dark hair. She was impetuous, always getting into trouble as a little girl." He paused for a moment, with a smile on his face. Zalia thought of her mom. The description didn't really match the picture of her mother.

"Evelyn was always into more trouble than Leidoch, her older brother," he continued with a smile, glancing at Prince Beckam. Looking back at Zalia, he continued. "She grew into a beautiful woman, one we were so proud of. A woman fit to be queen. With Leidoch as her older brother, she would never be queen in our kingdom, so we looked for an outside match for her. She met your father when we were invited to his father's kingdom for a ball. It was love at first sight for those two." She could hear the affection in his voice. "They danced all evening. I watched them together and knew he would be the one. They had a fast courtship and were married within the year." He looked down at Zalia. "Your father took over the kingdom as king. Then your brother was born. We would come visit your family, and sometimes your mother would bring your brother to us for a visit."

"Then, one day," he looked down at Zalia sadly, "the visits stopped. They ceased all contact with us. When we showed up for a visit, we were turned away by the guards. We sent letters and heard no response." He paused for a moment, lost in thought. "That was almost eighteen years ago."

Zalia felt sucker-punched. "They stopped communication after I was born?" she asked him, confused. He looked down at her sadly. "We never knew Evelyn had another child. I didn't know you existed until today. If I hadn't seen you for myself and saw your amazing resemblance, I would never have believed it."

"I don't understand. Why didn't they tell me about you? Why was I a secret? What did I do?" Zalia asked in despair. The King, well her grandfather, took her hand.

"I don't know. Something must have happened when you were born, or around the time you were born, something that…" he trailed off. "I just don't know," he said quietly.

The Prince took a step forward and cleared his throat in the silence. Her grandfather looked up at him and smiled. "Beckam, meet your cousin Zalia." Her grandfather smiled down at her. "Beckam is the son of Leidoch, your mother's brother, and your uncle. Leidoch was the first-born prince, slated to take over the kingdom one day, but he and his wife died several years ago," he said sadly.

Then his eyes brightened as he looked at Beckam. "So Beckam stepped into his rightful place as first-born prince, heir to the throne. You two are cousins." Zalia looked carefully at Beckam. He was looking down at her with calculating eyes, but he held out his hand to take hers.

"Nice to meet you, cousin," he said in a deep voice.

Zalia could hardly take it all in. She had extended family. She thought she had lost her only family, but now she had a grandfather and a cousin. Her grandfather looked at Beckam. "Keep our relationship to her quiet for now. I would like to see if we can find out why she was kept a secret. If there was a reason or is something else was going on." Beckam nodded.

The King took a deep breath. "We will need to place security around the clock on Zalia," he told Beckam.

"I will arrange it," Beckam said.

He looked back down at Zalia with a smile on his face. "Now, my dear, let's get you a room, clean clothes, and some food. You must be hungry and tired. Rest tonight. Tomorrow…" he looked at her sadly. He continued quietly, "Tomorrow, I will need you to tell me what happened to your family, but tonight you must rest. Beckam will lead you to your room. We will meet for supper in my quarters. Please bring your two friends. Beckam, please be sure to arrange that." Beckam nodded once. Her grandfather squeezed her hand. "I will see you in a few hours, Zalia." She smiled up at him. He left the room, and Zalia sat staring after him.

Then she swung her eyes towards Beckam's. "Let's get you to your room," he said kindly.

Zalia followed Beckam through a labyrinth of rooms and halls, not sure if she would ever find her way back again. Beckam didn't say anything, he just walked along beside her. He was intimidating, and Zalia couldn't think of anything to say to him. Finally, he stopped in front of a door and stepped back. "Here is your room. I will be back at dinner time to escort you to the King's quarters," he said and started to walk away.

"Thank you," Zalia called out after him. He turned back towards her, a small smile on his face.

"You're welcome," he said. With that, he turned on his heel and walked away.

Zalia took hold of the door handle, turned it, and walked into the room. She looked around in awe. It was magnificent. The windows were draped in colorful silks, the bedcovers were a beautiful indigo silk. Intricate tapestries covered the walls, and two ornate chandeliers hung low in the room lighting up both ends of the room. It was a beautiful room, fit for a princess. Zalia wondered for a moment if her mother had grown up in a room like this. She was turning around in a circle when she heard a soft tap at her door. Upon opening it, she was surprised but happy to see Raven.

"Raven, I wasn't sure where you had gone. Come in." Raven stepped into the room behind Zalia and looked around the room.

"This room is so beautiful!" she said reverently.

Zalia looked at her, "Isn't it? What's your room like?"

Raven continued looking around, "It's fine, but not this fine."

Zalia looked at her and blurted out, "You should stay in here with me." Raven looked at her in surprise.

"Your Highness…"

"It's Zalia. And we should stick together. We're all we have left. Will you please stay with me? I don't want to be alone," Zalia finished quietly.

Raven began, "I don't know that it would be appropriate."

Zalia walked close to Raven and looked her right in the eye. "We're equals now. We're friends. I don't really know what I am anymore, but I know you are definitely not a servant anymore. We're going to figure this all out together, as friends."

Raven still didn't look very sure, but she nodded. "All right," Zalia said. "We need to get ready for dinner. What to do first," she muttered to herself. Another knock sounded at the door, and both Raven and Zalia turned toward it. When she opened it, a guard was standing there. He held out a basket to her with a few gowns laid across the top.

"The King requested this be given to you," he said as he handed the large basket to Zalia.

Zalia pulled two beautiful dresses off the top of the

basket and peered into the basket. Inside the basket was a mix of beauty and bathing supplies, clean clothes, shoes, and more. The next two hours flew by as Zalia and Raven took turns bathing and getting dressed. After a week of traveling outdoors and only washing on occasion, they were both happy to rid themselves of their grime. Feeling fresh and clean, both girls put on a clean chemise and lay down on the bed and rested for about an hour before they had to finish getting dressed for dinner. Zalia stretched and sat up, feeling a little more rested. She walked over to look closely at the gowns the guard had brought them. Both dresses were the royal blue color the King and Prince wore. Raven stared in awe at the dresses. Each girl chose a dress and put it on, helping each other with the clasps in the back. Raven brushed her hair one more time, and Zalia ran a finger through her unruly curls. Both girls decided to leave their hair down.

Raven's eyes teared up. "I wish my ma could see me now," she said softly as she spun in front of the mirror.

Zalia's eyes filled with her own tears. "Me too. You look beautiful, Raven," she said and gave her a hug. Their hug was interrupted by a knock at the door. "That will be the Prince, looking to escort us to dinner," Zalia said to Raven. Then she swept her arm through Raven's and guided them towards the door to walk to dinner with Prince Beckam.

Dinner took place in the King's quarters. It was a relaxed and informal time. The King sat at the head of the table; at the other end was Prince Beckam. Zalia sat to the left of the King, with Raven next to her. Next to Raven sat another man. Zalia couldn't remember his name, but he was the advisor or something to the King. He maintained a lively conversation with Prince Beckam. Reid sat across from Zalia and Raven, and next to him sat one of the warriors from the greeting party that had detained them upon their arrival at the castle. The King introduced him as Kell, captain of the King's Guard. There was an empty chair at the table, but nobody mentioned anything of it. They began to eat their dinner. Zalia's stomach growled loudly as she took in all the amazing food on the table. There were lamb chops, stew, jellies, fritters, fresh bread, cornbread pudding, and dried figs set before them.

The King looked around the table. "A fine feast this is this evening. We celebrate our new friends' arrival. I keep things pretty relaxed in my private quarters. Please help yourselves." Zalia looked around in surprise. She was used to the servants serving dinner in her kingdom. She'd never been at a dinner where you served yourself. She grinned and began filling her plate. She liked it.

At the end of the table, Beckam saw her smiling and grinned at her mischievously. "Hungry?" he asked.

"Starved!" she replied. Zalia had just taken a massive bite of food, probably inappropriate for a princess, when the King looked up and said, "Oh, you made it. Our last dinner guest. Please come, join us, Prince Valen." Zalia looked up, wondering who this new prince was. She looked up and met the intense dark eyes of the man who had saved her life.

Thoughts flooded her mind, taking her back to those nightmare moments. Every emotion she had pushed aside suddenly came crashing forward with the force of a tidal wave. Fear, panic, grief, and loss suddenly overcame her. The fork she was eating with dropped to the table with a loud clatter.

Chapter Five

Everybody stopped eating and complete silence reigned for just a moment before Zalia practically jumped out of her chair. "What is he doing here?" she whispered hoarsely. The king looked from Zalia to the Prince and then back again, before sighing.

"Zalia, please sit down. Let's keep eating our dinner and we will talk this through." Zalia looked at her grandfather in surprise.

"I'm not sitting down to eat with him. He killed my fam...fam," she couldn't even get the words out for the horror she felt. She couldn't breathe, she couldn't think; she clutched her stomach, realizing in horror she was going to throw up in front of all these people. She ran from the room in absolute devastation, swallowing back the contents of her stomach. She ran down a series of halls trying desperately to remember her way back to her room.

Knowing she wasn't going to make it a step further, she bit back a moan.

At the last second, she ran smack into Beckam. He grabbed her arm and pulled her quickly into a room with a bathroom. She ran to the toilet and emptied her stomach of what little contents she had in there. When nothing else would come up, she dry-heaved several times into the toilet, shaking. She felt a cold rag on her neck and tried to think calming thoughts. That only made her think of her mom and that made her dry-heave again.

The cold horror of what had happened to her family had flooded into her mind upon seeing that tall soldier, and it was as if the wall she had set up around her mind to protect her from the grief had been yanked away. A torrent of emotion, emotions she hadn't allowed herself to feel came cascading in, drowning her in sorrow. Her body shook with sobs she could no longer contain. She couldn't breathe, her sorrow was so fierce. Anguished sobs and screams ripped from her throat as she saw in her mind's eye the family that no longer existed. She tortured herself with thoughts of their last moments. Had they felt pain? Had they wondered where she was? Had they called out for her? What would she do without them?

Zalia wept for her loss. She would never again feel the comfort of her mother's touch. She would never again laugh at her brother's silly antics. She would never again know her father's love. Why couldn't she just have died with her family? Why couldn't she have saved them? Her thoughts tormented her body. Her body, so weak from travel and lack of food, began to shut down. She heard low voices as somebody or somebodies entered the bathroom. She heard arguing, but all she knew was her grief. It was too much, and she soon sank into peaceful oblivion.

When Zalia awoke, it was dark out. She lay in the bed in the room they had assigned her. Raven sat in a chair next to the bed, sleeping. The nurse, Henrietta, who had helped her earlier, sat in a chair on the other side of the bed. Zalia sat up slowly in bed, feeling ashamed that both women were here because of her and not getting good sleep.

"Raven," Zalia whispered quietly. "Raven." Raven startled awake and looked at Zalia.

"How are you feeling?" Raven asked quietly. Zalia shrugged her shoulders, not really ready to think about anything right now.

Zalia looked at Raven. "Please get some sleep. Please don't stay awake on my account. Come on. This bed is huge. You can sleep on that side; I'll sleep on this side. You have to be just as exhausted as I am." Zalia waited for an argument, but Raven just agreed. She had to be so tired. She climbed in on the other side of the massive bed. Zalia turned to the other side to look towards the nurse. She was sitting up, looking at Zalia.

"How are you doing, dear?" she asked sympathetically. Again, Zalia didn't really know how to respond. "Are you feeling ill still?"

Zalia shook her head. "I'm okay. I'm just really tired. I can sleep now. You don't need to stay in here." Henrietta looked at her closely.

"Are you sure I can't do anything for you?" she asked.

"I'm sure. I just want to sleep," Zalia said. At this, Henrietta stood up and stretched.

"All right. Get some sleep, dear. I will check on you first thing in the morning," she said. Then she stepped closer to the bed and placed her arm on Zalia's arm. "You are strong. You will get through this. Give yourself time and permission to grieve. Our greatest strengths come from our deepest moments of pain. Don't give up."

Zalia nodded, too tired to unpack the wisdom found in her words. Henrietta looked down at her one more time, then stood and quietly let herself out the door. Zalia rolled over and relaxed and willed herself to go to sleep before her mind could start into gear again and the grief could overwhelm her.

As exhausted and overwhelmed as she was, Zalia had a hard time sleeping. She tossed and turned most of the night. When she did sleep, images of her family and servants and guards played out cruelly in her mind, making her cry out often in her sleep. Sunrise finally came and Zalia lay in bed, too exhausted and emotionally drained to get out of bed.

Raven woke up a little while later and sat up, looking over at Zalia. "How are you doing?" she asked quietly.

Zalia looked at her with despair in her eyes. "I don't know how to keep going. I just want the pain to go away. I feel like I can't face it," she said bleakly. Raven didn't say anything. She slid close to Zalia and wrapped her arms around her in a hug.

They stayed this way for a few moments before Raven said, "Let's get you something to eat."

"I don't feel like eating," Zalia muttered.

Raven looked at her. "I know, but you have to. You didn't get a chance to eat anything last night. You have to get some food in your system."

Zalia pulled away. "Please leave me alone." It was quiet for a moment, and then Zalia felt Raven get up from the bed. All that day, Zalia dozed, in and out of consciousness. She heard people coming and going, but she never responded to anyone. A few times, she heard a low voice talking, but she couldn't bring herself fully awake to make sense of the words. That night she slept fitfully again.

The next morning, she tried to stay in bed again, but Raven would have nothing of it. "Let's go," she said. "I'm not letting you stay in bed today. You have to get up. You must eat." Zalia opened her mouth to argue with her, but Raven wouldn't let her. "Nope. You're getting out of bed today. Let's go." She began tugging Zalia out of bed.

Zalia grumbled at her. She didn't feel like eating; she didn't feel like doing anything but pulling the covers back over her head and never getting out of bed again. Raven pulled her towards the bathroom.

"We will get you washed up, dressed and ready for the day, get you some food, and then you will feel better, you'll see." Raven kept pulling on Zalia's arm until Zalia finally relented.

"You're worse than my mom," Zalia muttered, then instantly teared up.

Raven saw her and gave her a quick hug. "Come on." With Raven pulling and prodding, Zalia finally finished bathing. In another dress with her hair freshly washed, she did feel a little better. She was still light-headed and weak this morning, but she figured she probably just needed food. A knock sounded at the door, and Raven went to answer it. She came back to Zalia. "It's Prince Beckam, ready to escort us breakfast."

Zalia felt her stomach roll and wasn't sure if she could

go. She didn't want a repeat of the other night. She looked at Raven. "You know, I'm not feeling too great. Maybe I'll just lie down..." She didn't finish her thought before Raven grabbed her arm and dragged her to the door.

"Nope. You need food. Let's go." At the door, Beckam smiled and bowed slightly to them.

"Good morning, ladies. How are you feeling today, cousin Zalia?" he questioned Zalia kindly, but his eyes were intense as he looked at her.

"I'm okay, Prince Beckam." She looked him in the eye. "Thank you for your help the other night." Zalia looked down at her feet, embarrassed. When she looked back up again, he was smiling.

"Please," he said, "it's Beckam. We're cousins. No need for formality and I was happy to be of assistance. I'm just glad you're smelling better this morning and clean now." Zalia's mortified gaze shot to his, but she relaxed when she saw his smile and the gleam in his eyes. She gave him a tentative smile.

Beckam looked at both of them. "Come on," he threw over his shoulder as he started walking away. "Let's go eat." The girls followed him, Raven with a smile and Zalia a little more subdued.

When they got to the King's chambers, Zalia's stomach began to growl when she smelled the food. It must have been instinctive because she didn't feel hungry. They walked in and Zalia pulled back hesitantly, her eyes searching the room.

Raven leaned in next to her ear and whispered, "He's not here." Zalia took a deep breath and moved with Raven into the room.

King Avery entered the room next. He looked at Zalia kindly. "How are you this morning?"

"I'm okay. Thank you," Zalia said. She wondered fleetingly if she should apologize for her behavior, but she decided against it. She wasn't going to apologize for her reaction. They had wanted her to sit and eat with the enemy. It didn't matter that he had saved her life; he was still the enemy. Zalia took a deep breath, trying to calm her stomach or she would have a repeat of the other night. As much as she didn't want to, she knew she needed to try to eat.

Breakfast was a quiet affair. Just Raven, Zalia, Beckam, and the King. Raven wondered fleetingly where Reid was but didn't ask. They all ate quietly.

Zalia managed to eat a small plateful of food. Begrudgingly she realized she did feel a little better and stronger now that she had eaten. After everyone had eaten, the King pushed his plate away. "We need to talk this morning, Zalia. Beckam, why don't you escort Raven to her room; then come back and join us."

Beckam nodded at the King and stood. Raven followed suit. "Thank you for breakfast, Your Majesty." It was quiet when they left the room. Zalia looked down at her plate. She didn't know what to say.

They sat quietly until Beckam came back to the room and sat down. Her grandfather looked at her and asked gently, "Can you tell us what happened?"

Zalia started at the beginning, with her being in the tower instead of with her family. She plodded through her story, ending with coming here to Cascadia.

During her explanation, neither man moved but listened carefully to every word. They exchanged glances a few times but didn't say anything. At the end of her story, her grandfather stood up and began to pace.

Zalia looked at him. "The soldiers acted like no one even knew I existed. Why would I be kept a secret? I don't understand. If I was a secret, then how does the King of Astra know I exist? I am so confused." She looked helplessly at her grandfather and cousin, but they seemed just as confused as her. "And why did that warrior help me? I don't understand. You called him prince. Is he the first-born prince to King Mylan?" she asked angrily.

Her grandfather stopped pacing and came back to his chair. Taking her hand in his, he told her, "Prince Valen is the first-born prince of Astra, Kingdom of the Dark Moon."

Zalia yanked her hand from his and stood up. "Then why in the world would you invite him to dinner and expect me to sit across from him?"

Her grandfather sighed. "That was a mistake on my part, Zalia. One I hope you can forgive me for. I wanted to know what happened, and I wanted to hear it from him. I should have thought how his presence would have felt to you, though. I'm sorry."

Zalia looked at him in confusion. "Is he a friend of yours?"

Beckam spoke up. "Mine actually. Valen and I have been friends since we were kids. We kept it a secret from our parents because of conflict brewing between the kingdoms."

"He's not evil like his dad?" Zalia asked.

Beckam smiled. "No, Prince Valen is not evil like his dad."

Zalia continued, "Then why did he help carry out the attack on my kingdom and kill my family?" Her voice broke on the last few words.

Beckam looked at her compassionately for a moment before his eyes hardened. He stood up and looked at her as he spoke. "King Mylan is an evil man. He was a hard man during Valen and Reid's childhood, but when their mom died, he became evil incarnate. He..."

Zalia interrupted. "Wait, Reid and Valen..." her voice died off.

"Yes, Reid and Valen are brothers," Beckam said. He looked at her confused. "You didn't know that?"

"No," Zalia said, exasperated. "Reid wouldn't tell me anything."

Beckam nodded. "That doesn't surprise me. Valen and Reid are pretty tight-lipped. They have been through a lot, and they don't talk about it much. Shoot, they don't really talk a lot, period. Anyway, their father turned maniacal after his wife died. Valen believes his father murdered his mother but doesn't have proof. King Mylan is cruel to his people, allowing horrible things to happen in their kingdom and doing nothing to stop it. Valen told me that his father spoke often of attacking other kingdoms, but never in front of Valen because he knew Valen was against it. Valen said he and Reid left on a trip on kingdom business when they heard news of the impending attack. He said they raced back, but they were too late to stop the attack." Beckam looked up at Zalia. "He didn't take part in the attack. He would have stopped it if he had known."

Zalia looked back at him. It was a lot to take in. "So, what happens next?" She asked the question of her grandfather.

He looked at her quietly for a few moments, then said,

"That's up to you, Zalia."

Zalia looked at him warily. "What does that mean?" she asked.

At her words, her grandfather nodded to Beckam and Beckam stood and left the room. Before Zalia could ask what was going on, the door opened and Beckam strode into the room again, bringing with him none other than Prince Valen.

Chapter Six

Zalia stared at Prince Valen in shock. Then she crossed her arms across her chest and looked to her grandfather for an explanation. Beckam and her grandfather both maintained that he was a good man, but it was hard to let go of her hostility toward him. It was his father, after all, that had engineered the attack.

"Prince Valen has agreed to help with your training," her grandfather said.

Zalia looked at her grandfather in shock. "My what?" Her gaze shot to Prince Valen's eyes. He stared at her, awaiting her reaction. She looked away from his dark gaze and back to her grandfather.

"Prince Valen and Beckam are going to start training you to defend yourself and then eventually take back your kingdom," her grandfather continued.

Zalia laughed. "Take back my kingdom..." She looked at her grandfather, then Beckam, and finally Prince Valen. None of them said a word. They just watched her.

"Wait. You're serious?" she asked incredulously.

"Absolutely," her grandfather replied.

"You think I can just waltz back into my kingdom and take it back from the evil King Mylan, from *his* dad?" she asked angrily, pointing at Prince Valen. She laughed again. "Oh, this is good. With what army?" When none of them responded, she stood up and glared at each of them. "Well, this has been enlightening, but I think I will be leaving now." She turned on her heel and moved towards the door.

"I didn't take you for a coward." The words were so quiet and low she almost didn't hear them. Zalia's head snapped up and she froze. She turned and looked at Prince Valen. *What?* She opened her mouth in shock, but he continued "I assumed you would have more of a fighting spirit in you after what happened. But if you want to just sit around and wait for my father to find you and kill you, and make no mistake he *will* kill you, then be my guest."

Zalia was flabbergasted at his cruel words. She stalked over toward him and shoved him as hard as she could in the chest. The stupid man didn't budge an inch. "How dare you!" she yelled at him. "You don't know anything about me! You took everything from me!" she spat the words at him. She made a move to push him again, and he grabbed her arms.

"No," he said quietly.

"No?" she questioned incredulously.

"I saved your life. I didn't do anything to you or your family," he said, still in his quiet low voice.

Zalia yanked her arms from his grasp, and he let go. "Oh, I'm sorry. Correction. Your *father* took everything from me," she said angrily. "I don't have to stay here for this." With that, she turned and practically ran from the room. She was angrier than she had ever been in her entire life.

"Zalia…" She heard the desperation in her grandfather's voice, but she didn't slow down. Prince Valen's cruel words burned in her mind.

She stepped into the hall and started walking. She didn't know where to go, she just knew she had to get away from everybody. Her life was literally falling to pieces around her.

"Zalia," she heard a familiar voice call out. She turned as Beckam came striding down the hall toward her.

"I really don't want to talk right now, Beckam," she said when he caught up to her.

"I know. Look, I'm sorry for what happened in there. Valen sometimes doesn't say things the right way," Beckam told her.

"You think?" she responded sarcastically. "I can't believe he said those things to me."

"Then prove him wrong," Beckam told her, crossing his arms over his massive chest.

Zalia just looked at him. "Beckam, I..."

Beckam interrupted her. "He's right, you know."

Zalia looked up at him. "About what?"

"His father will never rest until he finds you and kills you," Beckam said.

Zalia threw up her arms in exasperation. "Why? He has the entire kingdom of Arrosa now. Why would he possibly worry about me? I'm just a girl."

"A girl who is heir to the throne. He won't rest until he destroys anything and anybody in the way of him completely taking over the throne. He won't leave any loose ends." He paused for a moment, looking at her.

"Maybe he still doesn't know I exist," she said hopefully. She knew in her heart that was naïve.

"If he didn't know before, he knows now. You had a bedroom there, right?" he asked. At her nod, he continued. "Everyone will know now that there was a princess," he said.

Zalia groaned in frustration. She saw the look on Beckam's face. "What?" she asked warily.

"I think there may be more to you than meets the eye. I think there's another reason King Mylan invaded the Kingdom of the Red Rose, killed your family, and wants you," he said, still looking at her.

Zalia looked at him questioningly. "Why do you think so?" He was starting to make her nervous.

"When do you turn eighteen?" he asked randomly.

"What?" Zalia asked.

"When do you turn eighteen?" he asked again.

"Next month," Zalia responded. "But what's that got to do with anything?"

Beckam looked at her for a moment before answering. "Grandfather and I have been talking. There is obviously some reason your parents stopped all contact with our family after you were born. They had to have seen something or knew something that scared them into hiding you. Arrosa was once an open trading kingdom. Eighteen years ago, that all changed. And now, just weeks from your eighteenth birthday, King Mylan attacks your kingdom. We just don't think it's a coincidence. We need to get you ready for whatever is coming."

Zalia's mind spun with so many thoughts, she couldn't sort through them all. "But Beckam," she said, "even if I figured out what is so special about me and trained really hard, there is still no way I could take back my kingdom. That's not even possible. I'm just one person, and a female."

Beckam looked at her in surprise and said, "Zalia, you're family. You're my cousin. That was my aunt and uncle and my cousin who were murdered, even though I don't remember them. We will train you and when you're ready, Cascadia will fight with you to take back your kingdom and bring justice to your family."

Zalia's eyes widened. "I couldn't ask you to do that!"

Beckam smiled. "You're not asking. Don't count out Valen, either. He's amassed quite a following separate from his father. He would join forces with us, and there is not a better swordsman in the realm than Prince Valen."

Zalia didn't know what to say. There was so much to take in. She took a deep breath and looked at Beckam. "There are good people in my kingdom. They don't deserve to be under a wicked king like King Mylan." Beckam nodded. "And my family deserves to be avenged," she said tightly.

He nodded again. "Well," he smiled menacingly, "then I guess you need to start training. If you're going to take back your kingdom, you're going to need an army and an army needs a leader. And *you* right now are no leader." Zalia opened her mouth to snap at him, but he held up his hand. "You are no leader *yet*, but you could be. With the appropriate training, we could turn you into a fierce leader and fighter."

Beckam was silent for a moment. "We're going to take you to a location no one knows about and train you there. We will have to bring extra guards for security. We can't let anyone know where you are. We need to train you before King Mylan finds you. You can bet by now he is already on the hunt for the Princess who escaped," he said warily. Zalia shuddered at his words.

"We're going to ask Ryder and Adaire also to help. Ryder is the first-born prince of Verdia, Kingdom of Vines; and Adaire is the first-born prince of Sol, Kingdom of the Rising Sun. The four of us train together from time to time at our training center. It's hidden. No one knows about it. Just like no one knows of the alliance between the four of us. Valen will train you in swordsmanship, Adaire in archery, Ryder in knife throwing, and myself in hand-to-hand combat and daggers," he said as he wiggled his eyebrows.

Zalia grimaced up at him. "I think you are going to enjoy this way too much. Will it just be me and you and four princes? There won't be any other girls?"

Beckam was contemplative for a moment. "I didn't think of that. I guess you might want some female companionship over the next few months, huh?" he asked sheepishly.

"Could I take Raven?" Zalia asked him hopefully.

"I don't see why not," he said.

"When do we start?" Zalia asked reluctantly.

Beckam smiled at her. "That's my girl," he said and threw his arm around her shoulders. "I knew you would do the right thing. First thing tomorrow morning, we take you to the training center."

The next morning, Zalia was beginning to understand some of the power Beckam possessed. He started barking orders and quickly Zalia's world turned from upside down to right side up. All of a sudden, she had purpose again. Clothes and everything they would need for the next few weeks were packed and sent ahead with a few of the people who worked for her grandfather. Beckam had seen to it all.

Her grandfather came to see them off. After a hug, he looked directly into her eyes. "Zalia, I love you. Please be careful."

"I will," Zalia told him. He swallowed her up in a huge hug, then stood back to watch them leave. There were four guards traveling with them for protection, and Zalia, Raven, and Beckam.

Beckam looked at Zalia. "I'm assuming you know how to ride," he said. Zalia nodded. He looked at Raven.

"I've ridden a few times, enough that hopefully I won't fall off," she said ruefully. Beckam grinned at her.

Beckam helped Raven and Zalia mount their horses. Then he rode between them. After riding for just a few minutes, Zalia looked at Beckam. "I thought Prince Valen was coming with us," she said.

Beckam responded. "He will join us when he can. He had business to attend to," he said.

Zalia didn't respond to that. Instead, she said, "Tell us about the center, please."

Beckam looked at her and Raven. "After making our alliance several years ago, the four of us princes knew we wanted to train together. I talked to Grandfather about it because he was the only king at the time we could safely tell about our league. He arranged for a training center to be built. It's just a small center with an arena for training and several rooms for sleeping. It has a kitchen, bathrooms, everything we need to be able to live and train there for months at a time. Over the years, Grandfather brought in the best masters to train us in the arts of weapons and warfare."

Zalia stopped him a moment. "Will I have any masters

training me?" she asked.

Beckam answered, "Nope. We can oversee everything you need to learn."

Zalia glanced at him. "I can see you're humble."

Beckam grinned unabashedly.

Zalia thought about this for a moment. "Why didn't my brother participate in training with the other first-born princes?"

Beckam looked at her for a moment. "We tried years ago to get Kael to come join us. But he wouldn't; he didn't tell us why. We never asked him again." He grimaced. "I'm sorry, Zalia."

Zalia nodded. She understood, but she didn't really want to think about why.

"Tell us more about our training," Zalia requested of Beckam.

If Beckam noticed Zalia's changing the topic, he graciously didn't say anything. The trip took only a few hours, and he spent the rest of the trip telling them all about the training they would partake in.

When they got to the training center and dismounted, Beckam grabbed Zalia's arm gently. "Zalia, this is not going to be easy. Keep an open mind and trust us with your training."

Zalia nodded. She liked Beckam. Sure, he was a fierce

warrior and intimidating, but he was her cousin and had been nothing but kind to her since they first met.

"I'll do my best, Beckam. Thank you for all you have done for me." She turned to Raven. "Well, I have no idea what we're getting ourselves into, but here goes nothing. Are you ready?"

Raven slid her arm through Zalia's and gave her a timid smile. "I guess."

Zalia looked at the large building in front of them. When Beckam said a training center, she pictured a small building. This was like a miniature castle! Beckam began leading them towards the building. He led them inside a heavy iron door and into an entrance area. From there they followed him down a long hallway, passing several rooms. From a quick glance, Zalia surmised they were bedrooms.

The end of the hallway brought them to a large door. Beckam opened the door and ushered them inside. Inside, Raven and Zalia looked around the massive training room. As far as the eye could see were targets, an open track for running, an armory full of weapons, all kinds of training areas set up, and more.

Beckam looked around. "This is where we are going to turn you into a warrior, Zalia," he said with a smile. "You too, Raven."

Raven looked at him, surprised. "I thought I was just

coming to keep Zalia company."

Zalia laughed at her surprised expression. "Hey, if I have to learn all this, you do too," she said, linking her arm through Raven's.

Raven groaned, and Beckam and Zalia laughed. Beckam beckoned them back to the entrance. "Let me show you where you will be sleeping."

He led them back down the long hall and pointed to two rooms next to each other. "You can have these two rooms."

Stepping inside her room, Zalia looked around the sparsely decorated room. There was a small bed, an armoire for clothes, a washbasin, and that was it.

"Sorry it's not more fancy," Beckam apologized.

"It's fine," Zalia said with a smile. She noticed their bags had already been placed in their rooms. She and Raven could go through them later and split the contents between the two of them.

"Let's go and meet some of the people who work here, running the center," Beckam said.

Zalia and Raven followed him out the door. "I thought you said it was just the four princes who come here," Zalia said.

Beckam looked at her and nodded. "It is, but we need help running the center, especially when none of us are here. And we need a cook because God knows none of us can cook!" he said with a grin.

Zalia and Raven laughed as they followed Beckam to another area of the training center. They walked into a huge kitchen, complete with a large table and chairs.

They followed Beckam through the kitchen to a hallway with more rooms. Beckam knocked on one of the doors. "Mari, it's Beckam," he called out. The door opened, and a gray-haired woman opened the door with a smile.

"Is that you Beckam?" she asked with a smile. Beckam bent low to give her a hug. "You been eating good?"

Beckam smiled. "No, not at all. I need some of your cooking. Nothing tastes as good as Mari's cooking," he told Zalia and Raven. "Mari, these are my friends—Zalia and Raven. They are going to be joining us for the next few weeks for training."

If she was surprised at the news, she didn't show it. Beckam continued, "The other princes will be joining us at some point. I'll be sure to let you know."

"Sounds good, Beckam. I'll let Henry and Collette know too," Mari said.

"Thanks so much, Mari. We will see you at dinner," Beckam said and gave her a kiss on the cheek.

Beckam led the way back to their rooms, explaining on the way that Henry was Mari's husband and the groundskeeper, and Collette was their daughter and the housekeeper. "I'll leave you to unpack and get settled. We can meet in an hour for dinner and go over the schedule then. Tomorrow morning, we start training. So, sleep well tonight." He walked away with a smile on his face, and Zalia groaned as she closed her door. She was in so much trouble.

Chapter Seven

Dinner was a pleasant experience. Zalia discovered Mari really could cook. They had a delicious dinner of roast lamb, roasted veggies, and bread pudding for dessert. Mari, Henri, and Collette, and a few of the guards joined Raven, Zalia, and Beckam for dinner. They all laughed and talked their way through dinner. After dinner, Zalia and Raven said goodnight and headed to their rooms to get their clothes and supplies unpacked and put away in their respective rooms.

Zalia unpacked a few chemises and underclothing for her and Raven. She unpacked soaps, hairbrushes, hair ribbons, towels, tunic tops, pillows, blankets, and more. She found two beautiful pairs of tall leather boots. She tried a pair on and was amazed at the perfect fit. She handed a pair over to Raven, who was in Zalia's room helping.

Raven squealed as she put them on. "These are the most beautiful pair of shoes I've ever owned. They're so soft!" she exclaimed.

Zalia smiled at her. "They are really comfortable," she agreed. Zalia was pulling out more clothes. She pulled out several pairs of black leather leggings and held them up for Raven to see.

"Whoa," Raven said as she came over to feel them. "These are amazing," she said to Zalia. "Are these for us to train in?"

Zalia nodded. "I guess so. Beckam said Arrosa isn't as advanced as the other kingdoms because we've been closed off these last eighteen years. I guess this is one of those things. It makes sense. We wouldn't be able to do the training we need to do in dresses."

Raven nodded. "We are going to be amazing in these!"

Zalia laughed at her. "I think we're going to need more than nice pants to become warriors." They laughed together and finished unpacking everything and putting it away.

That night, Zalia lay in bed tossing and turning. She was nervous about the next day's training. She knew it was the next step on her journey, but she was scared about it. She finally fell asleep several hours later and slept fitfully. She dreamed of the night of the attack. She dreamed she couldn't get to her family to save them and they kept being killed over and over again in front of her. Crying out, she woke herself up. Sitting up in bed, she cried quietly to herself. After a few moments, she took several deep breaths, trying to calm herself. She was really unsettled but knew she needed to sleep. She slept off and on during the night and got up at daybreak to get bathed and ready for the day.

Standing in a towel, she surveyed her clothes. She had never worn a pair of pants before. She'd never had a need. Hesitatingly, she pulled them on. They were much softer than she thought they would be, and they were thick. She knew they would help provide protection for her legs. She picked out a long tunic top in a deep purple and pulled it on. Pulling her curls behind her, she put a long braid in her hair. She left off all her jewelry because she knew it would get in the way of training. She pulled on thick socks and her new leather boots. She looked at herself in the long mirror along the wall. She didn't recognize the princess in her anymore. She looked scary. All she needed now was a large sword on her back like Prince Valen and she would look like a warrior. Unbidden, an image of the Prince came to mind, and Zalia whisked it away. *Where did that come from? I need to focus. It's time to train.*

Zalia neatly made her bed and headed to the kitchen to get breakfast and hopefully some tea before training. She smelled fresh bread as she got close to the kitchen. When she got there, she saw Mari standing at the stove stirring a large pot.

"Good morning, Mari," Zalia called out. Mari whirled around to look at her.

"Mercy child, you scared me," she said placing a hand over her heart.

"Sorry," Zalia said with a wince.

"Never you mind," she said with a smile. "You're up early. Do you usually get up this early or could you just not sleep?" she asked.

Zalia shrugged. "A little of both, I guess," Zalia said. She walked over to the stove. "Can I help you with anything?"

"Do you have experience in the kitchen, Child?" she asked Zalia.

"Not really," Zalia said sheepishly.

"Well, it's time to remedy that then. Come on over here."

Zalia spent the next hour learning how to peel and cut potatoes and how to fry up thick slabs of ham in butter. She helped pull the bread out of the oven when it was done. She even learned how to boil water and make tea.

By the time Raven and Beckam came into the kitchen for breakfast, Zalia's cheeks were flushed from the heat of the kitchen, but she had a huge smile on her face. "Good morning," she called out as they entered the kitchen.

Raven smiled and came over to see what she could do to help. Beckam looked at her curiously. "You're working in the kitchen?" he asked.

"Yes," Zalia said defensively. "I'm helping."

Beckam smirked. "Do you know your way around the kitchen?" he asked as he pulled a cup of hot coffee to his mouth to drink.

Zalia scowled at him, but before she could say anything, Mari turned on him, waving her spoon at him. "Don't you be messing with my girl. She was a big help this morning."

Beckam held up his hand in a gesture of surrender and smiled. "Yes, ma'am."

After breakfast, Zalia and Raven both offered to help wash dishes and put the food away, but Mari waved them off. Beckam said, "Stop trying to get out of training. Let's go."

After hugs and thanks for breakfast to Mari, Zalia and Raven walked to the training hall, apprehensive.

When Zalia walked into the training center, she immediately saw the difference in Beckam. Gone was the fun-loving cousin. In his place stood the serious warrior.

"Let's go, ladies. Over here," Beckam called out. Zalia and Raven walked over to him. "Follow me and keep up," he threw out over his shoulder.

Raven and Zalia both looked at each other and then

followed Beckam over to the track running all the way around the training hall. He started jogging at a slow pace. Zalia just watched him.

"What are you doing?" she asked.

"I'm running at a nice easy pace for you two. Let's go." Beckam said as he ran backwards, facing them.

Zalia looked at Raven and then back at Beckam. "Okay," she said and started following him, running at a nice slow pace. When she caught up next to Beckam and matched his stride she asked, "Why are we doing this?"

Beckam grinned at her. "It's called conditioning."

Zalia scowled at him. "What does this have to do with training? I thought we were going to learn how to use weapons."

Beckam looked at her. "Part of being a soldier is developing endurance and strength. We have a lot of training we are going to do that has nothing to do with weapons. You have to train your body to be the weapon."

Zalia looked at Raven with a grimace. Raven grinned at her. "Ooo, our bodies get to be weapons," she waggled her eyebrows at Zalia. Zalia just laughed and kept running.

A few laps later, they were neither smiling nor laughing. Beckam finally told them to take a break. Zalia bent over, gasping for air, sweat dripping off her face. "He's trying to kill us," she gasped out to Raven. Zalia didn't know what to do with herself. Her heart was pounding out of her chest, and she was covered in sweat.

Beckam let them rest for a moment before he yelled, "Break's up. Let's go."

Both girls groaned and headed his way. When they reached him, they saw he had two dummies of hay standing up. He spent the next few minutes explaining the series of punches and kicks he wanted them to practice. He demonstrated the punches and kicks. He motioned for them to start.

Zalia stepped up and tried it, and Beckam just laughed. Zalia whirled around and glared at him. "Hey, I've never done this before. So instead of laughing at me, maybe you could show me what I'm doing wrong."

Beckam grinned at her and came over and corrected her stance and her motions. After several tries, she started getting a better feel for it. Then he walked over and helped Raven. After they both had the hang of it, he started to walk away.

Zalia stopped and asked him, "How long do we do this?"

Beckam kept walking. "Until I say stop." Zalia and Raven both groaned. "Start punching," Beckam yelled out.

Zalia punched her dummy. "I wish that was his face," she grumbled. Zalia punched and kicked until she couldn't feel her arms and legs anymore. Finally, Beckam told them they could stop. Zalia and Raven both collapsed on the ground. Beckam led them from there to some strength training.

After that, they stopped for lunch and then went back to the training hall again. Beckam led them in more training. He worked on some hand-to-hand combat with them. He gave them each a flat-edged dagger to practice with and began making them practice defensive and offensive moves. He taught them how to break a choke-hold, where to kick to do the most damage, and more. By dinner time, Zalia was ready to start crawling. Every muscle in her body hurt. She and Raven walked quietly to dinner.

Mari just smiled at them as they walked in and collapsed in chairs. Wisely, she didn't ask them how training was going. Henri and Collette joined them for dinner and kept the conversation flowing along with Beckam. After a quick dinner of beef stew and brown bread, Zalia and Raven bid everybody goodnight and went to their rooms.

After saying goodnight to Raven, Zalia headed into her room. She went right to her bathroom and had a long soak in the bathtub. After an hour in the bath, Zalia got dressed in her nightclothes and lay in bed. Exhaustion plagued her, and she fell right to sleep. Miraculously, she didn't have any bad dreams and even managed to sleep all night.

She woke up the next morning feeling well-rested, but when she tried to get out of bed, she realized she couldn't move. Gritting her teeth, she pulled herself out of bed and got dressed slowly. She couldn't believe how much her body hurt. It took her forever to get dressed. She finally made her way slowly to breakfast, just as Beckam walked in. He smirked at her when he saw her. Zalia wanted to throw something at him. "Not a word," she said with a growl and he laughed out loud.

"I hate you," she said, and he just laughed harder. She slunk into the kitchen and fell into a chair. Raven came in a few minutes later and looked as bad as Zalia felt.

Zalia made it through breakfast and then headed to the training hall. It was more of the same. More running, more hand-to-hand combat, training with knives, strength training, and more. Zalia fell into bed exhausted again that night. Two weeks passed with each day more of the same. She had a long way to go, but each day she was getting stronger. Her body didn't hurt as bad at night.

One night, two weeks into training, Zalia was feeling better. She had more energy than she had in the last two weeks. After dinner, when she and Raven walked back to their rooms, Zalia asked Raven, "Hey, can I come in your room and talk for a little bit? I'm not ready to go to bed yet."

"Me neither," said Raven. "Come on in." Zalia followed Raven into her room. They both sat on the bed and relaxed.

Zalia looked at Raven. "Why are you continuing to do this?"

Startled, Raven looked at Zalia. "Doing what?" she asked.

"Training," Zalia said. "Why are you putting yourself through all this? I have to because I have to take back my kingdom. Why do you?"

Raven was silent for a moment, thinking. "I've always only been a servant. I have never had a chance to experience the world or do anything with my life. I want to strengthen my body and become the strongest I can be. I want to make something of myself, not just be a servant. I need to be as strong as I can to be able to do that. And..." She looked at Zalia. "I don't want you to have to go through this on your own," she said with a smile.

Zalia looked at her. "You know you will never have to be a servant again, right? You are free."

Raven nodded. "It's an incredible feeling."

"Do you miss your family?" Zalia asked her after a moment.

Raven looked away for a moment and then back at Zalia. "I do," she said quietly.

Zalia placed her hand on Raven's arm. "I'm so sorry, Raven."

Raven looked away again. "It's okay. It's the life of a servant," she said.

Zalia looked at the wall for a moment, thinking. "Do you think they're still alive? You're from Sol, right?"

Raven nodded. "I am. I don't know. I hope so."

"Do you have any brothers and sisters?" Zalia asked of Raven.

"No," Raven responded. "Just Ma and Papa."

Zalia looked at Raven with a promise in her eyes. "When we get through this, I will get you back to your family. I give you my word. I will do everything in my power to help you find them and reunite them with them."

Raven had tears in her eyes when she hugged Zalia. "Thank you."

They both sat quietly for a few moments, lost in thought. Then Raven asked Zalia, "How are you doing? Do you miss your family?"

"Every day," Zalia responded. Then she sat quietly for a moment. "I wonder if I could have done something to help them. I wonder why I am still alive, and they aren't." She blew out a breath. "I miss my brother Kael teasing me.

I miss my mother's hugs. I miss my father telling me what to do. I miss seeing them every day. I miss them so much it hurts, but I also feel this strange aloofness. I feel like there is so much I don't know. I feel like my parents kept secrets from me, and now I may never know the answers. I don't understand why. It's all so frustrating," Zalia said as she looked at Raven.

Raven looked at her cautiously and then asked, "What happened to you that day? How did you survive?"

Zalia took a deep breath and blew it out. She told Raven the story from start to finish of the day her castle came under attack. When she finished, she lay back on the bed, exhausted. Raven said, "I didn't realize Prince Valen helped you so much. I thought that he just helped send you into the woods. I didn't realize he walked with you through the entire castle and all those soldiers. That's so romantic," she teased.

Zalia rolled her eyes. "That was not what I was feeling when my kingdom was under attack and my family was killed."

Raven put a hand to her mouth. "I'm so sorry, Zalia. That was so callous of me. I shouldn't..."

Zalia interrupted her. "It's okay. I know what you meant." After a little more time spent talking together, Zalia yawned. "Well, we had better get to bed. We have another full day of training tomorrow."

Raven groaned. "Don't remind me." She stood up and hugged Zalia, surprising her. "I'm so glad we're here together. I wouldn't want to do this with anybody else."

Zalia found that she had tears in her eyes as she hugged Raven tightly. "Me neither."

Zalia headed to her room, her heart heavy. She felt good talking to Raven, but she feared talking about the attack would bring on her nightmares again. Because of that, she was afraid to go to sleep.

Chapter Eight

As Zalia lay in bed that night, her mind kept returning to the conversation with Raven and the uncertain future they both had. Zalia had made a promise to return Raven to her family; she just hoped she could keep it. She worried about the days ahead. Would she really be able to lead an army against King Mylan to take back the Kingdom of Arrosa? It seemed so far-fetched. And what would she do if she defeated him? She supposed Prince Valen would take over Astra. But what would happen to her kingdom? She had no desire to rule over it herself. She thought of her dad and wished he could still rule the kingdom. She wished none of this had ever happened, putting her in this horrible position. Then she thought of her family, and her heart ached once again. She lay there for a long time before finally falling into an uneasy sleep.

Zalia was running. There was death all around her. Zalia ran faster and faster. She saw servants lying face down all around her. She saw Silas as he was struck down. He looked up at her and said, "This is all your fault." Zalia cried out and ran to help him, but he was dragged away by soldiers from Astra. They laughed at her as she tried to run after them but couldn't. She turned away. She knew she had to find her parents and her brother. She ran and ran but couldn't get anywhere to find them.

Finally, she made it to the throne room. She opened the massive door and ran inside, finding her mother and father. They were sitting on their thrones with smiles on their faces. Kael stood at their side. They talked as if they didn't have a care in the world. Zalia ran towards them, yelling, trying to warn them of the soldiers, but she couldn't get to them. They didn't hear her. She screamed as loud as she could and fought at the restraints that held her, but she couldn't get to them. Then the doors opened, and the soldiers came in. They ran to her parents and brother and drew their swords. Her father looked up at her then, right into her eyes, and she heard him say as clear as day, "This is your fault." And then the soldiers struck them down. Zalia screamed...

Zalia shot up in her bed into a sitting position, breathing hard. She was drenched in sweat and couldn't catch her breath. She heard her door close softly. "Raven? Beckam?" she called out, her voice filled with fear.

"It's Valen," she heard a low voice say.

Zalia was shocked. "Wh-what are you doing in here?" she hated that her voice quivered, but she couldn't help it. It was the aftermath of her nightmare.

"I just got in and heard you cry out. I thought you were in danger," he said, and she heard him quietly sheath his sword.

"I'm sorry," she said quietly. "It was just a dream. You can go now."

Valen stood there quietly for another moment as if unsure whether he should leave or not, and then in a whisper of movement, he was gone. The man moved like the shadows themselves. Zalia sat there for a few more moments trying to calm her racing heart. Then she finally lay down. After what seemed like several hours, she fell into a light sleep.

She awoke early. Unable to go back to sleep, she sat up on the side of her bed. She felt slow and heavy-hearted as she dressed. She needed to get out of her room and go help in the kitchen. Helping Mari always put a smile on her face. With that thought, she began to get ready quickly. She put on her black leather pants, pulled on a deep rose-colored tunic, and pulled her curls back into a braid. She quickly made her bed and straightened her room before heading to the kitchen for the day.

When she got to the kitchen, she pushed open the door and ran right into Prince Valen who was on his way out of the kitchen with a cup of hot coffee. The impact spilled coffee all over him, and Zalia shot startled eyes up to his dark ones. "I'm so sorry. I didn't even look where I was going. I'm not used to anyone beside Mari being in the kitchen this early." Zalia finally shut her mouth. She knew she was rambling. She looked away from his dark eyes and ran to the counter to grab a towel. "Here," she said, walking back to him. She began to wipe the coffee on his shirt, touching his stomach, before she felt a hand on her arm.

"I've got it," he said briskly before turning and walking out the door. Zalia stood staring after him, her cheeks burning in humiliation.

She groaned out loud and walked over to the sink to put the towel back. She looked over at Mari who had witnessed the entire episode and had a huge grin on her face. "Rough morning?" she asked.

Zalia groaned again. "My day is off to a great start," she grumbled. "Oh well. I'm not going to let a cranky prince ruin my morning. I'm here to help. Put me to work," she said to Mari. Mari put Zalia to work kneading bread for breakfast. Zalia got lost in her work, enjoying the quiet peace of the early morning hours. Two hours later, Zalia's cheeks were flushed and her hair was starting to come out of its braid, but breakfast was ready. As always, Zalia felt pride in her work in the kitchen. She was learning so much. Today she had made mutton, potatoes, fresh bread, eggs, and hot coffee. They had also prepped the veggies and meat for the evening meal, and Mari had taught Zalia how to make custard for the evening's dessert. All in all, it was a successful morning.

"You sure do good work," Mari said to her as they carried all the breakfast dishes to the table. Zalia smiled at the compliment.

She was still smiling when she turned around and saw Prince Valen standing over by the table watching her intently. She hadn't even heard him come him. She looked at him for a moment and then said, "Good morning again, Prince Valen."

He nodded. Zalia whirled back around to finish helping Mari finish setting the table. His presence unnerved her, but she was determined to not let it bother her. A few minutes later, Beckam strolled in.

"Valen," he said as he came in. The two men clasped hands and drew close for a shoulder hug. "When did you get in?"

"Last night," was Valen's low response. He looked up and caught Zalia watching them. She quickly spun away.

Beckam walked over to her and pulled her in for a side

hug. "How's my favorite cousin this morning?" he asked with a smile.

Zalia smiled up at him. "I'm good, no thanks to you."

Beckam laughed out loud. He was used to her ribbing him about training. Beckam gave Mari a hug next. "What's for breakfast? I'm starving."

Mari chuckled. "You're always starving. Zalia and I cooked up quite the feast this morning. Sit and eat before it gets cold."

Beckam turned back to the table. "You don't have to tell me twice," he said as he began filling his plate.

A moment later, Raven walked in with a smile on her face until she noticed Valen. She turned quickly to look at Zalia with a questioning look in her eyes. Zalia just shrugged her shoulders. Raven walked over to say good morning to Mari and give her a hug. Zalia tried to find more to do to keep busy so she wouldn't have to go sit at the table. Thankfully, Henri and Collette came in then and everybody started eating at the table. Conversation started flowing, so Zalia grabbed some tea and walked over to the table and sat down. She was across the table and a few seats down from Valen, so she didn't have to pay attention to him. She let the conversation flow around her. She filled her plate quietly; but when she looked down at it, she didn't feel like she could eat. Her stomach churned uneasily. She knew it was leftover from her dream. She just couldn't shake the horror. She tried to take a bite of potato. She put it up to her mouth, smelled it, and put it back down on her plate. It nauseated her; she couldn't eat. She just pushed the food around on her plate, hoping nobody would notice she wasn't eating. When she looked up, she caught Valen watching her, his dark eyes not missing anything. Zalia lifted her chin defiantly into the air. His dark eyes narrowed, but he didn't say anything.

Zalia pushed her chair back, picked up her plate and carried it over to the counter so she could begin cleaning up. Everybody left the kitchen, heading in different directions for the day. Zalia started washing dishes but Mari shooed her away. "I've got this, dear. You head to training." Zalia groaned quietly to herself. She hadn't thought about the fact that with Valen being here, he would start training her. With a scowl on her face, she headed to the door. Right before she reached the door, she looked up and was startled to see Valen standing in the doorway with his arms crossed.

"You need to eat," he said quietly in his low voice.

Zalia shook her head. "I'm good." She made a move to walk towards the door, but he didn't move from his position. He was effectively blocking her from going through the door into the hallway. Zalia looked up at him. "I need to get through."

He shook his head. "Not until you eat," he said.

Zalia just looked at him. "What, are you my mother? I don't want to eat," she bit out the words at him.

Valen looked down at her. "I'm training you today, and I don't want to deal with it when we have to stop training for you to throw up because you don't have anything in your stomach."

Zalia sneered up at him. "Well aren't you the kind and caring prince," she sarcastically shot at him.

He narrowed his eyes at her but didn't budge an inch. Exasperated, Zalia finally threw her hands up. "Fine," she spat, whirling around to go to the counter to get a plate. Mari was busy working quietly, acting as if she didn't hear their conversation. Zalia angrily grabbed a plate and put some eggs and potatoes on it. "See, I'm eating," she said angrily to Prince Valen. She shoved a whole forkful of food into her mouth and followed it soon with another. Zalia instantly regretted it. As soon as the food hit her rolling stomach, she knew she wouldn't be able to keep it down. She whirled around, put her plate down and ran towards the door. Valen wisely stepped out of her way this time. She made it all the way to her bathroom before emptying her stomach into the toilet. She threw up last night's supper and the few bites she had managed to get down at breakfast. Even after everything was out, she kept retching. She felt a cold rag on her neck but didn't look up to see who had placed it there. She was far too miserable. When she was finally able to stop and catch her breath, somebody held out a cup of tea to her. Instinctively, Zalia knew it was Valen. She waved his hand away.

"Drink it," she heard him say. "It will help settle your stomach." Zalia wasn't sure why Valen was helping her, but she was in no shape to argue. She took the mug and managed a few sips. Surprisingly, she felt the effect immediately in her stomach. It started settling. She took a few moments to finish the tea. She couldn't believe how much better she felt. She pulled the rag off her neck and wiped her mouth before turning her head to look at Valen. "What's in this? It really works," she said.

Valen smirked at her, and Zalia caught her breath. It was the closest thing to a smile she had ever seen from him. She hesitatingly smiled back. Apparently, he wasn't going to reveal what was in the mystery tea. Oh well. It didn't matter. She was just glad she felt better.

"Ready to eat now?" he asked.

"Ugh, again with the food?" Zalia groaned. He came forward and offered his hand to help her off the floor. Zalia grasped his arm and startled. It felt almost like a shock when their hands connected. His eyes widened just a fraction as he pulled her up from the floor. He quickly dropped her arm and strode from the bathroom without another word. "Well, I guess it's back to the mean prince," Zalia muttered after he left.

Zalia followed him wordlessly to the kitchen where she found him leaning against the wall. He motioned to her plate on the table. Zalia scowled at him as she walked over to the plate and managed to eat a few bites. When she finished as much as she thought she could handle, she stood up and took the plate to Mari. Mari grinned at her.

Zalia turned around to face the Prince. "Are you ready to train?" he asked.

Zalia cocked her head. "Are you going to try to kill me like Beckam?" Valen only smirked at her before turning and walking away in long strides to the training center.

"I'm in so much trouble. He's going to kill me," she groaned as she headed to the training hall for another day of training. She heard Mari chuckling behind her.

Zalia made her way to the training hall. When she walked in, Beckam yelled over to her. "Took you long enough. Let's go."

Zalia scowled at him and headed to the track where Raven was already running. After running for a while, Zalia was warmed up and sweaty. Beckam motioned for her and Raven to come over. "Zalia, you're going to start first with

Valen. Raven, you're with me. Then we will switch." He turned and walked away.

Raven walked over close to Zalia. "Will you be okay with him?" she asked in a quiet voice so that the guys couldn't hear. Zalia just nodded. Raven looked into her eyes and then gave her a quick side hug before walking over to where Beckam stood.

Zalia walked over to another part of the training center to find Valen. He stood by the armory, holding two swords. He looked up as she approached. "Have you ever trained with a sword before?" Zalia shook her head no. He walked toward her and handed her a sword with flat edges. "We'll start with this one," he said before turning and walking away.

Zalia followed him over to an open area. Valen spent the next hour teaching her the basics of how to hold the sword, how to position herself, where to place her feet, and simple basic moves. She finished by working through a series of moves before Beckam came over to them.

"Time to switch," Beckam said. Zalia handed the sword back to Valen.

"Thank you," she said quietly. He nodded. She followed Beckam over to the area he had set up for training.

"Okay," he said. "Let's see what you remember. Go ahead and do the series of punches and kicks you've been practicing, but this time do them on me."

Zalia looked at him. "You want me to punch you?"

Beckam grinned. "Yup. I'm pretty sure that's what you do when you fight."

Zalia scowled at him. "I know that. I just don't want to hurt you."

Beckam laughed in his deep voice. "Believe me. You won't hurt me."

That annoyed Zalia and she was ready to start hitting and kicking him. They started at a nice easy pace. Zalia used the moves she had been practicing for the last few weeks. He let her do the motions for a little bit; then he started deflecting her. Zalia had to start working harder. She was punching harder now, kicking harder. He had a cocky grin on his face like she couldn't possibly hurt him. They fought and fought until Zalia was breathing heavy and covered in sweat.

"Is that all you got?" he taunted her. "You couldn't take down an old lady, let alone a soldier with punches like that." His comments made Zalia angry. "Come on, Zalia. Stop being weak. Fight like a warrior, not like a princess." Zalia hit him again. "You think you're going to avenge your family fighting like that?" Zalia saw red. She changed up her hit then. She was supposed to do two punches then a sweeping kick. Instead, she did one punch, a sweeping kick, and another punch aimed at his face. The hit surprised him, but being the seasoned fighter that he was, he blocked it quickly. Unfortunately, his instinct made him hit her back and she went down hard.

"Shoot," Beckam crouched down beside her. "I'm sorry, Zalia. You surprised me. I didn't mean to hit you. I tried to pull back at the last second." He reached out his hand and pulled her up. The side of her face ached. She felt dizzy for a moment. She knew if he had hit her with his full force, she would be unconscious right now. She looked up at him, but he was staring at something behind her. Zalia turned around and saw Valen standing there with his arms crossed. His normally gray eyes were darker than usual, and he looked mad. Zalia glanced back at Beckam, trying to figure out why the Prince was so mad. Beckam was looking at her oddly and then back at Valen. He backed away slowly from Zalia, still looking at Valen.

Valen pinned her with a look. "Are you all right?" he asked in a voice lower than his usual voice. It sounded almost guttural.

Zalia looked at him in surprise and a little bit of fear. "I'm fine," she said in confusion. "We're just fighting. It's none of your concern," she said snippily. She didn't mean to act nasty, but she was tired and sore, and her face was starting to really hurt.

He narrowed his eyes at her and took a step towards her, then stopped. He shook his head slightly, then spun around and walked away. Zalia watched him in confusion. She turned back toward Beckam. He was still looking at her with an odd expression on his face.

"Well, that was weird," she said. "Let's get back to work."

Beckam shook his head. "We're done for now. Let's get some ice on that cheek and take a break for lunch." He put his arm around her and walked with her out of the training center, heading for the kitchen.

Chapter Nine

Zalia walked with Beckam to the kitchen. When she got there, she was surprised to see her grandfather sitting in a chair at the table, talking to Mari. "Grandfather!" she called out as she walked over to him and gave him a hug. "What are you doing here?

He stood up to accept her hug. "Hey Zalia, it's so good to... what happened to your face?" he asked.

"He did it," she said, pointing to Beckam. Zalia turned away with a grin.

Beckam looked at their grandfather. "In training. It was an accident," he said exasperated.

Her grandfather didn't look too happy with Beckam, and Zalia smiled. She winced, though. *Wow, that hurts*, she thought. She turned to go look for some ice to put on it when she felt a hand on her shoulder. She turned around and saw Valen holding out a rag with ice in it. She hadn't even heard him come in. "Thanks," she said, taking it from him. He dropped his hand from her shoulder and moved away from her. *Is it me? Or is he acting odd?* She didn't have time to dwell on it. She headed back toward the table and sat down, placing the ice on her cheek. She winced momentarily.

"So why are you here?" she asked her grandfather.

He looked at her with a smile. "I have a surprise for you."

Zalia smiled at him. "I'm not sure how I feel about surprises," she said cautiously. She looked around the table. Everybody was looking at her grandfather, waiting to see what he had to say. She met Valen's eyes for just a moment before she looked back at her grandfather. Valen always unnerved her.

"So, do I have to guess what it is?" she asked.

He sat back in his chair and looked at Zalia. "What takes place in three days?" he asked her.

Zalia sat back for a moment and thought about it. "My birthday!" She had forgotten all about her birthday. She looked back at him cautiously. *What is he planning?*

He took her hand and said, "We are going to have a party. There's going to be music and dancing, good food and drinks; it's going to be wonderful."

Zalia was so shocked she didn't know what to say. Beckam leaned forward, "What about keeping her identity a secret for fear of King Mylan?" he asked with a quick glance towards Valen. Valen said nothing. He took everything in, his eyes missing nothing.

"That's the best part," her grandfather said. "It's going to be a masquerade ball. Everyone will come in a mask, so no one will have to know your true identity. Our warriors will be there for security for the castle, and Beckam and Valen will be there for security for you, Zalia. It will be an amazing celebration for an amazing granddaughter. Obviously, no one will know the real reason we are celebrating, except for us." He continued to talk about the plans for the evening, but Zalia tuned him out.

She plastered what she hoped was a happy smile on her face. She knew she was having a bad attitude, but this just surprised her. She supposed she should be happy for a party, but it felt so wrong without her family. She hadn't thought about turning eighteen without Kael and her mom and dad. A wave of grief came over her quickly, and she knew she had to get out of there. She stood up and leaned down to kiss her grandfather's cheek. "Grandfather, that sounds so amazing! Thank you," she gushed. "I can't wait. If you will excuse me, though I think I need to lie down for just a few minutes. I guess that hit was harder than

I thought." With a fake smile plastered on her face, she walked toward the doorway. Right before she walked out, she looked up and met Prince Valen's eyes. His eyes were narrowed as he watched her walk to the door. He didn't look away. Too tired to hold the fake smile, she let it drop and just nodded at him as she left the room.

Back in her room, Zalia sat on her bed and tried to stop the tears from coming. It was useless. She let them come. She didn't know how in the world she would be able to celebrate her birthday when her family was gone. She heard a soft knock on the door and quickly dried her tears.

"Come in," she called out softly. She breathed a sigh of relief when Raven slipped inside. She didn't have to hide anything from Raven. Raven came over to the bed, wrapped her arms around Zalia, and just held her. Zalia started crying again.

Raven whispered soothing words to her. When Zalia finally had control over emotions, she pulled away from Raven. "I'm sorry," she said.

"There's nothing to be sorry for," Raven told her. "I'm sorry about the party."

Zalia nodded. "I know he thinks he's helping. I just don't know if I can do it, Raven. All those people...I mean, they won't know who I am, but still. How can I dance and have a good time when my family is dead? They were supposed to be here to celebrate my eighteenth birthday with me."

Raven nodded. "I know," she simply said.

Zalia knew there was nothing more she could do right now. She looked at Raven. "Did Beckam send you to fetch me for training?"

Raven looked at Zalia with a smile. "He did. Then Prince Valen told him to give you some time. To which Beckam didn't look very happy, but the Prince reminded him that he was the one who hit you. He said it was really Beckam's fault."

Zalia stared at Raven. "Prince Valen said all that?"

Raven nodded with a huge smile on her face. "It was nice to see Beckam put in his place for once!" Zalia and Raven both laughed at that.

Zalia stood up and straightened out her clothes. "Well, I guess we have put them off for long enough."

Raven put her arm through Zalia's, and they headed out the door and down the hall to train. When they got to the training center, they could see Valen and Beckam sparring against each other. Valen must have gotten to choose the weapon because they both used swords. Zalia knew Beckam preferred his daggers. Both men were bare-chested and covered in sweat. Zalia watched, mesmerized at the almost dance-like coordination. Valen's skills as a swordsman were greater than Zalia had ever seen. He moved his sword so fast, Zalia almost couldn't even see it. Beckam was exceptional too, but just not quite to the level of Valen. The girls watched for a few more minutes before Beckam made a tiny slip and Valen got in what would have been a killing blow if they had been fighting for real.

Valen smiled at Beckam's defeat, and Zalia caught her breath. That was the first full smile she had ever seen on the Prince. She couldn't imagine what would happen if he ever directed it full-on to her. It was devastating! She felt her heart rate pick up, before shaking herself. *What am I doing?*

Before she could turn away, Valen and Beckam noticed them and turned around. Valen instantly dropped the smile and his dark penetrating eyes met hers. She blushed and turned away, knowing he had caught her staring at him. She looked towards Beckam. When she looked at Beckam, she noticed the markings. They started on his chest, about two inches below his collarbone and wound up and over his shoulder. Zalia found herself walking toward him, mesmerized. "Beckam," she called and he looked up. "What are those symbols on your chest?"

Beckam looked down at his marks and then over at her. He held his shirt but didn't put it on yet. He looked at her questioningly. "They're my marks." At her look of confusion, he continued. "All first-born princes are marked with royal marks. It signifies they are of royal blood and will be king one day. Most get them when they are born; I got mine when my father died and I became first-born prince, heir to the throne." Beckam let Zalia study his markings. In the center was the symbol of his kingdom—two half circles. It was surrounded by other intricate markings. He pointed at Valen. "Valen has markings too."

Valen had already put his shirt on, but he slipped it off and turned around. Zalia saw his marks started on his back right below his right shoulder. They spread from his shoulder down to the middle of his back. It was an intricate marking of a crescent moon surrounded by other decorative markings. It was beautiful and somehow masculine at the same time. Zalia had a crazy desire to touch it. She lifted her hand but caught herself at the last moment. Her cheeks burned with embarrassment. Thankfully, nobody seemed to notice.

Both men put their shirts back on, for which Zalia was very grateful.

Beckam looked at Zalia in confusion. "Didn't Kael have markings?"

Zalia thought for a moment. "I honestly don't know. Maybe he did, and I just never noticed. I mean, I don't think I ever saw him with his shirt off."

Beckam shrugged. "The marks can be anywhere on the body. Maybe he didn't get so lucky with placement," he said with a chuckle. "Well, enough talk," Beckam said. "Let's get to work." And they did. For the rest of the afternoon, Zalia trained with Beckam, working with daggers. She worked again with Valen on sword-wielding abiliites, then more strength and physical training. When they finally finished, Zalia was sore but not as sore as she had been before. Every day she was getting stronger.

At dinner, Beckam talked about the plans for the next few days. "We have two more full days of training. Three days from today, we travel to the castle for Zalia's party. You girls will have a day to rest and prepare, and the next evening will be the ball. After that, it's right back here for training. Understand?"

Zalia and Raven nodded. After dinner, Zalia helped Mari put away the food and wash the dishes. Finally, she left the kitchen intent on heading to her room for a relaxing soak in the tub and to bed. She walked quickly to her room with her head down. She was tired after the emotionally draining day. She slowed her steps when she got close to her door because Valen was leaning against the wall next to her door with his eyes closed and his arms crossed. Zalia tiptoed past him, trying to slip into her room. Without opening his eyes, he said quietly, "You don't have to go to the ball if you don't want to."

Zalia looked up in surprise. *How does he know I don't want to go? He doesn't miss anything!* She was still standing there, unsure what to say when he opened his eyes and leaned his shoulder on the wall so he was now facing her. She let out a deep sigh. "I don't want to hurt my grandfather's feelings. This relationship is so new to both of us. It will be fine." She didn't even try to pretend with him. He obviously knew she didn't want to go, so why pretend?

He stared into her eyes for a moment, then nodded. He turned to walk away. Zalia couldn't help herself. "Valen," she called out. He turned back to look at her. "Thank you," she said simply, knowing he knew what she meant. He nodded again and turned and walked away. *Hmm, maybe the Prince isn't stonehearted after all.* Zalia smiled to herself and went into her room to take a long bath and go to sleep.

That night, Zalia fell right to sleep but knew it would be a long night when her dreams started right away. They were always the same.

Zalia was running through the castle trying to find her family. She couldn't find them. Where were they? There was death everywhere. Everywhere she looked, servants were being cut down. She saw Silas killed right in front of her. His eyes remained open, staring up at her as she ran past.

She had to get to the throne room. Zalia ran harder and hard-

er. She got to the throne room and threw open the door. There at the front of the room stood Kael. He was talking to Mother and Father. They laughed and smiled as if everything was okay. Zalia opened her mouth to scream at them to run, but nothing would come out. She ran towards them, but she couldn't reach them. She watched in horror as soldiers surrounded them. She screamed as her parents and brother were cut down in front of her. "Zalia," she heard them call one last time. Sobbing she tried to reach them but couldn't. "Zalia... Zalia," she felt somebody shake her. She was too weary and heartbroken to open her eyes. She felt a hand reach up and push her hair out of her face. She heard a low, soothing voice speaking quiet words to her. Her mind didn't register what the voice was saying, but she felt safe for the first time in a long time. She relaxed back into her sleep and slept the rest of the night.

Zalia awoke the next morning feeling rested for the first time in a long time. She thought through her night. She remembered having the nightmare, and then she thought she remembered someone being in her room. Or had she only imagined it? It couldn't have been Valen right? Was it Beckam? She didn't want to ask because she didn't want to humiliate herself. She wouldn't be able to look at Valen all day if she knew it was him.

Zalia shook it off and focused on getting ready for training. She only had two more days until the small break for her party. She finished getting dressed and headed out the door to start her day. She didn't look Valen in the eye when he came in for breakfast. She held her breath when he glanced towards her, but she released it when he didn't say anything. Maybe it *had* been Beckam. That day and the next flew by as Beckam and Valen tried to fit in as much training as possible. Both nights she slept fitfully, like she had too much energy, but she didn't have her nightmare. She was grateful for that.

The morning of her birthday, Zalia woke up early and got dressed quickly for the day. She was eighteen today. She should be happy, but all she could feel was deep inner sadness at reaching this milestone without her family at her side. She shook it off and decided to do her best to not think today. She headed towards the kitchen but was intercepted by a smiling Raven. "Happy birthday, Zalia," she said and gave Zalia a huge hug.

"Thanks, Raven," Zalia said with a smile.

Raven looked down. "I'm sorry I don't have anything to give you," she said sadly.

Zalia smiled at her. "Your friendship is the best gift I could ever have," Zalia told her truthfully. They walked arm and arm towards the kitchen. Breakfast was a special affair. Mari had gone all-out making a spice cake, fresh fruit, cheese, sausage, and eggs for breakfast.

"You are so amazing, Mari. Thank you for making my morning so special," Zalia told her and gave her a big hug.

"Happy birthday, Zalia," Mari said.

Beckam came in next, calling out loudly, "Happy birthday, cousin!" He strode towards her and placed a narrow box in her arms.

Zalia looked up at him. "What is it?" she asked.

He laughed "You have to open it."

Zalia opened the box. She caught her breath. Inside lay a beautiful ruby-jeweled dagger. Zalia caught her breath. "Beckam, it's beautiful. Thank you!" She stretched up on her tiptoes to give him a hug. He hugged her in return and smiled down at her.

"Do you feel any different?" Beckam asked Zalia seriously.

"No, should I?" Zalia asked.

Beckam shook his head. "I was just wondering if anything would happen to you on your eighteenth birthday." Zalia pondered this for a moment.

"I don't think anything is different. I'm sorry," she said to Beckam.

"It's okay," he said. "We'll figure it out. Let's eat this delicious birthday meal."

Zalia knew what he was referring to. They still didn't know why Zalia's birth had been kept a secret and why no one knew she existed. Zalia let out a quiet sigh and picked up her fork to try and eat.

Everyone began to eat the wonderful food Mari had made. Valen was quiet and didn't say anything to Zalia, not that she was expecting him to. But she couldn't help feeling disappointed.

After everyone finished eating, Beckam looked at the girls. "We need to get packed up and leave in an hour, okay?" Both girls nodded and started to head towards their rooms.

"Zalia," Beckam called out. Zalia turned to look at him. "Can you come with me to the training center for a moment?" he asked.

"Sure," Zalia said as she followed him to the armory where Beckam stood. When she got close to him, he said, "We need to fit you with a sheath for your dagger. Here, try a few of these."

Zalia took the sheaths and set two of them on the ground, so she could try on the third. "Where does this go?" she asked, looking at it.

"On your thigh," Beckam said. "That way, even if you're wearing a dress, you have protection."

Zalia sputtered up at him. "I'm supposed to strap a knife to my thigh under an evening gown?" she asked incredulously. He just grinned at her.

"That's the idea. Now stop stalling and try it on," he said.

The first two didn't fit at all, but the third one seemed to work. Beckam didn't look at her when he said, "You'll have to try it when you don't have your pants on and see if it still fits."

Zalia felt her cheeks burning, so she thanked him quickly and left.

When Zalia got to her room, she saw a small white box sitting on the middle of her bed. There was a small note sitting on top of it. It read,

I believe these belong to you. I'm happy to return them to their rightful owner.

Happy birthday, Zalia.

-V

Zalia couldn't imagine what was in the box. Her hands shook as she carefully opened it. Immediately she recognized her mother's ruby earrings. Zalia lovingly picked them up out of the box, her hands shaking. Silent tears coursed down her cheeks. These had been her mother's favorite earrings, a gift from Zalia's father. Zalia had never been so grateful for a gift. She couldn't believe Valen's thoughtfulness. He must have found them when they raided her kingdom, and he brought them to her. It was the nicest thing anybody had ever done for her.

She sat still a few more moments looking at her mother's earrings before getting up to pack. She didn't have long before it was time to head to the castle for a party she didn't want to take part in. Maybe she could talk to her grandfather while she was there and see if he had any leads on why her parents had hidden her away.

Chapter Ten

Zalia packed her bag and headed to the front of the training center. She was nervous to see Valen, unsure of what to say to him. She shouldn't have worried because when she got out front, it was just Beckam and Raven and a few guards for protection. Zalia noticed there were only three horses saddled. "Is Prince Valen not coming?" she asked, trying to keep her voice neutral.

Beckam shook his head. "He had business to attend to. He said he would try to make it back in time for the party tomorrow night."

Zalia knew he probably wouldn't. She couldn't imagine that he had any desire to hurry back for a party that consisted of socializing and dancing. He was more a fighting kind of guy. She couldn't tell if she was relieved or disappointed.

They began the ride back, talking as they went. Well, Beckam talked; Raven and Zalia listened. A few hours later, they arrived back at the castle. They were greeted by Kell and the other members of the king's guard and escorted into the King's chambers.

"Beckam, Zalia, and Raven, it's so good to see you. I've missed you." Her grandfather came forward, giving them all huge hugs. He hugged Raven as if she was one of his grandchildren. Zalia grinned. She loved that about her grandfather. He treated people so well. He grabbed Zalia's hand and kissed it. "Happy birthday, Zalia."

Zalia smiled at him, "Thank you, Grandfather. And thank you in advance for my party," she said graciously. She meant it too. It was kind of him to go through all this just for her.

He smiled down at her. "Your birthday present is on your bed. I'm sure you ladies are looking forward to some relaxing and resting today before the big party tomorrow." Zalia and Raven nodded and started heading towards the door. "Zalia, I would like to have a quick word with you first before you go. Raven, you will find your room ready for you."

Raven said, "Thank you, Your Highness." Then she left quietly. Her grandfather waved Beckam and her over to the sitting area.

"So Zalia," he began, "how is training going?"

"Well, other than the fact that Beckam is trying to kill me, great," she said with a smile.

Beckam and the King let out a laugh. Beckam looked at her fondly. "She's doing a great job. Actually, she has surprised me a bit. She's picking up on things faster than I thought she would."

Zalia beamed with pride at his kind words. Her grandfather looked over at her. "I knew you would, Zalia. You're so much like your mother." Zalia felt a pang of sadness hit her, but she managed a small smile. "So," he looked at Zalia, "Anything new today? Do you feel any different today?"

Zalia's smile fell. "No; I'm sorry. I don't feel anything." She felt so bad disappointing them. She knew her grandfather wanted an explanation of why his daughter and son-in-law ceased all contact when she was born. She was disappointed too. She wanted to know what was wrong with her.

Her grandfather smiled brightly at her. "Well, today is a day for celebration. It isn't every day that you turn eighteen," he said with fondness. "Zalia, you're free to go. Enjoy your day off. Get some rest, and I will see you at dinner tonight." Zalia walked over and gave him a hug before leaving. At the last second, she turned back and walked over and gave Beckam a hug too. He smiled as he pulled her in for the hug.

When Zalia found her room, she walked in and stopped inside the door. Laying across her bed was the most beautiful dress she had ever seen. It was a deep red, the color of her kingdom. Zalia went over to the bed and lovingly touched it. It was beautiful and so elegant. It had layers of red silk. The top was intricately designed with jewels sewn into the bodice. Next to the dress lay a beautiful pair of soft leather shoes. Zalia slipped them on. They felt heavenly on her feet. She could dance all night in these, and her feet would never get sore. Zalia took off her clothes, so she could try on the dress. After getting it on, she knew she would need help with all the tiny clasps behind her; but she held it on to be able to look at herself in the mirror. She caught her breath. It was a bit more revealing than she was used to, but she was turning eighteen after all. It wasn't inappropriate, just lower than she was used to. She couldn't wait to wear it. She slipped it off and put her clothes back on so she could go check with Raven.

She went to Raven's room and knocked on the door. Raven opened the door, and Zalia could tell she had been crying. "What's wrong?" Zalia asked her anxiously. Raven opened the door all the way and pointed to her bed.

Zalia looked toward the bed and saw a gorgeous yellow dress laying on her bed. Looking back at Raven, Zalia smiled with tears in her eyes.

"It represents your kingdom," Zalia said. Raven nodded. "Oh Raven, you're going to look so beautiful in that dress."

Raven said, "I can't believe he got me a dress in my kingdom's color. That's the nicest thing anyone has ever done for me." Zalia loved her grandfather even more. He was so considerate and kind.

"You are going to look like a princess by the time we get done with you, Raven!" Zalia said with a smile. She was excited for her friend. She would do her best to enjoy the party if not for her own sake, but for that of her best friend.

Zalia and Raven parted ways after that. They both wanted to get some rest while they could. Their bodies were tired and sore from all the training they had endured. After a restful afternoon, they met up with Beckam and Zalia's grandfather for supper. It was a casual affair. They talked and enjoyed each other's company. Zalia and Raven didn't stay long afterward but went back to their separate rooms to get some good sleep before the big day tomorrow.

Zalia prepared for bed but was uneasy about going to

sleep. She felt worked up and nervous, and that always led to her nightmares. She had snagged a few books from her grandfather's library earlier in the evening and she tried reading to tire herself out. Finally feeling tired, she fell into an uneasy sleep.

She ran and ran, sobbing as she saw her guards and servants killed before her eyes. She had to get to the throne room.

She burst into the throne room and saw Kael and her mother and father laughing and talking. Didn't they know they were in danger? Didn't they know that they were going to die? Zalia tried to scream, but nothing came out. She tried running to them, but invisible forces kept her from getting there. She watched in horror as the soldiers came and surrounded them. She cried out again. She tried to run harder; she had to stop them. She saw as they were struck down. "No!" she screamed. She knew what would happen next. She fell to her knees in agony. As the soldiers moved in, her brother turned and looked directly at her. Then he was struck down.

Zalia shot up out of bed, crying softly, covered in sweat. She tried to get control of her breathing. She stood up on shaky legs and walked around her room for a few minutes trying to get herself under control. She finally sat back down on her bed. She didn't want to sleep. She was terrified of going to sleep. She hated this feeling of fear. Her nightmares robbed her of peace. She got out of bed and lit the lantern on the end table. She pulled out the book she had been reading earlier and started it again. She read for a long time.

Zalia opened her eyes and looked around. It was morning. She had finally slept. She sat up, and the book toppled off her chest. She carefully picked it up and placed it on the table. She walked over to the water basin and splashed water on her face. She looked in the mirror and saw the dark shadows under her eyes. It was a good thing everybody would be wearing masks tonight. Zalia slowly got dressed for the day and headed to breakfast.

Breakfast was a quiet affair as it was just Zalia and Raven. Her grandfather had left a note saying he and Beckam were busy attending to kingdom business. It looked like it was just Zalia and Raven for the day.

After breakfast, Zalia and Raven headed to their rooms. When they got there, Zalia asked Raven to come into her room. They both walked in and sat on the bed. "What are we going to do all day?" Raven asked as they lay back on Zalia's bed.

"I don't know," Zalia said. Zalia sat up. "I borrowed some books from Grandfather's library. Would you like to look at them and see if you want to read one?" she asked Raven.

Raven sat up immediately, her eyes sparkling, "Really?

Could I read one of them?"

Zalia laughed at her enthusiasm. "Of course." She walked over and grabbed the three titles she had and gave them to Raven. She watched as Raven held them reverently before her. Zalia asked her, "Have you never read books before?"

Raven looked at her. "I know how to read but I've never had books like these to read. I'm going to be busy the rest of the day!" she said with a huge smile.

Zalia smiled back, happy for her. Now she just had to figure out what to do for the day. She lay there for a moment longer before deciding to do something she hadn't done since that fateful day when she lost everything. She got up and walked over to her bag and pulled out her sketchbook and pencils. She looked up at Raven and looked down again at her book. She wanted privacy but didn't know how to ask without being rude. Just then, Raven stood up. "Do you mind if I take these to my room? I'd like to lie down in my bed and read for a while," she asked Zalia.

"Of course," Zalia said with a smile. "Come back this afternoon and we can get ready together." Raven agreed and headed out the door with her treasures. Zalia walked over and sat down on her bed. She sat there for a moment without opening the book. She thought back to the last time she had drawn. She had no idea that her life was going to change forever. She wasn't sure if she was strong enough to look through the pages, but she opened her sketchbook slowly. She turned through the first few pages, seeing pictures of the ocean, flowers, and other random pictures. She kept turning pages, then stopped. She stared down at her book. She was looking at a picture of her mother. Zalia reached out her hand to touch her mother's face. "I miss you, Mother," she said as tears began to track down her face. Next, she saw a picture of Kael. More tears poured down her cheeks. She kept flipping through the pages, looking for a picture of her father. She never found one. Sorrow overcame her as she realized she didn't even have a picture to remember him by. He had been hard on her, but she had known he loved her. Zalia turned to a new page and began drawing her father.

The hours flew by as Zalia got lost in her work. She hadn't realized she missed lunch and it was now late into the afternoon until Raven knocked quickly on her door and came flying in. "Zalia, we only have an hour until the guests start arriving!"

With a yelp, Zalia jumped up from her bed. "Oh my goodness! I completely lost track of time." Both girls started moving in a frenzy. They spent the next few minutes taking turns in the bathroom getting washed up and putting their underclothes on. Raven helped Zalia do her hair first, managing to wrangle all Zalia's curls into an elegant pile on top of her head. She left a few curls hanging down around her face, softening the look. Then Zalia helped Raven with her hair. They decided to leave it down. Zalia brushed it several times until it shined. She then pulled the sides up and twisted them, pinning them in the back. When they finished, they were ready to step into their beautiful dresses.

Zalia picked up Raven's and walked towards her. "Let's get you into your dress first," she said. She helped Raven step into it and then went behind her to fasten all the clasps. After finishing, she directed Raven over to the mirror and stood beside her. "Raven, you look absolutely stunning," she said. Raven blushed. Zalia meant every word. Her yellow dress complimented her bronzed skin and dark hair.

Raven turned toward Zalia, "Your turn," she said.

"Wait a second," Zalia said. She walked over to the table beside her bed and pulled out the drawer. Inside lay her new dagger from Beckam and her sheath. She quickly placed the sheath around her leg and slipped her dagger into it. It felt weird, but she figured she would get used to it. When she turned back to Raven, she grinned at the look on her face. "What? I want to be prepared," she said.

Raven shook her head. "Come on, let's get you into your dress, Warrior Princess," she said teasingly.

Raven picked up the beautiful deep red dress and brought it over to Zalia and helped her slip into it. Zalia pulled it up around her chest while Raven started the tiny clasps in the back. Zalia looked in the mirror for a second.

"Raven, this isn't going to work," she said in a nervous voice. Raven stopped what she was doing and came around to look at the front of the dress.

"You're right. Your chemise is showing. Oh well, you're just going to have to go without it," Raven said nonchalantly.

"Go without it?" Zalia squeaked. "I can't do that."

Raven looked at her and looked at the dress. "Well, you don't want to wear it looking like that. It will be fine. You will be plenty covered. Come on, I'll help you take it off."

Zalia stood there a moment longer pondering. "You're right. Okay. I'll do it."

Raven chuckled and helped her step out of the dress. Then she came around to the front of Zalia. "Okay, we have to do this carefully so we don't ruin your hair." Together they worked carefully to pull Zalia's chemise off. Then Zalia stepped into the dress for the second time.

Zalia held the dress up around her chest as Raven walked behind her to help fasten the clasps once again.

Raven stepped behind her and gasped. Zalia's head shot up. "What is it?" She turned around and looked at Raven. Raven stared at her speechless. Zalia felt dread pool in the bottom of her stomach.

Chapter Eleven

"When did you get these marks?" Raven asked.

Zalia looked at her in confusion. "What marks?"

Raven stared at her, then put her hand over her mouth and shook her head.

Zalia looked at her like she'd lost her mind. "Raven, what is the matter with you? You aren't making any sense."

Raven marched Zalia over to the tall mirror and went to the bathroom and came back with a small mirror and shoved it in Zalia's hand. "Look!"

Zalia was almost too scared to look in the mirror. She wasn't sure what she would find. With shaking hands, she held up the mirror and gasped, almost dropping the mirror. She stepped closer to the mirror to look at her back.

There, just under her shoulder blade and trailing to the middle of her back were the exact markings that Prince

Valen had on his back. Zalia stared at the crescent moon surrounded by other intricate markings. Zalia couldn't breathe. Her heart began pounding loudly in her chest. She shot panic-stricken eyes to Raven. "I don't understand. What does that mean? How did this happen?"

Raven reached out and grabbed both her hands. "Zalia, look at me. Don't panic. It's okay. We will figure it out. We will just ask..."

"NO!" Zalia shouted. She looked Raven right in the eye. "You can't tell anybody! Promise me you won't."

Raven looked at Zalia. "It will be okay..."

"Promise me," Zalia said again.

Raven took a slow breath. "Okay, I promise I won't tell anybody." They both stood there silently for a moment, lost in thought. Then Zalia walked over to the mirror to look at it again.

"It really is beautiful," she said softly. Then she moaned. "I can't even wrap my head around what this could possibly mean. I mean, I'm obviously not a first-born prince. Do you think I got this because my father and brother died, but why would it be the same as Prince Valen's? I am so confused right now," she finally said. She was working herself into a panic again.

Raven came over and grabbed her hands again. "We will figure it out, I promise. But right now, you have to calm down. We need to get you to the party. *Your* party. We will have time later to sort this all out. The best thing would be to just not think about it." She finished fastening the back of Zalia's dress and started to turn towards the door. She stopped and turned back. "Oh, and don't show anyone your back."

Zalia sputtered. "How would I show anyone my back? I'm not going to be getting undressed at the party!" Raven laughed and stood at the door waiting for her.

Zalia took just a moment to look at herself in the mirror. The deep red dress from her grandfather looked more beautiful than she thought it would. Her mother's earrings hung from her ears. Zalia couldn't believe how they complemented her dress perfectly. Her soft leather shoes lay beneath the satin folds of her dress, safely covered but oh so comfortable. Looking in the mirror, Zalia felt she looked older, more mature. She looked away from the mirror to where Raven stood.

"You look beautiful, Zalia. Like the princess you are," Raven told her. They smiled at each other and jumped when they heard a knock at the door.

Zalia looked in the mirror one last time, wondering what the marks meant and what in the world she was going to do about it.

Raven turned and opened the door. Beckam stood there,

dressed in his royal dress clothes. He wore a white tunic top with black pants. Over that he wore his royal blue robe with gold buttons running all along the left side and gold cuffs on his wrists.

"Beckam, you look so handsome. How come you haven't made some lucky girl a princess yet?" Zalia asked.

He grinned with a cocky smile. "Haven't met her yet."

Zalia grinned at him. "You haven't found *one* girl that you liked enough to make her your princess? Maybe you're being too picky," she said with her hands on her hips.

Beckam looked at her for a moment. "You know I can't just pick any girl, right? Never mind. Now is not the time for this discussion. We have a party to get to. You both look beautiful."

Both girls smiled and said, "Thank you." He put out an arm to both girls. They each put an arm through his and floated down the hall to the ballroom. Beckam explained that when they got to the entrance of the ballroom, there would be a basket of masks to choose from.

Zalia started getting nervous. She wasn't used to being around a lot of people. She had never been allowed to be around visitors in Arrosa, and they certainly had never hosted any balls or parties that she could remember. She did know how to dance. She had a private tutor to thank for that. She knew she could dance well, but she had only ever danced with her tutor. What if she couldn't dance well with other partners? She started getting worked up, and Beckam must have noticed.

He looked down at Zalia with a smile. "There's nothing to be nervous about. Your mask will cover your eyes and most of your nose. No one will know who you are." Zalia tried to return his smile but was sure she failed miserably.

They came near the entrance to the ballroom and just as Beckam said, there were several baskets of masks. Zalia and Raven started looking through them. There were so many, and Zalia had no idea which one to choose. After a few minutes of looking and getting more confused by the moment, Beckam held up a mask. "This one, Zalia." He handed her a beautiful silver mask that looked as if it were decorated with tiny diamonds. It sparkled in the light. A single red feather adorned the side.

Zalia caught her breath. "It's beautiful," she whispered.

"For a beautiful princess," Beckam's deep voice said as he helped her put it on. It took a moment to get used to, but it wasn't as bad as she thought it would be. Actually, it was kind of fun. She felt like she could be in plain sight and yet hidden all at the same time.

"I should wear one of these all the time," Zalia said and Beckam smiled. Zalia looked over at Raven. "Raven, I love yours," Zalia said. Raven's mask had yellow butterfly wings that perfectly complemented her outfit.

Beckam smiled at them both. "All right. Let's get you two lovely ladies to this party." He walked ahead of them and opened the door.

"Wait, why aren't you wearing a mask?" Zalia asked.

"I'm here for security. I will be watching over you for the evening, and I don't want a mask to get in my way," he said with ease. Zalia wasn't sure what to say. Beckam turned around and opened the doors. "After you, ladies."

Zalia felt as if she were entering a fairy tale. Everywhere she looked, ladies in beautiful gowns and glittering masks stood eating and talking. The men were all impeccably dressed and wearing masks as well. Tables loaded with food and drinks were lined all around the room. Musicians played music off to the side, and couples were already dancing on the dance floor. Zalia felt immersed in this fairy tale.

Raven put her arm on Zalia's and Zalia could feel her shaking. She was just as nervous as Zalia. "Let's get some food," Zalia suggested. Raven nodded.

Zalia and Raven headed towards the food, but before they got there, a man with a gold mask stepped into their path.

"Good evening, beautiful ladies. I am looking for a dance partner. Can I interest you in a dance?" He asked the question of both of them but looked at Zalia as he asked.

Zalia hesitated for a moment, and Raven whispered in her ear. "I'm fine. Go ahead." She turned to walk away, leaving Zalia all alone with the man.

She took a deep breath. "I would love to," she told the man. She took the arm he offered and walked toward the dance floor. They began to dance. The song and the movements were well known to Zalia, and she began to relax.

Her partner looked into her eyes. "My name is Hadden. What's your name?"

Zalia froze for a moment. She was sure she wasn't supposed to give her name, but was she supposed to make up one? She looked up at him and smiled. "I can't tell you my name. This is a masquerade ball after all, right?" she managed, smiling sweetly at him. He threw back his head and laughed.

"You are right," he said graciously. They danced a little longer; then the song finished. Zalia thanked him for the dance and was going to make her way over to the food when another man asked her to dance. This continued on for quite some time. Zalia was never able to take a break long enough to get food before someone would ask her to dance again. She enjoyed the dancing, but she was starting to get weary. She had seen Raven several times on the dance floor, so she must have been kept busy too. Zalia was just about to head towards the food table when she felt arms circle her waist and pull her back to the dance floor. She gasped and turned around to see her next dance partner.

"Hi gorgeous, we haven't had a chance to meet yet. With a body like yours, I would have known if we had. I'm Jasper. What's your name?" Zalia took in a quick breath and looked up at her dance partner. He was tall and well-built. Even though he was wearing a black mask, she could see his eyes leering at her. "Cat got your tongue, beautiful?" he asked.

Zalia looked up at him and tried to smile. She gave him the line she had been giving out all night. "I can't tell you my name. This is a masquerade ball after all, right?" He looked at her as if angered by her response.

Annoyed, he looked at her again. "No, seriously, what is your name?" When Zalia didn't respond he continued. "What kind of a game are you playing?" he asked.

Zalia looked up at him in surprise. "I'm not playing any games, sir." In response, he tightened his hold on her.

"Stop playing around and tell me your name," he said almost angrily.

Zalia looked at him. None of the other men she had danced with had given her any problems when she didn't give her name, but this guy seemed angry with her. Zalia stopped dancing and made a move to pull away. He didn't let go but rather held on to her tighter. His arms were strong, and he was grasping her arms really hard now. She was going to have bruises if he didn't loosen his grip.

He shook her angrily. "I'm done playing your games. Tell me your name or..."

Strong arms wrapped around her waist and pulled her against a hard chest. "Or what?" she heard a low voice say behind her. Zalia stiffened as she recognized Valen's voice, but it was cold and deadly now. Zalia stared at the man in front of her.

The man instantly took a step backward when he saw who held her. "Your Highness, I didn't know you were here." Beckam appeared at his side a moment later and yanked his arm, pulling him away from Zalia and toward the door. The man didn't make a sound but allowed Beckam to pull him from the room. A moment later Kell, the captain of the King's Guard, grabbed the man from the other side.

In one fluid movement, Valen turned Zalia gently around and held her in his arms as he guided them effortlessly through the dance moves for the next song. "Are you okay?" he asked in his quiet low voice.

She looked up at him. His eyes were darker now, a sign that he was angry. She tried taking a step backwards, but he tightened his hold on her. "Did he hurt you?" he asked in a deadly calm voice.

"N-no," she stuttered. Her heart was still beating hard in her chest. "He just was really insistent on getting my name. Why do you think that is?"

She saw his jaw tighten. "That's what Beckam's going to find out." He looked down at her arms and saw the bruises beginning to form, and his eyes grew darker. She could see his jaw clench.

Zalia looked up at him and gently said, "I'm okay." He looked down at her and their eyes met.

His eyes were almost black now. "I'm sorry I didn't get to you sooner. I'm sorry he hurt you," Valen said angrily.

Zalia smiled at him. "You saved me. I'm good now. Hey, how did you recognize me with my mask on?" she asked.

He was silent for a moment. "I would recognize you anywhere," he said. She almost didn't hear the words; they were so soft and low. Zalia didn't know what to say to that. They danced for a few moments when Zalia remembered the earrings.

"Thank you so much for the earrings. They were my mother's. It means so much to me that you found them," she said with tears in her eyes. He simply nodded. She rambled on. "I can't believe how perfectly they go with my dress. I wasn't sure if they would match but they do."

She caught herself and stopped rambling. She stopped dancing and put her hand on his arm. "Are you okay?" she didn't understand why he was so angry. He didn't say anything as he looked down at her.

Seeing she wasn't going to get anything from him, Zalia decided to just try to move on and put the unpleasant episode behind them. "All right. I need a favor from you. Can you help me?" Zalia asked. She continued without waiting for his reply. "I need you to protect me so I can get food. I'm starving and exhausted. Every time I try to get a bite to eat or sit down, someone else asks me to dance. My feet are going to fall off," Zalia finished with a laugh. She looked at him. He wasn't laughing. If anything, he looked even angrier. "Come one," she tugged at his arm. "I'm going to fade away from starvation," she said with a mischievous smile. He looked down at her and smirked. Zalia turned away from him with a smile on her face. *Mission accomplished,* she thought smugly to herself. Now she just needed to spend time with the Prince without making an idiot out of herself. *That might not be as easily accomplished,* Zalia nervously thought to herself.

Chapter Twelve

Zalia felt Valen close behind her as they made their way to the table. Before she could get there, another man stepped in front of her. Zalia nearly groaned out loud.

He bowed before her. "May I have the pleasure of this next dance with you?"

Zalia opened her mouth to respond, but Valen cut her off. He came up to stand next to her and placed his arm around her shoulder. "She's with me," he said in his no-nonsense voice. The man in front of her stepped back quickly.

"Of course, Your Highness. I didn't realize." He almost tripped, trying to get away so quickly.

Zalia put a hand to her mouth to cover her laugh. She looked up at Valen. "That wasn't exactly what I meant, but it worked. Thank you." He nodded. She expected him to remove his hand from around her, but he didn't. He guided her toward the table. As she picked out food, he stood behind her with his back to her. She couldn't see what he was doing but he must have been sending out daggers with his eyes because nobody approached her. When she had a plate of food, he led her towards a door on the side of the room. On the way, he turned away four more men asking to dance with her.

When they finally made it to the door, Valen pushed it open and allowed her to walk through ahead of him. Zalia took a breath of fresh air and sighed. "This is just what I needed." She walked over to a chair and sat down. She finally had a chance to eat. She bit into an apple tart and moaned. "This is so good." She looked over at Valen, who was smirking at her. "What?" she asked.

"I don't think I've ever seen somebody enjoy food as much as you," he said, still smirking at her.

"Did you try any of this food? It's amazing!" He shook his head no. "Here." Zalia stood up and picked up the apple tart she had been eating. "Taste this." She held it up to him and watched as he took a bite. "Isn't that amazing?" she asked, smiling up at him. His eyes intensified as he watched her.

"It is," he said quietly. Zalia felt her heart rate pick up and she noticed for the first time how intimate she was being with him. She stepped back quickly and walked back to her seat, heat fusing her cheeks. She had just sat down when pandemonium erupted.

Three soldiers appeared out of nowhere with swords drawn. Valen was instantly in front of her, pulling her to her feet and behind him. Zalia's food plate fell to the ground, forgotten. Valen kept one arm on her behind him, and the other on his sword.

"Prince Valen, we just want the Princess. Surely you know of the reward for her. King Mylan wants her dead or alive. I'm sorry, but we can't pass this up," one of the soldiers said.

"Over my dead body," Valen spoke the words quietly but she felt the deadly calm in them.

"Well, so be it then," the soldier said. All three soldiers stepped forward, fanning out around Valen with their swords drawn.

Zalia gasped behind Valen and hung on to his robe. They were going to kill Valen. It was three against one, and these soldiers looked terrifying.

She tried to step out from behind him. "It's okay, Valen. I'll just go with them."

"Don't move," he growled out.

"Valen, it's three against one. Please don't do this." He didn't pay any attention to her, and she let go of her hold on him. While she was talking, she had discreetly pulled her dagger out of the sheath on her thigh, hidden under her dress. She clasped it in her hand and readied herself. She squeezed his hand; hopefully, he would know that meant she was armed.

There was a stand-off for only a moment before two soldiers lunged forward in an attack on Valen. The other soldier moved towards Zalia. Zalia wanted him to believe she was the helpless female. As soon as he moved towards her, Zalia met him halfway. Swords clashed and clanged around her. Zalia wanted to look away but she made herself focus. She stared at the soldier in front of her. He swung at her and Zalia whirled away from him, swiping his arm in the process. He let out a curse in anger. He lunged again, and Zalia barely missed getting sliced by his blade. She moved in and got another good swipe on his arm. A moment later, as he made a brutal frontal attack, she slid in and thrust her dagger up and into his heart. He looked at her, his eyes wide with shock. Then he dropped to his knees and keeled over. Zalia couldn't look away from his lifeless body. Valen grabbed her hand and pulled her away. Zalia was too much in shock to notice the other bodies Valen had killed.

"Let's go," he said in a dark voice. Zalia was too shocked to move. He yanked on her arm and pulled her after him.

He picked up his pace and headed toward the front of the castle. On the way, they ran into Beckam. He came running from the direction in which we were headed.

"Zalia!" he called out and pulled her in hard for a bear hug. "I'm so glad you're okay." He looked at Valen. "It was a coordinated attack. They hit three different places at once. We lost four guards." Beckam ran his hands through his hair in frustration. "I don't understand how they knew she was here?"

Zalia felt like she was going to be sick. This was all her fault. She placed her hand on Beckam's arm. "I'm so sorry. This is all my fault. I should have stayed at the training center and..."

Beckam interrupted her by pulling her close to his chest. He looked right in her eyes. "This is not your fault." Before she could say anything else, he grabbed her hand and began pulling her towards the front of the castle. "We need to get you out of here. Come on." Valen followed quietly behind them with his sword in his hand. They rounded a corner and saw Kell. He hurried toward them. "Princess, I'm so glad to see you're..." He never finished his words.

Zalia watched in horror as he sank to the ground, an arrow protruding out of his back. Zalia screamed. Valen slammed her down to the ground, and chaos ensued once again. Soldiers swarmed them from all directions. Valen rolled off her in one fluid movement and pulled her up and behind him. Beckam and Valen made a wall in front of her, both of them cutting down anyone who got too close. Zalia held her dagger close and prepared to step up beside the guys. She paused for just a moment to take in the scene around her. It was absolute chaos. She recognized some of Beckam's warriors in the mix now. It seemed the numbers were more even now. Zalia took a step back and tripped over something. She looked down and realized it was Kell.

She immediately dropped to her knees. She bent down to feel his pulse. It was light, but it was there. He was still alive. Zalia crawled over to his side where the arrow was sticking out of his back. She pulled with all her might. It was stuck. She couldn't get it out. She stood and tried again, gritting her teeth. Bracing her feet on him, she gave one more heave. It came out, but the wound started gushing blood. Zalia instinctively put her hands there, trying to staunch the flow. As she put her hands over the wound, she started to get a horrible burning sensation in her hands. She wanted to pull them away, but something instinctively told her not to. Zalia looked at her hands in shock. A faint blue light was coming from where she held her hands over the wound. But the craziest part was that Kell's wound seemed to be closing up right under her hands. Zalia hung on as the burning sensation got worse. She gritted her teeth through the worst of it. Then it seemed to be letting up. Once it was completely closed and the bleeding stopped, Zalia lifted her hands to look at them. Little wisps of blue light danced off her hands. She didn't know what to say or do. She shook her hands and the light dissipated. She looked down at Kell, but he still didn't move. Glancing around, she saw the downed soldiers. Valen and Beckam still had their backs to her. They were okay. She breathed a sigh of relief. As the last of the enemy was destroyed, she looked back down at Kell, just as he opened his eyes.

She didn't know what to say. "Um, how do you feel?" she asked him awkwardly. He stared at her.

"What did you do to me?" he asked her in a weakened voice.

"Well, you were shot with an arrow, and I pulled it out. Um, then I, uh sort of healed you?" she finished quickly, really unsure of herself right now. He didn't say anything, but just stared at her with a dazed expression. "Here," she said offering him her hand. "Let me help you up." He was a little unsteady on his feet, and she put his arm around his shoulder.

Just then, Beckam turned around to check on her and saw Kell leaning on her. He moved toward them quickly. "Kell!" He came around to help hold Kell's weight.

Kell looked at him. "I'm fine, Your Highness. She healed

me," he nodded at Zalia.

Beckam looked at him. "What are you talking about? Zalia, help me get him inside."

Zalia looked at Beckam, "He's telling the truth. He's healed."

Beckam looked at her like she had grown two heads. Zalia noticed that Valen had stopped what he was doing and was looking over at them, his eyes narrowing. He strode toward Kell and approached him from behind. Zalia watched as Valen took in the hole in Kell's jacket but saw no wound. He looked at Zalia in confusion. "He's right," Valen said to Beckam. "There's nothing there."

Beckam let go of Kell and turned him around. "What do you mean there's nothing there? I saw the arrow enter his body myself. He should be dead." Beckam looked at the hole in Kell's tunic, then said, "Take it off." Kell quietly obeyed. Zalia turned her eyes away for a moment, but curiosity got the best of her. She turned around and stepped close to Beckam and Valen, looking at Kell's back. You could see the dried blood, but there was nothing there. Not even a scar marked the place where the arrow had entered his skin.

Beckam and Valen stared at Zalia. Zalia tried smiling and said, "So, um, I guess I'm a healer." She waited and when nobody said anything, she awkwardly laughed,

"Surprise," she finished lamely.

Kell put his shirt back on and grabbed both of her hands. "Thank you, Princess." Zalia didn't know what to say. "My wife and children thank you," he said with tears in his eyes. "I pledge my life to you, a life for a life," he said earnestly. Zalia felt her own eyes moisten with tears. She couldn't say anything around the lump in her throat, so she just nodded. He stepped a step closer. "I won't tell anyone your secret," he said in a quiet voice.

"Thank you," Zalia managed to whisper. He touched his hand to his heart and then stepped away.

"Okay," Beckam drew out. "Well, we will deal with this later. Right now, we need to get you out of here, Zalia and to safety. How do you feel?" he asked.

She took stock of how she felt. She still felt a little bit in shock. She felt a little dizzy and weak, but nothing too bad. Just the kind of weakness you feel when you haven't eaten for several hours. "I'm good, just a little weak and dizzy. I'm sure it will pass," she said. She had the starting of a headache, but she kept that to herself.

She glanced at Valen for a second. He stared at her, but his expression was inscrutable.

Beckam took charge. "Kell, you get Valen and Zalia on horses and get them out of here." Kell nodded and headed off. "Valen, you take Zalia and get her to the training center. I'll send extra guards with you." He sounded weary.

Valen nodded and grabbed her arm, pulling her in the direction Kell had taken. He sheathed his sword and looked around for her dagger. He found it and brought it to her.

Zalia grimaced. "I'm sorry. I must have dropped it when I, uh, helped Kell." She stumbled over the words, not really knowing what to say. She walked quickly, following Valen's long stride.

In just a few minutes, Kell had sent Valen and Zalia on their way to the training center. There were two guards riding along with them, one on either side of them. They rode quickly in silence, giving Zalia time to think about everything that had just happened. She couldn't believe she had healed Kell. Before she had left the castle grounds, he had given her a huge hug and thanked her again. Zalia hadn't known what to say, so she just hugged him back. Now she sat thinking about it as she rode quietly through the forest.

Was that why she was hidden away? Had her parents known she would have healing powers? But how would they have known, and what did that mean? Zalia had more questions now than she had before. She so desperately wished her parents were around to answer her questions. Ugh. The more she thought about it, the more of a headache she got. She rode on quietly, trying to relax; but her head kept getting worse.

Valen didn't say anything for a while. He rode next to her, his eyes watching carefully around them. He glanced her way. "Are you okay?" he asked.

Zalia nodded and then grimaced. The action hurt her head. "I'm good," she said. "My head just hurts, but I think..." her voice trailed off and she groaned in pain. Clasping both hands to her head, she tried to apply pressure to get the pain to stop. Nothing helped. A ringing started in her ears and she felt like she was going to be sick to her stomach. Dark spots started dancing before her eyes. "Valen," she called out weakly, hoping he would hear her. Just as she started to lose consciousness, she felt herself being pulled from her horse and into the air. The movement made her head hurt worse. She couldn't hold on any longer. Blackness closed in around her, and she blissfully fell into its waiting arms.

Chapter Thirteen

Zalia slowly opened her eyes. Looking around, she realized she was in her room at the training center. It looked like it was light out now. She must have been out for several hours if it was already morning. She tried to sit up and groaned softly. Everything hurt.

"Easy there," she heard a voice say. Looking over, she saw Reid sitting in a chair by her bed.

"What are you doing here?" she asked with a smile on her face.

"I heard you were busy trying to get attention again," he said with a slight grin.

Zalia reached behind her and threw her pillow at him. "Hey," he yelled as he ducked. "You missed me," he taunted. Zalia just laughed at him.

"It's so good to see you. Where have you been?" she

asked him.

He scowled at her. "I had to return to my father's kingdom on business, but Valen called me back here. Enough about me. How are you doing? Valen wouldn't tell me what happened. He just said you passed out. Are you still weak?" he asked with a smirk.

Zalia stuck her tongue out at him. "I am not weak. I've been working really hard at my training. I just..." she fell silent. She wasn't sure if she was supposed to tell anybody her secret. In that moment, she decided to tell Reid. He had risked his life before to save her, and he was Valen's brother. She was sure she could trust him. She met his questioning eyes. "I healed somebody, and then I passed out," she told him quietly.

His eyes rounded. "Really? You're a magical healer? That's incredible!"

She nodded. "I guess my power came to me after I turned eighteen; I don't really know."

"So, you've only done it once. Was it a fluke?" he questioned.

"I don't know," she said. "It just happened today, and now I'm in this bed. So, I'm sort of overwhelmed at the moment."

"We need to see if you can do it again," he said.

Zalia looked at him. "Well, yes probably at some point

but... What are you doing?" she cried out in alarm. She watched in horror as he took out the sword he carried on his waist and held it up to his wrist.

"Now's as good a time as any," he said and sliced through his wrist.

Zalia stared at him in shock for just a moment before her senses kicked in. She launched herself from the bed at him. She watched the wound on his hand instantly gush blood, and she knew instinctively that it was a deep cut. She reached out and tried to stop the blood with her hands. "I don't know what to do. I've only done this once before!" she said, her heart pounding in her chest. As soon as she touched his wound, her hands started getting that tingly feeling again. She breathed a small sigh of relief. Hopefully it would work just like last time. As she sat there holding her hands on his wrist, her door crashed open and hit the wall. Valen came storming in, sword drawn.

He took in the scene in front of him. He stalked toward his brother. "What's going on?" he asked.

Reid looked up at him, his face now white and sweaty, "She wanted to know if she could do it again," he said in a weaker voice.

Valen scowled at him. "So, you just decided to try to slice your wrist off?"

Reid nodded with a small grin.

"You're an idiot," Valen angrily told him. "Of all the irresponsible, stupid things to do!" Valen fumed.

"I'm fine," Reid told him. "Nothing to worry about."

Valen glared at him, "I'm not worried about *you*. I'm worried about her. She just woke up from the last healing she did that she PASSED OUT FROM," Valen bellowed at Reid.

Zalia kept focusing on what she was doing. The burning got worse, then finally weakened. The wound was completely healed now. She took her hands off of Reid and stared at the blue wisp. She looked up and saw Valen and Reid both staring at her hands in wonder. She shook them slightly and the light dissipated.

She looked up and met Valen's angry eyes. "It's okay." She looked down at Reid. "You're healed. Now, we tested it; we know it's not a fluke. Please don't ever do that again or I might just let you bleed."

Reid looked up at her and started to say something when Valen growled, "Out. Get out now." Reid looked up at his brother, took one look at his face, and scrambled out of the room.

Zalia looked up at Valen and saw he was really angry, his eyes shooting daggers at her. He took a step towards her, and she automatically took a step back. That made him pause. He closed his eyes and took a deep breath. When he looked at her again, he seemed a little more in control. "Are you okay?" he asked in a low voice.

Zalia was still frightened of him, so she just nodded her head. He stepped closer, and she managed to stay perfectly still. He took hold of her arm gently. "I'm sorry my brother did that to you. I'll kill him later."

Zalia let out a laugh. "I'm fine, Valen. Seriously. It's no big deal. He just..."

Valen interrupted, "It *is* a big deal. I just carried you in here a few hours ago. Don't tell me it's not a big deal," he said angrily.

Zalia could see he was really worked up. She reached up and put her hand on his bicep. "I'm okay," she said softly. He seemed to calm at her touch. He closed his eyes and took in a large breath of air. He calmed down and asked how she was feeling.

Zalia took stock of her body. "Honestly, I feel a little weak and dizzy, but I don't have the headache I had earlier." She dropped her hand from his arm. "Maybe because it wasn't as big of a healing, it didn't take as much out of me. Kell's wound was much more serious than your brother's."

Valen looked thoughtful for a moment. "Maybe," he said.

Zalia looked up at him. "Do you know anything about

magical healers?"

He shook his head. "I don't, but Beckam asked your grandfather to talk to you. He may have knowledge of healers in the past. He will be coming in a few days."

Zalia nodded. "That's good. Then maybe we can find out what's going on," she said worriedly.

Valen looked down at her. "Everything will be all right. We will figure it out." Zalia smiled up at him. It was sweet of him to act like it wasn't just her problem. Zalia's stomach chose that moment to make a loud noise. He smiled down at her. "Come on. Let's get you fed." He walked over to the door and opened it for her, letting her go ahead of him. Once in the hallway, he put his hand on the small of her back, directing her towards the kitchen.

When she walked into the kitchen, Mari turned and saw them and cried out. "Oh, my dear, how are you?" She walked over to Zalia and pulled her gently into a hug. "You gave us such a worry!" she said.

Zalia hugged her back. "I'm okay."

Mari pulled back and asked her, "What happened to you? They told me you passed out. Did you not eat dinner?"

Zalia opened her mouth to answer her, but Valen stepped in instead. "I think she just did too much dancing on an empty stomach," he lied smoothly.

Mari smiled slyly at Zalia. "Ooo all those handsome men. You just couldn't take a break for food. Sit down. Tell me all about them. Who was the most handsome? Did you kiss any of them?"

At this, Zalia laughed, even while she felt her face heating up. She looked away for a moment in embarrassment and happened to catch Valen's eye. He was glaring at her with his arms crossed. Zalia didn't know what his problem was but didn't have time to think about it. She loved to get Mari stirred up. "Well, there was this one guy," she said as she looked once again at Mari. "He was really tall and incredibly good looking. I wanted him to kiss me, but..." A door slamming against the wall cut her off. She whipped her head around in time to see the door bounce off the wall and come back to a close. Valen was gone, and he was madder than mad.

Zalia looked back at Mari in shock. "What's his problem?" she asked.

Mari grinned. "Oh, I think I might know what the Prince's problem is."

Zalia looked at her blankly. "Well, what is it?"

Mari moved back to the stove. "Nope. It's not my place to butt in. You have to figure this out all on your own."

Zalia sat there a moment longer before she decided to get up and help Mari.

She spent the next hour talking with Mari as they made breakfast for everybody. They made boiled eggs, pottage, bacon, jelly, and fresh bread. As they were putting the finishing touches on all the food, people started trickling into the kitchen. Henri and Collette came in, followed by Beckam and Reid. They all sat down and started eating. Zalia noticed Valen wasn't present. She looked around, but nobody seemed bothered by the fact that he wasn't there. Zalia wasn't sure if he was upset with her still. She wasn't sure if he would still be angry, but she grabbed a cloth and put some bread and bacon and a few boiled eggs in it while everybody was busy eating and talking and slipped quietly out the door.

She walked towards the training hall, figuring that's probably where he was. She walked inside and didn't see him immediately. She walked further into the great room and finally saw him in the corner in his training area. His back was to her, and he was bare chested. As she got closer, she stared in fascination at his mark. Then she watched him work. He had a sword in each hand and was doing a series of lunges, pivots, stabbing, and fancy footwork. He was so fast, Zalia could hardly see his movements. When he paused for a moment, she called out to him quietly.

"Valen?" she called softly. He froze. He didn't turn and look at her. He stared straight ahead, ramrod straight. Zalia took a step closer. "I, uh, didn't see you at breakfast, so I brought you some food. I wasn't sure what you liked to eat, so I brought some bread, a few eggs, and some bacon. But I can see you're busy, so I'll just leave it here for you." Zalia stopped rambling, mortified. *What is it about him that makes me ramble like an idiot!* Zalia set the food down and turned and practically ran out of the training center. She was so embarrassed. He obviously wanted to be alone. He didn't even say thank you.

Zalia went straight to her room and got ready for training for the day. She was looking forward to getting back to it. She had so much to learn. By the time, she made it back to the training hall, she was more composed and ready to forget about Valen and get started with her training. She just hoped she didn't have to work with Valen much today.

Beckam made her run laps and do some strength training. Then he worked with her on her fighting form. He also spent time training her with her new dagger. They took a break for lunch, and Zalia saw that Valen wasn't at the table again. She hadn't seen him all morning. When she asked Beckam about him, he just said that Valen had business to attend to.

In the afternoon, Reid trained with her. Surprisingly, she enjoyed it. They worked hard but laughed and had a good time together. Zalia was happy they had finally forged a friendship.

The next few days flew by. After dinner one night, Zalia was heading towards her room when she saw Raven coming towards her. She broke into a run and threw her arms around Raven, both of them laughing. "I missed you so much!" Zalia said. "It's so lonely here without you."

Raven smiled at her. "I missed you at the castle. I thought I would die of boredom! I never thought I would say this, but I am so happy to be back at the training center," she said with a happy sigh.

Zalia grinned at her. "I will be reminding you of that tomorrow morning."

Raven laughed. "Your grandfather is here too," she told Zalia.

"Oh good," Zalia said. "I need to talk to him." Raven nodded. Zalia put her arm through Raven's arm. "Let's get you settled, and you can tell me everything that I missed at the castle after my party."

They walked together to Raven's room. Zalia sat on Raven's bed while Raven unpacked her bag. They laughed and talked for a little bit before they heard a knock at the door. Raven went to answer it and found Beckam standing there.

"Welcome back, Raven," he said with a smile.

"Thank you, Prince Beckam," Raven returned his smile.

"Beckam," he corrected her. Then he looked at Zalia. "Grandfather would like to talk to you."

Zalia nodded. "I'll see you later, Raven." Raven waved, and Zalia headed into the hall with Beckam.

As they walked next to each other, Beckam asked, "How are you doing?"

Zalia looked up at him. "I'm feeling fine, just confused. I feel like there is so much I don't understand. I have so many questions that nobody has any answers to."

Beckam looked at her in sympathy. "It does seem that way. I'm sorry; we will figure it out. I promise." He pulled Zalia under his arm. Zalia smiled up at him. Beckam led her into the kitchen. Her grandfather was sitting at the long table, nursing a cup of hot tea. He looked weary.

"Zalia," he said as she walked in. He stood up and came over and gave her a long hug. He kept his hands on her shoulders and looked into her eyes. "How are you doing, my dear?"

Zalia smiled at him. "I'm not going to lie. I'm really confused right now. I have so many questions."

Her grandfather nodded. "I'm sure you do. Let's sit down. Do you want some tea?"

"No, thank you," Zalia said. Zalia followed her grandfather to the table and sat next to him, with Beckam across from them.

Her grandfather folded his hands and placed them on the table. "Okay. Let's start at the beginning. Zalia, please recount to me everything that happened with Kell."

Zalia told him every detail she could think of. Then she went on to describe what happened with Reid. Her grandfather listened the entire time. When she finished, he looked at her. "And you have never done this before, correct?"

"Correct," she answered him.

He sat there quietly for a few minutes. Beckam looked at him. "What are you thinking?" he asked.

Her grandfather paused a moment longer, then began slowly. "I don't know what to make of it. You have to be a magical healer, but how? We haven't had magical healers in hundreds of years. If you had other signs, I would think that maybe..." He shook his head. "I just don't know."

Beckam looked at him. "What signs?"

Her grandfather shook his head again. "There's a really old prophecy that exists about four marked royals. But nobody really believes prophecies like that anymore. They're archaic."

Zalia had stopped breathing when he said marked. Taking in a large breath, she asked quietly, "What do you mean by marked?"

Her grandfather explained patiently, "You know about

the marks on a first-born, right?" Zalia nodded. He continued, "The prophecy states that four marked royals will lead the five kingdoms into a peace treaty that will finally last. The first is said to be a magical healer. Nobody ever believed the prophecy because there have always been five kingdoms in our realm. Why would there be only four mentioned in the prophecy? And there have never been four first-born royals at one time.

Beckam looked at her and then back at his grandfather. "And now, Zalia is a healer," he said quietly.

Her grandfather nodded. "But it doesn't all fit. Zalia's not marked. Her brother Kael was marked. Once he died, the marks would have passed on to the next generation or died out. They don't skip to a sibling; they can only skip generationally. I just don't understand. She doesn't have any markings."

Beckam looked at his grandfather again. "What about if they were the markings of the prince—you know, the true mark. That would make sense. Maybe they are not first-born royals. Maybe it's the ones who bear the marks of the royals."

Her grandfather nodded slowly. "I guess that could work. Most people have always believed they would be first-born princesses or princes. But it still doesn't work. Zalia doesn't have true marks."

Zalia had sat absolutely silent during this whole exchange, trying to regulate her breathing. Her heart was pounding hard, and she felt sweat breaking out on her forehead. "Um, I have something to show you," she said quietly. Her grandfather and Beckam stared at her. Zalia carefully pulled her tunic top up her back all the way above her shoulder blade, exposing the marks on her skin.

Beckam shot out of his seat. "Those are Valen's marks! Has he seen those?"

Zalia shook her head fearfully. She was absolutely terrified of what it meant; she was afraid she knew all too well.

Her grandfather stood up and came over to her and gently pulled her shirt down. "Do you know what those marks mean, Zalia?" He asked so gently that Zalia felt tears pool in her eyes. She had so much pent up emotion from everything going on, that once she started, she couldn't stop. Her tears began flowing freely, and soon sobs started shaking her body.

"Oh Zalia," her grandfather whispered as he pulled her close to his chest and wrapped his arms around her. Zalia cried into her grandfather's chest. She cried out her overwrought emotions of fear of the unknown, confusion, rejection, and most of all her deep sense of loss. "So much loss, so much pressure for someone so young. Oh, my sweet Zalia. I'm so sorry." He held her and talked soothingly to her. When she finally pulled herself together, she pulled back slightly and looked up at him. He had tears in his eyes and on his cheeks. She hugged him tightly. He was such a precious gift to her. To have gained a grandfather, after she had lost so much was a miracle in and of itself. He hugged her a little while longer. Then he pulled back. "We will talk more tomorrow. Tonight, you need sleep. Let me walk you to your room." He began to lead her from the room. She looked over her shoulder and saw Beckam still sitting at the table watching them.

"Beckam?" she called out. Her grandfather stopped with her. Beckam looked at her. "I know Valen is your friend. Please don't tell him. Not yet. Please."

Beckam looked like he was about to argue, but her grandfather stepped in. "Nobody will tell Valen anything until we talk all this through." He looked pointedly at Beckam. Beckam finally nodded. He stood up and walked over to Zalia. He reached out and gave her a big hug.

"Goodnight, cousin. Get some rest. We will figure all this out. I won't tell Valen. I give you my word," he said as he kissed her on the cheek.

Zalia turned away to start walking out the door with her grandfather when she heard Beckam say, "But Zalia..." he waited until she turned around. "Don't wait too long to tell him." Zalia nodded and turned back to walk with her grandfather to her room. Zalia was not looking forward to the conversation with Beckam and her grandfather tomorrow, but she was dreading the conversation with Valen even more.

Chapter Fourteen

Zalia hugged and kissed her grandfather goodnight. After he left, she climbed into her bed. She was so weary, but she knew it would probably be a long night. She knew with the attack, her healing, and everything going on, her nightmares would probably be plaguing her for the next several nights again.

Zalia sighed as she lay there thinking. There was so much racing through her head, she would never be able to sleep. She held her hands up in front of her face, even though it was dark, and thought of her healing powers. *Why now? Why couldn't I have gained this power earlier? Would I have been able to save my family?* Zalia shut down those thoughts. It was too painful; she felt the tears pool in her eyes. She turned her mind to think about something else.

Her mind turned to the marks on her back. There was

no mistaking that they were Valen's marks. She had never heard of a true mark, but she could only guess if she had Valen's marks on her back what that meant. She groaned aloud. "Why him? He hates me!" Zalia couldn't believe her rotten luck. Why did it have to be Valen? She couldn't imagine what would happen when they told him. She would never be able to face him again. He would hate her. And what of her kingdom? Would she have to give up her kingdom and go with him to his? There was so much she didn't know.

Zalia groaned again and rolled over, willing her mind to shut down and stop thinking. She finally fell asleep, but slept fitfully. Her nightmares returned, plaguing her from getting good sleep. After the last one felt so real, she decided to just get up for the day. She got out of bed, got dressed, and took her sketchbook with her to the kitchen.

When she got to the kitchen, it was too early for Mari to be working yet, so Zalia had the kitchen all to herself. She didn't mind. She sat down at the table and opened her sketchbook to a blank page. She couldn't decide what to sketch. Her mind was overwhelmed this morning, too many thoughts on her mind. The leftover fear from her dreams was still raw. Without even realizing what she was doing, Zalia started sketching Valen. She drew him in his black cloak with a sword at his waist and one on his back. It was the warrior version of him, the one that somehow made her feel safe. It was his eyes, though that she couldn't quite capture. There was so much depth to his eyes and something she couldn't quite put her finger on.

Zalia was so lost in her work she didn't hear anybody come in. "Hmmm, I see who you've been thinking about early this morning." Zalia jumped in her chair, startled. She turned around to see Mari standing there with a huge grin on her face.

Zalia squirmed in her seat. "No, I'm just... it's not like that, I... oh never mind." Zalia closed her book, flustered. She stood to her feet. "Let me help you with breakfast."

Mari looked at her. "You sure you don't want to continue your drawing of Mr. Tall, Dark, and Handsome?"

Zalia could feel herself blushing furiously. "It's just a drawing," she mumbled.

Mari laughed out loud and then took compassion on her. "Come on. Let's get breakfast going." Zalia worked happily with Mari for the next hour, smiling when Raven came in to help them.

Raven smiled at Zalia. "How did you sleep?"

Zalia shrugged. "Okay," she said noncommittally.

Raven looked at her with understanding in her eyes. "Nightmares?"

Zalia nodded. Wanting to change the subject, she started telling Mari all about the dances and the food at her party. Raven joined in and told her about the handsome men she had danced with. The time flew by, and soon it was time to eat. The kitchen filled up. Zalia noticed that Valen was still absent, and she couldn't help but feel a little down because of it. She knew it was totally irrational. She figured it was just because she was tired, and her emotions were all over the place.

After breakfast, her grandfather asked to speak with her again. She and Beckam followed him to another small room to be able to talk privately.

"Zalia, did you sleep well last night?" her grandfather began.

Zalia shrugged. That seemed to be her response of late. Her grandfather looked at her astutely. "Do you always have a hard time sleeping?"

Zalia nodded, afraid if she said more, she would share everything about her dreams. She was too tired and overwhelmed emotionally for that this morning.

Her grandfather seemed to catch on and moved along in the conversation. "All right. Well, let's move on to what we talked about last night. Let's talk about what we know. We know that you turned eighteen, and your healing powers manifested. We also know you have markings on your back. So, with all that in mind, it could be possible for you to be one of the marked mentioned in the prophecy," he said thoughtfully.

"What exactly does the prophecy say again?" Beckam asked.

"I don't exactly remember it word for word. I've only heard of it passed down from one generation to another. It says something along the lines of four marked will become allies. They all have special gifts. One is a healer, one is a seer, another is an abjurer, and the last is a telepath. Together, they will unite the kingdoms of the realm and destroy the darkness. Or something along those lines."

Zalia looked at her grandfather and questioned, "Destroy the darkness. What does that mean? What darkness?"

He shook his head. "I don't know. I honestly never took the prophecy literally. Nobody did. There have always been five kingdoms; and nobody has seen a magical healer or telepath in hundreds of years, even longer for a seer and an abjurer. Most people just think it's a fable. I always did too, until now. I put my people to work finding everything they can about the prophecy and about magical healers. We will find out what we can, Zalia, and go from there. They did find a few interesting facts about healers, though." He stopped and looked at Zalia.

"What is it?" she breathed.

He looked at her carefully. "Well, first of all, when a healer is born, the baby comes out of the birth canal wrapped in a soft blue light. The light dissipates almost immediately. It's a way of marking the child so that the parents know the future of the child," he said gently.

Zalia stared at him in surprised silence. "So, my parents would have known at my birth that I was a healer?" she questioned her grandfather.

"They might not have known at the moment they saw the blue light because it has been so long in our history since there has been a healer. But I can guarantee your father sought out the answer. When he found out what you were, they cut off all trade and locked all outsiders out," he finished quietly.

"Protecting me," Zalia said softly. Her grandfather nodded.

"If anyone found out, they would have tried to take you. A magical healer is a rare gift and truly an invaluable resource to any kingdom," he said. Zalia didn't say anything as she tried to take it all in.

He continued. "My researchers found out something else interesting. They discovered that when healers heal, they are essentially giving their life essence to keep someone alive. That's why you passed out after healing Kell. It took so much from you. A really hard healing could wreak havoc on your body. Over time, your body will weaken from giving so much of your life source away."

Zalia felt lightheaded at his words. Beckam looked at her, worried. "Is there nothing she can do?"

Her grandfather looked at her again. "We did find something," he paused and looked at her, unsure.

"What is it?" Zalia asked softly.

"A healer can be grounded by completing the bond with someone of royal blood. Only a source of great power, such as that found in royal blood can keep the healer from giving too much of their life's essence away. The bond with royalty gives you strength and protection," he finished quietly.

Nobody said anything. It was absolutely quiet for a moment. Then Zalia spoke quietly, "What am I going to do? He will hate me for this."

Beckham's head jerked up. "Valen?" he questioned. Then he started laughing.

Her grandfather looked his way. "Beckam," he said in a warning voice. "This is between Valen and Zalia, and we promised we wouldn't interfere."

Beckam grinned. "I just want to be there when you tell him," he grinned.

"Beckam," her grandfather warned again. Beckam didn't say anything more; he just grinned.

Zalia looked back and forth between the two in confusion and decided it was time to move on. "How exactly does a true mark work?" she asked.

Her grandfather explained. "The first child of a king and queen becomes the first-born royal. It can be a prince or a princess. The first-born royal bears the mark of their kingdom. At birth, it's small. Once they turn eighteen, the mark spreads more, making it complete. A first-born has a lot of power because he or she will be king or queen one day. The only way to balance the power is to share it with another. The true mark of the first-born will be found on the person that completes them. The bearer of the mark does not receive it until they turn eighteen. Once the first-born and the person bearing the true mark are bound, the power flows between the two of them, keeping the first-born royal in a healthy place."

Zalia jumped in here. "Does the first-born have to marry the person carrying their mark?"

Her grandfather looked at her solemnly. "No, but it is dangerous not to." He paused for a moment. "I probably shouldn't be the one to tell you this, but that is why King Mylan is so wicked and not right in the head. He didn't marry his true mark. I don't know if he never found her, or if he simply chose not to complete the bond with her. He loved Cherish and made her his queen. They were happy for a lot of years, but eventually the power began to destroy him. After she died, he lost all sense of right and wrong. The power is destroying his mind," he finished sorrowfully.

Zalia looked at him. "So Valen doesn't have a choice? He has to marry me?" she asked in a small voice.

Her grandfather paused slightly before answering her. "He doesn't have to, but it would be really unwise for him not to." He looked at her again solemnly. "Zalia, nobody will make you bond with Valen if that's not what you want. I would never let that happen."

"But you said he would turn into his father if I don't."

"We don't know what would happen. Valen is strong, and he is a much better person than his father. He might be strong enough to handle it," he answered her.

"So basically, we don't have to bind to each other; but if we don't, Valen will go crazy from his power and I will die from healing people?" she looked incredulously at her grandfather. Her grandfather didn't respond; he just looked pained.

Zalia didn't say anything. She looked to Beckam. He was frowning but looked away when she met his eyes. Zalia's head was beginning to hurt. This was so much to take in. "I need a break from this. Beckam, can we train now?" she asked him.

Beckam stood up quickly turning into trainer mode

quickly. "Let's go."

Zalia turned back to her grandfather. "Thank you for not being afraid to tell me everything. I appreciate it."

He stood up and pulled her close. "Oh Zalia, I see so much of your mother in you. I miss her, but I'm so glad God brought us together. We will work through all this, I promise."

Zalia tightened her hold on him. "I know. Thank you." She reached up on tiptoe and kissed his cheek, then left to go train.

In the training hall, she saw Raven sparring with one of the guards here on protective duty from her grandfather's castle. Zalia bypassed them and walked over to where Beckam stood. Beckam led her over to his training area and got started on training. He worked with her on how to get out of several different holds, how to strike up close, everything she needed for self-defense. He drilled it over and over again with her. When Zalia was exhausted, he finally called it quits. With limbs shaking from exhaustion, Zalia headed out of the training center back to her room, but on the way, she stopped when she heard yelling. She heard a huge commotion near the entryway, so she turned that way. When she heard Beckam bellow, "Zalia!" she took off running. When she got to the entryway, she saw the guards, her grandfather, and Beckam all kneeling on the floor gathered around something. Stepping closer, Zalia gasped. It was Valen! She couldn't see his face, but his torso was covered in blood.

She ran towards him. The guards got out of her way when she got closer, having seen what she could do when she had helped Kell. Zalia fell to her knees next to Valen. Beckam was leaning over him. He turned to Zalia with his hands covered in blood. "Help him," he ordered. Zalia was already reaching out to find the source of his wounds.

She stood up and moved around to the other side. Taking control, she commanded, "I have to be able to touch the wounds. Get his shirt off."

Beckam yanked out his dagger and cut off Valen's shirt. Zalia gasped and her eyes filled with horror as she took in his torso. He didn't have one wound, he had several. They were all severe cuts. She took a deep breath and bent over him. Finding the deepest one, she started there first. As soon as she touched the wound, her hands started tingling. Then it abruptly stopped as someone grabbed her hands and pulled them away.

"Do not heal me," Valen ground out through clenched teeth. His hold on her was surprisingly strong.

"Valen, let go of me," Zalia demanded of him. Two of them could play this game.

"Don't touch me," he said. His eyes were dark with

pain and something else.

Zalia straightened her back. "Beckam, you hold his arms down." She looked up, and her eyes landed on Reid. He was looking fearfully toward his older brother. "Reid, you hold down his leg. Conlyn," she looked at one of the guards. "You hold down his other leg. Now! We go on one, two, three."

Everybody grabbed a part of Valen and held him down. She reached in again and started on the first wound. He fought against her. It took all of them to hold him down. He was so strong! Zalia didn't look up again at his face, because she couldn't afford to let him distract her. He was not happy. He kept yelling at her and everyone holding him down. More than once, he was able to get an arm or leg free. Beckam finally had enough. Holding down Valen's arms under his knee, he rose up over Valen and knocked him out. Valen went slack, and everybody was finally able to relax their hold on him.

Beckam looked at Zalia. "I'm sorry I had to do that, but he's too strong. He has to heal." Reid and Conlyn nodded their understanding. Beckam looked at each of the guys. "Stay close. I don't know how long he'll stay out. Probably not long. When he comes to, he's going to be a bear. And he's going to be stronger because his wounds are getting healed. So be ready." Each man stared grimly at the Prince.

Zalia kept moving. She healed two of the worst cuts. She had several more to heal. His cuts were healing nicely but she wondered about his blood loss. He had lost so much blood. Would he be strong enough to heal? As Zalia continued on, she found herself getting weaker. Her movements were starting to slow down. The healings felt like they were taking longer now. Beads of sweat started trickling down her forehead. She kept moving, hoping she could finish before she passed out. She was too weak to engage in conversation, and she needed to focus on what she was doing. Vaguely, she was aware they were discussing what had happened to the Prince, but she couldn't focus on it.

"Zalia, are you okay?" Zalia looked up at Beckam. He was looking at her with worried eyes. She wasn't sure how long he had been trying to get her attention. She felt like she was slowly fading away. She took a deep breath, trying to hang on to her consciousness. She only had one cut left to heal. She could do this. Taking another deep breath, she moved on to the last wound. She watched as it healed under her hands. She started seeing dark spots and hearing a ringing sound in her ears. She knew she was going to go under soon. She watched as the final wound closed up. She pulled her hands off and watched the dancing blue sparks. Usually, they dissipated right away, but they seemed to linger this time. She tried to shake her hands to rid herself of the lights, but she didn't have the energy. She couldn't do anything more. She fell into the soft blackness waiting for her.

Chapter Fifteen

Everywhere she looked, servants were lying face down. Zalia ran to the throne room. She had to get to her family. She opened the massive door and ran inside. She stopped when she saw her father and mother and her brother Kael. They were okay, but they wouldn't be soon. She had to warn them. She tried screaming, but they wouldn't listen. She tried to run to them, but she couldn't ever reach them. Soon they were surrounded by soldiers. She watched in horror as they killed her family. She screamed. Then she felt the soldiers close in around her. They grabbed at her arms, trying to kill her too. She fought them. She used all of her training to fight them. They laughed at her and called her name. "Zalia, Zalia..."

"Zalia." She felt herself being shaken. "Zalia," the voice called again. "Come on. Wake up, Zalia."

Zalia tried to open her eyes, but they felt like someone

had glued them shut. "Why isn't she waking up?" she heard. She wasn't conscious enough to recognize who was speaking. She spiraled right into another dream.

Zalia looked around her. She didn't recognize where she was. It was a beautiful meadow with green grass, purple wildflowers, and a beautiful cloudless sky. Zalia felt such peace. She looked around and saw someone sitting across the meadow from her. Zalia made her way over there. As she got closer, she recognized her mom. Zalia cried out and ran to her. As she got closer, her mother stood up and walked away from her. "Mother," Zalia cried out, running faster. "Mother," she cried again. Her mother stopped once and looked back at her. "I'm sorry," she said softly and then she walked away. Zalia ran after her, begging her to come back. It didn't make any difference. The harder she ran, the further away her mother got. Zalia sobbed. She felt strong arms come around her and soothe her. It didn't take the pain away but at least she wasn't alone anymore. She cried and cried until she had nothing left. Then there was nothing.

Zalia opened her eyes slowly. Looking around, she realized she was in her room. She looked down. She was still wearing her training pants and shirt. She couldn't tell what time of day it was because the curtains covered the windows. There was a lantern on low, casting shadows around the room. Zalia turned her head away from the wall and saw the legs of somebody sitting in a chair near her bed.

Rolling all the way over, she looked up and saw Valen. He had his head against the wall and appeared to be sleeping. He had a clean shirt on, and Zalia scanned him from head to toe. He seemed to be fully recovered from his injuries. *I wonder what he's doing in my room.* Zalia was slowly straightening and started to pull herself up into a sitting position when she felt Valen's eyes on her. She looked over at him and met his dark eyes. He just stared at her for a moment.

"How are you feeling?" he asked. His voice was a little gravelly, like he hadn't used it in a while.

"I'm fine," she said, though even as she said it, she ached all over.

"Why did you do it?" he asked angrily. "I told you not to."

Zalia just looked at him in shock. "Valen, why wouldn't I? You were dying!"

"Three days!" he said in his deadly calm voice. She could only tell he was upset by looking at his eyes. They were dark black. "I sat by your bed for three days, wondering if you were going to wake up. I hated myself because you were in that position because of me!"

Zalia looked up at him and just said softly, "I'm okay." She hated that he felt guilty because of her. He stared down at her. He made a move towards her, then abruptly stood up and backed away. "Thank you for healing me, but don't ever do that again," he said. Then he was gone.

Zalia just stared after him. *What just happened?* Zalia sighed. She was too tired to think about it. She sat on her bed, trying to get the motivation to get up and get going when she heard a knock on the door. "Come in," she called out. Raven came in with a smile.

"I heard you were awake. How are you feeling?" she asked Zalia.

"You know, I feel like all anybody says to me anymore is 'How are you feeling'?" Zalia said.

Raven looked at her with sympathy. "I'm sorry. Come on. Let's get you cleaned up. You haven't had a bath in a few days, and it shows," she said as she grimaced.

Zalia looked at her in alarm. "Really? Valen was just in here!"

Raven burst into laughter. "Oh, girl, you've got it bad."

Zalia just glared at her. "No, I don't. I would feel that way no matter who was in here."

Raven grinned, "Whatever you say. Now, come on."

An hour later, Zalia felt more human again. She had taken a bath, washed her hair, and put on fresh clothes. In leather pants and a tunic top, she felt confident again. She pulled her still damp hair back into a braid. "Come on. Let's go get some lunch."

Raven and Zalia sat with Mari for lunch. Everybody else must have been out training. After talking and laughing together, Zalia looked at Raven. "Do we get to have the rest of the day off?"

Raven smiled. "If you show up in that training hall, I think everybody will demand you go back to bed."

"Well, I guess I will go back to my room and rest then," Zalia said with a small smile.

———————

The next few days flew by as Zalia threw herself back into training. Valen trained her when it was his turn. Other than that, he mostly kept his distance. Sometimes she would catch him watching her, but he would look away when her eyes met his.

One afternoon, when Beckam and Zalia were training together, Beckam signaled to take a break. Zalia walked over and grabbed some water to drink and a rag to wipe the sweat off her face. While they were standing together, Beckam looked at her.

"What?" Zalia asked.

Beckam just looked at her. "This last healing, you were out for three days," he said quietly.

"I know," she said defensively.

"It's getting worse," he said. "I talked to Grandfather, and he said that everything they have found in old history books and documents says that the healer's powers continue to weaken the healer until they can tie it to a source of power."

Zalia looked at him. "I'm fine," she said.

"For how long?" he shot back. "What about the next time or the time after that? When will it be too much, and your body can't take any more?"

Zalia tried to tamper her frustration. "What do you want me to do, Beckam? I can't exactly control what it does to me. Would you like me to just stop healing people? Because I can tell you right now that's not going to happen!" she responded angrily.

He looked at her coolly. "Maybe you could stop hiding from your future."

"What's that supposed to mean?" she shot back at him.

"It means that Grandfather told you the solution to your problem, but you won't act on it. I don't know why you won't stop hiding from him and just deal with it."

"Because I don't want to," Zalia bit out.

"Well, maybe it's time you grew up a little bit and stopped being a coward," he said as he stepped close and glared into her eyes.

"How dare you!" Zalia shot at him.

Beckam just scowled down at her. "You have the answer to all your problems on your back. Just deal with it."

Zalia gritted her teeth. "Just because I have markings on my back does not mean that I am going to give myself over to a total stranger. Besides..." Zalia stopped what she was saying because Beckam had stopped looking at her and was now staring over her shoulder. Zalia closed her eyes and took a deep breath, hoping against hope that Beckam was not looking at who she thought Beckam might be looking at.

She turned around slowly and saw Valen standing close behind them with his arms crossed over his chest. He did not look happy! Nope; she would say he looked downright angry. And lucky her; it seemed his anger was directed at her again. Zalia looked up into his eyes that were utterly black now.

"Whose markings, Zalia?" he said through clenched teeth. His jaw was so tight, she thought he was going to break it.

Zalia scrambled, trying to get control of the situation. "Uh, how much of our conversation did you hear?" she asked him.

His eyes got even darker, if that was possible. "Enough of it," he said. He just stared at her; then took a step closer. "Whose marks?" he asked slowly and deadly.

Zalia turned around to look at Beckam for support and realized he was gone. "Ugh!" she threw her hands up in frustration. She was going to kill him. She couldn't believe he left her here to face Valen alone. She turned back to face Valen. He stalked her, like a predator. She knew never to run from a predator, but she was about two seconds away from doing just that.

Valen stopped right in front of her and looked down at her. "Whose marks?" he asked with his jaw clenched tight.

Zalia looked up at him with an apology in her eyes. "I'm sorry," she said quietly.

She watched him visibly react. He tightened his fists at his side, and she saw a muscle tick in his jawbone. His eyes were completely black now, a sign he was barely in control.

Zalia turned around and pulled the back of her shirt up and over her shoulder and stood there shaking, scared to death of what his reaction would be. As soon as she uncovered the marks, she heard his sharp intake of breath and felt him move closer to her. She shuddered as she felt his hand touch her marks ever so gently. He didn't say anything for what felt like forever. Finally, when she felt like she couldn't take it a moment longer, she felt him pull her shirt carefully back down. Then he placed his hands gently on her shoulders and turned her around. Zalia couldn't bear to look up into his face. She wasn't sure if she would see anger, or rejection, or even pity, but she wasn't brave enough to find out.

He gently placed a finger under her chin, forcing her to meet his eyes. He took a step closer, putting them really close. She couldn't get a read on him. His eyes were still really dark, but he didn't seem angry anymore. There was something else there; she couldn't put her finger on what it was. He looked into her eyes. "Those are *my* marks," he said quietly.

"I know," she whispered. "I'm sorry."

He looked at her questioningly. "Why are you sorry?" he asked just as quietly. "Do you not want my marks?" he asked, his body stiffening.

"No, I mean yes, I mean... I don't know. I just... you hate me," she fumbled around with her words. She was so confused.

His eyes just darkened further while she fumbled around. "How long have you had my marks?" he asked.

Zalia looked down. "They showed up on my birthday."

He looked at her. "Why didn't you tell me? Don't you think this is something I had a right to know?"

Zalia stiffened her back. "I was going to tell you in time. I just needed the time to..."

He cut her off. "To what?" he snapped at her.

"Beckam said..." she stopped when she saw his eyes

flash.

"Beckam knew and didn't tell me?" he growled out. "You talked to Beckam about *my* marks on your back, yet you couldn't tell me?" his voice was getting lower and calmer. That was always a really bad sign with Valen. The calmer he got, the angrier he was. He whirled away from her and started striding out of the training hall.

Zalia was right behind him. The situation was quickly spiraling out of control. "Where are you going?" she called out to him, running to keep up with him.

"To deal with Beckam," he growled.

"Shoot!" she said to herself. "Valen, stop," she called out. He didn't stop moving, and she was following right behind him. "You're being ridiculous!" she snapped at him. That was the wrong thing to say!

He stopped so suddenly, she slammed into his back. He whirled around, his eyes shooting fire. He opened his mouth to talk to her, then looked up and around the room. Then he grabbed her arm and pulled her with him from the training room, away from prying eyes. He walked from the training room into the hallway, still pulling her with him.

He stopped at a room and pulled her inside and shut the door. He dropped her arm and looked down at her. She wasn't going to be intimidated. She raised her chin at him and glared up at him. "Beckam has nothing to do with this. Just leave him out of this," she said angrily.

Valen stepped closer to her. "Beckam has everything to do with this! He knows how I have been killing myself trying to stay away from you. He knows how much I hate you being hurt and not being able to do anything to help, but I did everything I could to not be attracted to you and to not develop feelings for you." His voice got quieter and lower. "And how I was failing miserably." He reached up pushed her hair gently behind her ears. Then he got angry again. "He knew all that, yet he didn't tell me that you bore my marks. So yes, he has everything to do with this."

Zalia just stared up at him at a complete loss for words. "I thought you hated me," she whispered.

Valen just smiled ruefully. "No, I just wanted you to think that so I could try to stay away from you. You have to understand, as a first-born royal, I can only marry the one who carries my marks. I've seen first-hand what happens to someone who doesn't. As much as I wanted to develop a relationship with you, I would never do that to you." He looked away for a moment, then looked back at Zalia. His eyes darkened. "My mother didn't bear my father's marks. He fell in love with her and thought that would be enough, but it wasn't. My father grew more and more unbalanced over the years. He became increasingly difficult and very angry. My mom was the one who paid the ultimate price," he said rigidly. "I promised myself I would never develop feelings for anyone besides the one who bore my marks." He looked down at her. "These last several months have been hell for me. Beckam knew all of that, and *that's* why I'm going to kill him." He took a step back.

"No!" Zalia grabbed his arm. "Don't! It was my fault. I told him not to say anything."

Valen paused and looked at her. "Why? Why wouldn't you tell me? Why did you hide it from me? They're my marks!"

"On *my* body!" she snapped right back at him. He just smirked at her.

Then he turned serious again. "Do you know what the marks mean?" he asked her gently.

Zalia nodded. "I didn't until my grandfather and Beckam enlightened me."

He scowled again. "Your grandfather knows too?"

Zalia grimaced. "I'm sorry. I had to confide in them. I didn't know anything about the marks. Besides, I didn't bring them up. Grandfather was explaining to me about my healing powers and how they would get worse. He told me the solution was..."

"What do you mean worse?" he interrupted, stepping closer to her.

Zalia bit her tongue. *Why do I talk? I just keep making matters worse.* Out loud she said, "He was just telling me more about my healing powers."

Valen frowned at her, then grabbed her hand. "Come on. Let's go." He began pulling her towards the door.

"Wait, are we going to kill Beckam, because I don't want any part of that!" she said, desperately trying to get out of the iron grip he had on her wrist.

He just laughed at her. "*We* won't kill him."

Zalia relaxed for a moment. *Did the solemn prince just laugh?* Then she tensed up again when he said, "Just I will."

Chapter Sixteen

Zalia tried unsuccessfully to pull her hand from Valen's. He kept his grip tight enough that she couldn't escape, but not so tight that it hurt her. "You know I've been training really hard. I could take you down if I wanted to," Zalia said with attitude in her voice. She was not happy about being dragged to see Beckam.

Valen laughed. "I'd love to see you try!"

Zalia just huffed at him and started plotting all the ways she could hurt him. He looked back at her after a few moments of silence. "Did you give up already?"

"No," she said. "I'm just plotting all the ways I can hurt you."

He laughed again and kept walking. He stopped in front of a door and used his other hand to bang on the door. "Beckam, open up!" he ordered.

A second later, Beckam opened the door. Valen shoved the door and Beckam back as he strode into the room, dragging Zalia behind him.

Beckam looked from Valen to Zalia, then to their joined hands. Then he had the audacity to grin. "I see you found out she has your marks," he said happily.

Zalia stepped up next to Valen and looked at Beckam. "You know, he came here to beat the crap out of you. I tried to stop him, but you know what? I think I'll join him."

Beckam just laughed harder. Zalia was annoyed. She looked up at Valen and saw that he also had the audacity to grin. She tried to pull her hand from his, but he wouldn't have it. She put her free hand on her hip and said, "You're supposed to be beating him up now," she said to Valen.

Valen smiled down at her. "You're right." Then he turned back to Beckam and managed to lose the grin. All of a sudden, he turned menacing again. "Why didn't you tell me she had my marks? You know what I've been going through."

Beckam shrugged. "She told me not to tell you. I said I wouldn't, and I always keep my word."

Valen pulled back and slammed his fist into Beckam's nose. Zalia winced when she heard the crack and saw blood spray.

Beckam cursed, and Zalia stood there in shock. "I can't

believe you did that!" she said angrily to Valen.

Valen just shrugged. "He deserved it," he said.

Zalia moved towards an angry Beckam and reached for his nose. He backed away from her. "I'm just going to heal it," she said. Beckam didn't fight her and Zalia reached up and healed his nose quickly. Muttering under his breath, Beckam turned away to go get cleaned up.

Zalia turned around to scowl at Valen. "Was that necessary?" she asked him.

"Absolutely," he replied. "He'll understand when he meets his girl someday," Valen said.

Zalia stopped breathing for a second. *Did he just imply that I am his girl? No, obviously not. He was just making a point. Nothing to get all hyped up about, Zalia,* she thought to herself.

When Beckam came back with a clean shirt on, Valen looked at Beckam and pulled Zalia slightly closer to him. "Tell me about her healing powers. What did you mean when you said that they are getting worse?"

Beckam sighed. "This really is a conversation we should be having with our grandfather. He knows way more about it than I do, but I can tell you what I know. Are you going to hit me again?" he asked Valen darkly.

Valen replied, "That depends. Are you going to be an idiot again?" Zalia smacked Valen's arm.

"Valen!" she said angrily. To her surprise, Beckam laughed.

"Come on. Let's at least sit down while we have this conversation," Beckam said easily.

He led them over to a sitting room area, adjacent to his room. He sat down, leaving a small couch as the only available place for Valen and Zalia to sit. Valen finally let go of Zalia's hand, and she glared at Beckam as she sat down as close to the end of the couch as possible.

She grimaced as Valen sat down next to her, close enough that their thighs were touching. If he was aware of how close he was, he didn't show it. Meanwhile, Zalia couldn't seem to breathe. She wasn't used to being this close to Valen. He was intimidating from far away. Up close, he was deadly.

Oblivious to Zalia's distress, Valen sat back and crossed his arms over his chest. "Tell me," he ordered Beckam.

Beckam leaned forward. "Like I said, Grandfather knows more than I do, but we have talked about it several times." He let out a deep sigh. "Every time Zalia heals, she is giving away her life's essence. That's why she is able to heal, but it's also why she passes out once she finishes. The harder the healing, the longer it takes for her body to recover. Over time, her life's essence will be damaged too much to recover fully."

"How do you stop it?" Valen growled. Zalia looked up at him. He was angry again.

Beckam looked from Valen to Zalia, then back to Valen again. "Apparently the only way to stop it is to bond with someone with royal blood, like a first-born prince. The power of the royal blood grounds a healer. It also helps her heal faster after a healing, and ultimately keeps her from giving too much of her life's essence away because it's tied to the first-born."

Valen just nodded. "Okay. Then we will bond right away."

"What?!" Zalia almost shouted at him as she shot to her feet. Beckam covered what sounded like a laugh with a cough. "You can't be serious!" she said to Valen.

Valen was on his feet in a flash, towering over her. "I'm totally serious," he said in a calm voice.

"Well, you can't... I'm not... we don't..." Zalia sputtered. He smirked, infuriating Zalia more. "Well, we're not doing... that," she finally spit out.

Valen cocked his head to the side, "Do you know what the bonding process entails?"

Zalia looked down for a moment, blushing furiously. "Not exactly," she finally said, absolutely mortified. She felt a finger under her chin as he tipped her head up. She looked down for as long as possible, then finally met his eyes.

To her surprise, she didn't find any humor or mocking in his eyes. He was totally serious. "It's not as bad as whatever it is you're thinking to make you blush like that." Then he smiled slightly. He reached down and grabbed her hand. "Come on. We have a lot to talk about." Zalia allowed him to pull her. She was so past thinking right now. Her mind had officially shut down.

Valen looked at Beckam. "I'll deal with you tomorrow," he said without any emotion. Beckam full on grinned back.

"I'll be looking forward to that," Beckam told Valen. Zalia didn't know what to say, so she allowed Valen to pull her out the door. Glancing over her shoulder, Zalia caught Beckam's wink. Zalia just rolled her eyes, causing Beckam to laugh out loud.

Zalia's mind was muddled as she followed Valen out the door and into the hall. He led them down a few doors and opened a door and walked in. Zalia was so lost in thought that she didn't realize at first where they were. She walked in and sat down on the bed. *What in the world is going on? I am so confused right now. I thought he hated me. And now he wants to bond? Yeah right. He's just confused; he doesn't really know what he wants. Right? Right! I just need to show him...*

"Zalia," Valen called out, and Zalia realized he must

have been trying to get her attention for a little bit.

"Oh, sorry," she said. She finally looked around and realized they were in a very masculine room. A bedroom, and she was sitting on the bed. His bed!! Zalia shot off the bed. "We're in your room!" she said, completely startled. He just gave her his infamous smirk.

"Yes, we are," he said, clearly amused.

"We can't be in here!" she said.

"Why not?" he asked. "We're just talking. Unless you had something else in mind?" he asked her with a glint in his eyes. He was purposefully trying to get her riled up.

"No!" she almost shouted at him. Then she tried to get herself under control while he laughed out loud at her. She was so overwhelmed right now. Her thoughts were a scattered mess.

He took compassion on her and showed her over to a sitting area. He sat on a chair and left the couch for her. She looked around for a moment. "How come you and Beckam have awesome rooms with a sitting area?" He shrugged.

"Zalia," he called her name gently. "We need to talk about all this. I know you're nervous, but it's going to be okay. We will figure this out together."

Zalia looked at him helplessly. "I don't even know where to start. You hate me." She felt stupid saying that, but she didn't know what else to say.

Valen walked over to where she was sitting on the couch and sat next to her. He took both her hands in his. "Zalia, I have never hated you. I have spent the last few months of my life trying to convince myself that I did because it was dangerous for me to be around you. I couldn't let myself feel anything for you. The only way I could accomplish that was to try to ignore you and act like I didn't like you, but I didn't even do a good job of that. I have thought about you nonstop ever since I first saw you in your father's castle. I couldn't get you out of my mind. I was doing an okay job of it until the night of the masquerade ball. After that, I couldn't keep my distance. I told Beckam I had to leave. I left because I couldn't stand to be around you and not be able to be near you. I know that it must seem so sudden to you, but it's not to me at all."

Zalia just looked at him, unsure of what to say. He continued on. "We don't need to rush into anything. We can take our time, get to know each other. We don't have to get married right away, but..." He stopped for a moment because she had choked on the word marriage. He didn't say anything, just waited for her to recover. "But as for the bond, we won't wait on that. I will not sit by and watch you suffer when we could do something about it. Before you argue," he said as she opened her mouth to argue with him. She frowned but closed her mouth as he went on.

"Let me explain the bond to you. Do you know anything about it?"

"Not really," she said quietly. "Grandfather explained a little bit, but I'd like to hear it from you."

Valen looked into her eyes as he began explaining. "The bond takes place between a royal first-born and the one who carries his or her marks. Royal blood is incredibly powerful. Without a way to balance the power, it will destroy the king or queen. The only way to balance the power is to share the power with someone else. When a royal first-born and the carrier of his or her marks bond, the power distributes between both of them. The bond is a blood bond. When the time comes, we will each cut our wrists. Another royal will say the enchantment. In this case, your grandfather. Then we mix our blood and the bond snaps into place."

Valen continued, "When the bond is complete, we will have a mental connection. Simply put, we will be able to hear each other in our heads without talking out loud. Secondly, we will be able to feel each other's emotions. These are measures of protection. A bonded pair is harder to kill because they know when the other person is in danger or in pain."

Zalia's attention was locked on Valen. While it was insane to even think about bonding with him, she found the entire concept of a bonded pair absolutely fascinating.

He continued on. "The act of bonding is not intimate at all. We can do the bond without being married, but the feel of the bond is very intimate. I wouldn't suggest that we wait a very long time after bonding before getting married."

And just like that, the conversation went from absolutely fascinating to utterly terrifying. Zalia looked up at Valen. He was quiet now, just looking at her. She could tell he was trying to get a read on her. *Well, just keep trying,* she thought to herself. *She* didn't even know what she was thinking!

He stayed silent, and Zalia felt like she was supposed to say something, but she didn't know what. She decided to just be honest. "I really don't know what to say. This is so much to take in."

He nodded. "I know." He let go of her hands and ran his hand through his hair. "If this was a normal situation, I would never push you into this. But with your healing powers being a danger to you, I have to push you into this for your own safety. I won't let you continue to hurt yourself. If somebody got hurt, would you be able to withstand the pressure to heal them?" he asked.

Zalia thought for a moment. "I don't think I could. It's hard to explain, but it's almost like a compulsion. It's like I can't *not* heal. Does that make sense?" she asked. He nodded. "I'm sorry," she said quietly and looked down.

He gently tipped her head up until her eyes met his. "Why are you sorry?"

She just looked at him helplessly. "I'm sorry that because of the marks, you feel like you have to marry me; and because of my healing powers, you feel like you have to bond with me right away. If I didn't have the marks and my healing powers, we wouldn't even be having this conversation. You wouldn't even be interested in me."

He was quiet until she finally stopped and took a breath. Then he said, "I obviously didn't explain myself very clearly to you." She opened her mouth to argue with him. He held up his hand, and she closed her mouth. "I am very interested in you and was long before I knew about your marks or even your healing power. But I can't talk you into believing that. I'll just have to show you. I will take my time winning your heart. I will be gentle and kind with you. But make no mistake, you are mine now. We will be bonded and will get married when the time is right, and nobody will stand in our way!"

Zalia felt a wave of emotion run through her. She felt she was on the verge of tears and wasn't sure why. It was just so much to deal with. She closed her eyes, wishing she could process all this.

"Come on," he said gently. He took her hand and pulled her up to stand next to him. "Let's head to dinner." Zalia allowed him to guide her out the door for a moment before reality set in. She stopped and he looked down at her, puzzled. "I can't," she moaned. "I can't face everybody. Beckam and Raven and Mari... Oh, Mari will give me such a hard time. And Reid, oh your brother! I can't. I can't face everybody," she finished mournfully.

Valen took compassion on her. "Don't worry about it. You go to your room and relax. I will go to dinner and deal with everybody. I will tell them what's going on, so you don't have to. I'll bring dinner back to my room. We can eat in here."

Zalia shook her head. "You don't have to do that. I'm not hungry. Don't worry about me. You can just eat dinner with everybody else. I don't want you to miss that."

Valen looked down at her. "Let me deal with this. You go rest. I'll see you in a little bit." Zalia didn't know what else to say, so she just walked numbly to her room. "Zalia," he called a moment later. "Everything will be okay. I promise." Zalia nodded and walked away.

She walked into her room and collapsed on her bed. *What in the world have I gotten myself into?*

Chapter Seventeen

Zalia didn't realize how tired she was until she woke up. She looked next to her bed and saw the plate of food on the table. A cloth was covering it, and above the cloth was a small note. She picked it up and read it.

I'm glad you were able to get some rest.
Come find me when you wake up.
-V

Zalia's heartrate picked up just reading the note. She lay back down and threw her arm over her eyes. I'm in so much trouble, she groaned to herself. She lay there a few more minutes, then sat up. She pulled the plate of food into her lap and picked at it. She wasn't really hungry. Her stomach rolled at the sight of food, but she ate a few bites because she knew she needed to. After she finished eating, she decided to stop hiding in her room. She didn't know what to do about Valen yet, but she wasn't a coward. She needed to keep moving forward in her training. She'd missed a lot lately. She decided to head to the training hall. Absently, she thought about the other princes and wondered why they hadn't shown up yet. She would have to ask Beckam about it.

She walked into the training hall a few minutes later and heard sounds of training going on in Beckam's corner, so she headed there, and saw Beckam and Valen training together. They both had their shirts off and were covered in sweat. When they heard her approach, they stopped and looked toward her. Zalia wasn't in the mood to be babied. "Valen, I haven't worked on my sword fighting skills for a while. Will you train me for a little bit?" He looked at her for a moment, then nodded. Without waiting for either of them to say anything, Zalia turned away to retrieve a sword from the armory.

She met Valen in his training area. He had put his shirt back on, and once again she was very grateful. He looked at her questioningly when she walked in. She didn't want to talk about anything. She just wanted to lose herself in her training and hopefully tire herself out enough to sleep without nightmares tonight. Valen seemed to understand her need to train and not talk. He led her in a grueling practice. They trained together for two hours, with the only communication between them being a few comments from Valen strictly on training. After two hours, Valen finally said. "Okay, we're done for the night."

Zalia argued with him. "Let's keep going. I'm not tired yet," which wasn't exactly the truth. She was starting to shake with fatigue. She was afraid to stop training though, for fear he would talk again. She didn't think she could handle any more tonight.

Valen shook his head. "Nope. We're done. Come on." Zalia wanted to argue but found she didn't have the energy. She simply nodded. Then she walked over, wiped her sword down and put it away. She was surprised to see Valen waiting for her when she turned around. He didn't say anything; he just waited for her and then walked next to her. When they got to her room, Zalia rushed because she didn't want an awkward goodnight. "Thanks for training me and thanks for the food. Have a good night," she said quickly then slipped inside her room and closed the door. She leaned her head against the door quietly and heard him chuckle softly as he walked away.

Zalia let out the breath she didn't realize she had been holding. She drew in a shaky breath. What a day! She didn't even know what to think. Before she had a chance to move, she heard a knock on her door. Fearing it was Valen, Zalia stood frozen to her spot. Then she heard Raven's voice, "Zalia, it's me."

Zalia opened the door. "Quick, let me come in before he sees me," Raven said as she pushed her way inside. Zalia looked out into the hall.

"Before who sees you?" she asked.

"Prince Valen," Raven replied.

Zalia stared at her in confusion. "I don't understand."

Raven explained. "Valen came to dinner tonight and told everybody that you bear his marks. He said that because of your healing powers, you two would bond sooner than later. Then he threatened everybody and told them that you don't want to talk about it and that we are all supposed to leave you alone. Now, tell me. What is going on?" she squealed.

Zalia laughed at her. "You just said that Valen said not to talk to me about it."

Raven shrugged it off. "He wasn't talking to me, of course. You're my best friend!"

Zalia couldn't help it. Tears sprang to her eyes. She knew her emotions were overwrought because of everything going on.

Raven looked at her in surprise. "Zalia, what is it? Aren't you happy that you are going to bond with Mr. Tall,

Dark, and Dreamy?"

Despite her tears, Zalia laughed. "Really? That's what you call him?"

"Yep. Mari and I both do," she said unapologetically. Zalia smiled again. Raven walked over to her. "What's wrong?"

Zalia just reached out and hugged her. "I never had a best friend before," Zalia whispered quietly. "It just made me happy to hear you say that."

"Happy? You have a funny way of showing it," Raven said teasingly. "Seriously, you've never had a close friend? You're a princess!"

"A princess who was never allowed to be around anybody," Zalia said sadly.

"Well, enough tears," Raven said. "You have lots to talk about. Details, please," she said as she sat on Zalia's bed.

Zalia looked at her warily. "What do you want to know?"

"Everything!" she said. "Don't leave out anything. Did he kiss you?"

Zalia gasped. "No!" It was going to be a long night! Zalia had just opened her mouth to start her story when another knock sounded at the door. This time both Raven and Zalia froze. Then Zalia heard Valen's low voice.

"Zalia, it's Valen." Zalia turned quickly to Raven who

sat on her bed with huge eyes. Zalia pointed to the bottom of the bed and Raven nodded. She quickly climbed off the bed and slid underneath. Zalia straightened the bedding, so Raven was completely hidden underneath. Then she walked towards the door. Taking a deep breath, she opened it.

Valen stood there holding her dagger. "You left this in my room," he said.

"Oh," Zalia said as she reached for it. "I forgot I set it down in your room," she said and looked away. She was pretty sure she blushed over saying "his room." "Thank you," she said to him. He nodded. "Well, have a good night," Zalia said as she started to close the door.

"You too, Zalia," he said in his low voice, the one that made Zalia melt. Then just before the door clicked shut, she heard, "You too, Raven." Zalia heard his quiet chuckle in the hall. Zalia smiled ruefully and walked over to her bed.

"You can come out now," she told Raven.

Raven slid out from under the bed. "How did he know?"

Zalia laughed. "I don't know. Maybe he knows us too well. He knows you wouldn't have stayed away."

Raven scowled. "Well, anyway, spill it. Tell me what happened."

Zalia started with her fight with Beckam and told Raven everything. When she finished telling her about how Valen said they would bond, eventually get married, and nobody would stand in their way, Raven sighed.

"That's so romantic," she said.

Zalia laughed at her. "You're a mess," she said with a smile.

Raven looked at her. "So, what happens next?"

Zalia thought about it for a moment, "I guess we will bond."

Raven looked at her. "Are you okay with that?"

Zalia sat in contemplation for a moment. "I honestly don't know. It's so much to take in. I like Valen; I really do. It's just, I thought for so long he didn't like me. Now it's kind of hard to change my thinking. I mean I know he told me, but I guess it's going to take some getting used to."

Raven nodded. "Let him work for it," she said.

Zalia just smiled. "I love you, Raven."

"I love you too," Raven said.

They finished talking a few more minutes later, and Raven headed to her room for the night. Zalia didn't waste any time getting ready for bed. She fell asleep with a smile on her face, thinking about Valen. It didn't take long, though, for her nightmare to take hold.

She walked through the castle with terror shaking her insides. All around her was death. She heard a voice cry out, and she looked over in horror to see her guard killed. She cried out and tried to help him, but it was to no avail. He was too far away from her and she couldn't get to him. She kept moving towards the throne room, knowing that she was running out of time. Her feet felt like lead, but she kept pushing forward. She had to get to the throne room.

She finally made it there and threw open the heavy door. Inside she found her family. They talked and carried on as if they didn't have a care in the world. She opened her mouth to try to warn them, but nothing would come out. She had to get closer. She tried to move forward, but invisible forces held her back. She opened her mouth to try to scream, and again nothing came out. She watched in horror as soldiers surrounded them. One by one, they killed her family. Zalia couldn't take the pain in her chest. She screamed until her throat was raw.

Slowly the dream faded, and Zalia felt somebody sitting next to her on the bed. Her dream was still too real to her and she cried out in fear and lashed out at the person. She felt her arms held down and heard a low voice in her ear.

"It's Valen. Shh. It's okay. I've got you. You're safe." He kept murmuring soft reassuring words, and Zalia stopped fighting him. She clung to him, and he shifted her over and then climbed into her bed and lay beside her. He drew her into his arms and began to rub her back and speak soothingly to her.

For the first time in a long time, Zalia felt safe. She fell asleep in his arms.

———————

She awoke the next morning and looked over to where Valen had laid during the night. His spot was empty. She wasn't sure when he had left during the night, but she had slept without any nightmares the rest of the night. She sat up and stretched and climbed out of bed.

She needed to get a bath and get dressed for a full day of training. If she moved quickly, she would have time to help Mari get breakfast ready.

Zalia headed to the kitchen a little while later. She was greeted by a smiling Mari and a big hug. Mari pulled back and looked at Zalia. "So..."

Zalia looked at her innocently. "So what?"

Mari gave her a knowing grin. "So, you and the Prince, huh?"

Zalia blushed. "I guess," she said.

Mari was gracious and let the matter drop. They worked together in happy silence until Valen came in a few minutes later. Zalia had just picked up a heavy pot of potatoes and was carrying it to the stove. Without saying a word, Valen took it from her and set it on the stove. He turned back to her.

"Thank you," she said quietly. He nodded and stepped closer, gently pushing back a few of the curls that had escaped her braid.. Then he left her and walked over to get coffee. Zalia could feel that her face was red. She just kept working, trying to ignore Valen. Finally, he left, and she was able to take a deep breath. When she looked at Mari, Mari was grinning at her from ear to ear.

Zalia turned back around to focus on the jam she was making. A few minutes later, Raven came into the kitchen and joined them. Mari kept a lively conversation going with the two of them. They worked hard, and soon everybody started joining them for breakfast. Zalia found herself getting nervous. What if somebody says something? How do I act normal? Will he expect me to sit by him?

By the time Valen came back into the kitchen for the second time, Zalia was a ball of nerves. She had just decided she would skip breakfast and was heading towards the door when Valen came in. She froze. He looked at her and stepped close to her. Talking in a low tone so nobody but Zalia could hear him, he asked, "You weren't leaving just now were you?"

Zalia lifted her chin into the air. "Maybe," she said.

He smiled and pulled her chin back down. "Don't point your chin up defiantly at me like that or you might not like the consequences," he said.

She opened her mouth to argue with him, but he leaned even closer.

"I didn't say I wouldn't like the consequences," he whispered suggestively next to her ear. Then he turned and walked away.

Zalia felt her face turn red. She knew she was lit up like a Christmas tree. That man knew how to get to her! She looked up and saw him sitting at the table smirking at her. She wanted to throw something at him. She swallowed her frustration and walked over to the table, only to realize the only available seat was next to Valen. She groaned quietly and went to sit next to him. As she got closer, he pulled her seat out for her. She noticed he pulled it slightly closer to him as he pulled it out.

She sat down stiffly. "Thank you," she said quietly.

He leaned towards her and spoke softly. "You're welcome and thank you for making breakfast. It looks amazing, as always."

His compliment sent pleasure rushing through her. She smiled. She looked up just then and saw Beckam watching the two of them with a big grin. She had the sudden urge to wipe the grin off his face. She was still mad at him from yesterday. She stuck her tongue out at him, and he laughed out loud. She knew it was childish, but she couldn't help it.

Valen leaned really close. "I wouldn't stick that tongue out at any other men if I were you," he growled low in her ear.

Zalia choked on her food. Beckam just laughed louder.

Chapter Eighteen

Zalia finally made it through breakfast. She stood up and pushed her chair back. She was ready to get away from Valen. "Raven," she called out. Raven looked up at her. "Are you ready to get training for the day?" Zalia asked her. Raven just grinned at her, knowingly.

"Sure," Raven said as she stood up and picked up her plate. They both put their plates away and headed towards the training hall. Zalia stopped in the hallway. "Shoot. I forgot my dagger in my room. Do you want to go on ahead without me? I won't be far behind you."

Raven nodded. "Sure. I'll see you in there"

Zalia turned and walked back to her room. Once she was inside, she grabbed her sheath and wrapped it around her leg. Then she put her dagger in. She walked to the bathroom to touch up her hair before heading to the training hall. She stepped inside and moved towards the washbasin. She heard the door close softly behind her. She whirled around, but it was too late. Rough hands grabbed her. Zalia screamed, but it was muffled against the hand over her mouth. Her captor put a knife to her throat, and Zalia froze. "You're coming with me," she heard a menacing voice say in her ear. He started dragging her to the door.

Zalia panicked for a moment, before calling on her training. She allowed him to drag her to the door because she needed to be in the hallway to be able to attract somebody's attention. She thought it through carefully and quickly. She would get one chance at this. Her room was not too far from the entryway. If he got her outside, she was done for.

Once they got to the hall, Zalia feigned a trip and let her weight fall on him. For just an instant, he had to adjust to her added weight and moved the knife a fraction away from her throat.

Zalia didn't think. She just acted. "Valen!" she screamed as loud as she could while simultaneously ripping her dagger from her sheath. She pulled it up and plunged it into the arm holding the knife. Cursing, the man dropped the knife. Zalia made a move to stab him with her dagger, but he surprised her with a high kick. His kick knocked the dagger out of her hand and out of her reach. A second later, he punched her abrasively in her stomach. Zalia bent in half, trying to catch her breath. He wasn't done. With the arm that was still gushing blood, he pummeled her again. This time, Zalia fell to her knees. He kicked her in the ribs once before Zalia managed to roll away. She flung herself at her dagger and grabbed it. As he came at her from behind, she turned and stabbed him, catching him in his side.

Screaming in rage, he tackled her to the ground. He managed to grab his own knife and plunged it into her shoulder. She couldn't move. She watched as his hand raised again, knowing this was going to be a killing blow, but he never made the move.

Zalia heard a roar of rage, and the man was suddenly ripped away from her and thrown into the wall. An enraged Valen stabbed him before he even had a chance to defend himself. In a rage, Valen stabbed him again and again. Beckam came racing down the hall, followed by two of the guards. They took in the scene quickly. Beckam fell to his knees beside Zalia. "Zalia," he breathed. He made a move to touch her and heard a roar behind them. Beckam froze.

Zalia looked up in fear and saw Valen in full battle mode. He was standing in a ready position to fight. His sword was out and his eyes were so black, Zalia couldn't see the pupils anymore. She had never seen him so angry. It scared her to death.

Beckam made a show of putting his palms up in the universal sign of surrender. He began to back away slowly. Zalia made a small sound of protest. Without ever looking away from Valen, Beckam began talking to Valen in low, quiet terms.

"Look, I'm moving away. I'm not here to hurt her or take her from you. See, I'm moving far away." Zalia watched in confusion as the other two guards did the same.

Still without ever taking his eyes off Valen, Beckam said in a low, urgent tone. "Zalia, listen very carefully to me. You need to talk Valen down. He's in a full fury. He will kill anybody that gets near him or you right now."

Zalia looked at Valen. He hadn't moved a muscle. Zalia shook her head at Beckam. "I can't. If he'll kill you, he'll kill me."

Beckam said quietly. "No, he won't. You are the only one safe right now."

Zalia tried to sit up but couldn't. Gritting her teeth, she called out in a low soothing voice, "Valen, please stop. I'm hurt. I need you to put down your sword and help me." When he didn't move, Zalia put authority into her voice. "Valen, I need you now!"

His head moved slightly in her direction, and Zalia

could see he was trying to come out of it. He shook his head once. Then he shook his head again and started stalking towards her. He took in the blood all over her and grit his teeth. She could tell he was going to go all crazy again. He was close enough, so she reached out and grabbed his hand. She pulled him down until he was sitting next to her. She reached up and grabbed his face. "Valen, I need you now. Please come back to me." As soon as she touched his face, she could see the crazed look fade from his eyes.

He looked down at her and oh so gently pulled her into his arms. He looked down at her with anger boiling in his eyes, but he spoke to her gently. "Can you heal yourself?" Zalia was starting to fade from the loss of blood. She reached up and touched her wound. She felt nothing. She looked up into his eyes and confirmed that it wasn't doing anything.

"It's okay. We will just heal it the old-fashioned way." Valen whipped his shirt off and pressed it against her wound. Then he turned into full prince mode and started barking out orders at the guards. "Gregory, get Collette to get washcloths and hot water. Conlyn, find Mari and tell her to prepare a tea with healer's brew." He looked down at Zalia.

Zalia started to move around, trying to get away from the burning pain in her shoulder. "Try not to move, sweetheart. That will make it worse. Just focus on breathing for me. Okay? Deep breath in, deep breath out." Valen gently picked her up and carried her to her room, gently placing her on the bed. "Here you go. Everything is going to be okay."

He turned away for a moment, and in a panic, Zalia reached out to him. He turned back to her. "Shh. It's okay. I'm not leaving." He used his thumb to carefully brush the tears from her cheeks.

Zalia was in so much pain. She had never felt anything like this before. She wondered how in the world Valen had survived all the wounds he had sustained. Zalia started fading as people began coming in and working around her. She couldn't pay attention to details. She only knew that Valen had her hand, and she was hanging on to it for dear life.

Mari brought a cup of tea up to Zalia's lips. Valen held her head up, so Mari could gently help her drink the tea. Zalia took a small sip and gagged on it. It tasted awful. She tried to pull her head away, but Valen wouldn't let her.

"I know it tastes horrible, but it will help to take the pain away and heal your wound. Please drink it," Valen spoke to her softly.

Zalia didn't think. She just drank until it was gone. "That's my girl," she thought she heard Valen say. She must have been getting groggy because that didn't sound like him at all. He was usually angry.

She felt someone start touching the wound, putting some kind of ointment on it. She felt like she was going to be sick. She felt pressure on the wound, and that was enough to send her over the edge into the waiting blackness.

When Zalia awoke, she opened her eyes slowly, taking in the room. She saw Valen sitting in the chair next to her bed. It was DeJa'Vu. She tried to turn to look at him and say something, but the movement caused her shoulder to move and pain erupted. Zalia couldn't help herself. She cried out in pain. Valen was instantly there. "Shh. It's okay. Here." He lifted her head gently and helped her drink the awful healer's brew. She dutifully gagged it down. "That's good," he said as he pulled the cup away and set it down on the small table next to her bed.

Zalia wanted to thank him, but she felt the medicine begin to work quickly. She just stared up at him. "Just rest now," he said gently. Soon Zalia couldn't keep her eyes open. She closed her eyes and fell into oblivion once again.

The next time she opened her eyes, she instantly looked for Valen. He came towards her as soon as he saw she was awake. He helped her drink more of the healing drink. She went back to sleep moments later. Each time she woke up, it was the same thing. It didn't matter what time of day it or night it was, Valen was always there to take care of her. If Zalia was more with it, she would probably think about it more. But she couldn't. She just kept sleeping.

Finally, Zalia woke up and felt like she was starting to recover. She looked around for Valen but didn't see him. She swallowed her disappointment.

Shutting down her emotional thoughts that would only get her into trouble, Zalia looked around her room. She wondered how long she had been sleeping and healing. The sleeping aide in the tea had knocked her out every time she drank it. She knew she needed it to help her body heal. With the rest and the healing power found in the herbs of the tea, she couldn't believe how much better she was feeling already. "Well, I guess I should try getting up," she mumbled to herself. She was in desperate need of a bath.

Very slowly, she worked herself into a sitting position. It was painful, but she was able to do it. The effort cost her, though. Already, she had sweat breaking out on her forehead; but she was determined to get a bath. Laboriously she moved and soon she had her legs over the side of the bed. The last thing now was standing up. She stood up slowly and took a few steps towards the bathroom. Instantly, she knew it was the wrong decision. She was so dizzy and weak. Her legs were shaking, her arm was aching, and she felt like she was going to fall over.

Just then, her door opened and Valen walked in. He took one look at her and stepped forward and gently grabbed hold of both of her arms. "Why are you out of bed?" he asked in a low voice.

Zalia couldn't seem to form a coherent thought both because of her weakened state and his nearness. He started to move her gently backwards to the bed. She suddenly remembered. "I need a bath," she blurted out, then blushed furiously.

Valen stopped moving her backwards and looked down at her. "Do you think you're strong enough for a bath?" he asked.

Zalia nodded. She had no idea if she was or not, but she needed a bath desperately. Seeing her nod, he turned her and began leading her to the bathroom. Apparently, Zalia wasn't moving fast enough, because he moved behind her and swooped in and picked her up. The move surprised Zalia and she gasped. He looked quickly down at her. "Did I hurt your shoulder?"

"No," Zalia said quietly. He moved with her carefully into the bathroom. He set her down where she could lean against the wall. Then he walked over and started the bath for her. When he walked back over to her, she just looked up at him.

"I'm going to grab Mari to help you, okay? I'll be right back," he said and headed for the door.

Zalia got to work undressing. She didn't want to undress in front of Mari. She tried to undress but found she simply couldn't because of her arm. By the time Mari got to her, Zalia was all worked up. She was angry because she couldn't get undressed with her arm, she was in pain, and she was tired again.

Mari walked in, took one look at her, and said, "Oh my dear, let me help you." She came over and helped Zalia get undressed and into the tub without making Zalia feel awkward or embarrassed. She helped Zalia wash her hair and her body. Then she helped her climb out, get dried off, and into fresh underclothes. She pulled a clean soft blue dress over Zalia's head. Then she guided her to her bed and made her sit while she took a comb through her curls. When she was finally done, Zalia was exhausted, but she felt good. It was so good to be clean finally. She lay back on her bed and rested while Mari went to go get her some food.

She must have dozed off because when she awoke, Valen was back in her room and Mari was nowhere in sight. When she saw she was awake, he came over to her bed and sat on it. "How are you feeling?" he asked in his low soothing voice.

Zalia took stock of her pain. "Not as much pain as before," she said simply.

Valen nodded. "Are you hungry? Mari left some food for you." He indicated the plate. Zalia nodded, not because she was hungry, but because she knew she needed to eat to be able to heal completely. He helped her sit up and get settled, then handed the plate to her. She ate a few bites and then asked him a few questions.

"How long has it been since..." she trailed off.

Valen knew exactly what she was talking about. "Four days," he said darkly.

She didn't want to talk about it, but she felt she needed to for closure. "Who was it?" she asked quietly. She didn't think Valen was going to answer her. He was quiet for several minutes before he finally started speaking in a voice that sounded like rage under control.

"He was from my father's kingdom. He came into the training hall by himself. We found two other soldiers working with him outside the training hall. We think he meant to grab you and get you outside. He wasn't expecting much of a fight from a princess. We got rid of him and his friends, so they couldn't report back to my father. He will know something happened to them, but he will not be able to confirm your existence yet. I'm sure he will try again, but we will be ready." He said these last few words so deadly and calm that Zalia knew he was really upset. She lay her hand on his arm but didn't say anything. She ate a few more bites, then handed it back to him.

"Thank you," she said. "And thank you for telling me about the attack and for saving me that night," she said, shuddering as she said it.

He looked down at her, his eyes dark with anger. "That attack should never have happened. As soon as you are healed, we are bonding," he said. Then he stood up to go back to his chair.

Zalia was going to argue with him but knew right now was not the time. He was angry, and she was weak. That was not going to be a good combination. She knew he would never hurt her, but she needed him to be in a good frame of mind when they talked about bonding.

Chapter Nineteen

Zalia spent the next few days recovering. Each day she got stronger, and she had mixed emotions about that. She was happy she was healing and getting her strength back, but each day brought her one step closer to bonding with Valen. Thinking of Valen, Zalia sighed. He was strung so tightly right now. He'd ordered protective guard on her 24/7. When he wasn't around, one of the other guards shadowed her. During the night hours, somebody stayed awake outside her room. She was never left without a guard. It made her feel like she was going crazy. She was no longer a helpless, weak princess in her father's kingdom. She didn't need all the extra protection!

Valen was gone a lot. She wasn't sure where he kept going, because nobody would answer her questions. Whenever he came back, he always came to see her; but he was always vague about where he had been.

Today she woke up, tired of resting and feeling ready to get back to her life. She got up, took a bath, and got dressed. It took her a while because she was slow. She finally finished. With a smile on her face, she stepped out into the hall ready to take her life back. She came face to face with Conlyn, one of the guards.

"Princess Zalia, how are you feeling?" he asked politely.

"I'm doing well, thank you for asking." She stepped around him. He stepped into place right behind her. Zalia looked back at him. "What are you doing?"

"I'm your protection, Princess," he said.

Zalia bit back her frustration. "Yes, I know; and you have done a great job of protecting me. But I am back on my feet now. I'm going to the kitchen, so you don't need to follow me."

Conlyn didn't budge. "Prince Valen said that you are to be under protection every moment of the day."

Zalia frowned. "Is Prince Valen here right now?" He shook his head. "All right then. I can give my own orders. I don't need protection right now. Thank you." He opened his mouth to argue, but Zalia was not in the mood. "That's an order."

"But Prince Valen..." he argued before Zalia cut him off.

"I will deal with Prince Valen," she bit out. Then before she could get more frustrated, she walked towards the kitchen. Inside, Mari was busy cooking breakfast.

She looked up as Zalia entered the kitchen. "Zalia, oh my dear. How are you?" She walked over and gave Zalia a gentle hug. "Come sit down," she said, indicating a chair to Zalia.

"Mari, I have been in bed for days. I am going crazy. I have to get back to my life. Please let me help you, and don't baby me," Zalia implored her.

Mari looked at her for a moment, then said, "What are you standing there for? We have work to do."

Zalia smiled and got busy. She worked with Mari for the next hour. They laughed and talked and had a good morning together. Zalia was feeling tired, and her arm was starting to get achy. She pushed it aside because she felt so good being out of bed and getting back on track with her life. Everything was going perfectly well until she turned around and nearly ran right into a scowling Valen.

"Valen," she exclaimed, "you scared me!"

Valen looked at her with that intimidating look he had perfected so well. "What are you doing in here?" he asked in a clipped voice.

Zalia looked over at Mari for a fraction of a second and saw her grinning. "Busted," she mouthed to Zalia. Zalia frowned at her and turned back to Valen.

"First of all, I don't answer to you. Second, I am busy getting breakfast ready. I am sure you could see that," she said haughtily as she turned and moved away from him. Valen moved right in step with her so that he was blocking her path again.

"I can see that you are making breakfast," he said slowly and calmly. "I am asking *why*. Why are you in here making breakfast when you're supposed to be in bed? And why did you tell Conlyn not to worry about protecting you?

Zalia realized she needed a different approach. Swallowing her irritation, she tried to soften her approach. "Valen," she put her hand on his arm. "I have been in bed for far too long. I am going crazy. I have to start getting back to my life, and you have to let me," she said sternly.

He opened his mouth to argue, but she reached up and put her finger on his lips, effectively quieting him. "No. I have to do this. I need to get back to training and get strong again. How will I ever be ready to head back to my kingdom if all I do is sit around?" At her mention of her heading to Arrosa, his eyes darkened with anger. She dropped her hand and took a step back from him. "Please?" she implored him.

He relaxed slightly and some of the anger drained from him. "Fine, but you have to keep a guard on you at all times. I am not willing to give on that." Zalia started to argue with him, but he cut her off. "I need to know you're safe. I'm sorry, but I can't budge on that."

Zalia looked up at him. He was trying to compromise; she could compromise too. "All right," she said quietly. They both stood there for a moment. He reached down and gently touched her shoulder. "How are you feeling?" he asked.

"It gets better every day," she said.

"Are you sleeping?" he asked. Zalia knew he was referring to her nightmares. Zalia just shrugged. His eyes narrowed at that.

"I'm fine," she said softly. "Can I get back to work now?" she asked with a grin. She was about to step away from him when she really looked at him. "Are you okay, Valen? You look exhausted."

"I'm fine," he said briskly.

Zalia looked up at him and then at Mari. "I'll be right back, Mari," she called out. She grabbed Valen's hand with her good arm and pulled him into the hallway. He allowed her to lead him. She led him right around the corner to an empty room. "Where have you been?" she asked. Before he opened his mouth, she said, "And don't try to get around the truth. Just tell me what's going on."

Valen ran a hand through his hair. "I'm just trying to take care of business. Nothing you need to worry about."

Zalia frowned up at him. "When was the last time you slept?"

Valen shrugged. Zalia looked up at him. "Valen, you're not invincible, you know. You have to get rest."

"I will," he said, aggravation creeping into his voice.

"When?" Zalia pushed him.

"When what?" Valen growled at her.

"When will you sleep?" Zalia knew she was pushing him, but she was trying to get him frustrated so he would just tell her what he was up to.

"When I can!" he snapped at her.

Zalia's heart hurt for him. He carried the weight of the world on his very capable shoulders, but he was still human. She took a chance and reached up to palm his cheek. He instantly stood utterly still, his eyes darkening. "I'm just worried about you," she said quietly. "Please let me into your life. I want to know what you're doing."

Valen didn't say anything for a moment. Then finally he said in a quiet low voice, "My father has plans to move on Verdia.. I'm trying to stall the plans without him figuring out it's me.

"Oh Valen, I'm so sorry," Zalia said softly.

He blew out a frustrated breath. "The realm is in total disarray. Verdia and Sol are the closest kingdoms geographically. I can only assume if my father attacks Verdia,

Sol will unite and stand with them. In the meantime, your kingdom is being controlled by my father's guards. I have other soldiers in my father's kingdom to keep me apprised of his actions. I feel like it's all on the tip of falling apart, and we are precariously close to falling into an all-out war among the kingdoms. On top of all that, I hate leaving you here. It kills me to not be here to protect you." He sighed. "I feel like everything is spiraling out of control."

Zalia's heart broke for him. He had so much pressure on him. It was too much! The fate of the entire realm couldn't depend on one person. She didn't know what to say, so she just stepped forward and wrapped her arms around his middle in a hug. It took a moment for him to respond. Zalia smiled. She had surprised him.

His arms came around her, and he held her ever so gently against his chest. She felt him relax after a moment and rest his chin on her head. "I'm sorry. You have the weight of the world on your shoulders." She pulled away from him and looked up at him. "What can I do to help?"

He looked down at her. "Stay safe," he said. Zalia just shook her head. She was already running through a hundred different scenarios in her mind. She looked up at him. "I could travel to Arrosa." He was already shaking his head, but Zalia carried on. "If I took control there, that would be one less kingdom you have to worry about. You could focus on..."

"Zalia, no," he said angrily, cutting her off.

"But Valen," she got out before he interrupted her again.

"No," he said.

"But," she tried again.

"It's not going to happen. I can't risk anything happening to you. Arrosa is in chaos right now. I'm not sending you there by yourself. It's just not going to happen. I wouldn't know if you were safe or not, and it would kill me," he growled at her.

"Then go with me," Zalia said. "Help me establish my rule over my kingdom. We can do it together. If we gain control of Arrosa, we can invade your father's kingdom and overthrow his rule there. You would control Astra. When we, uh, move forward with things, we could establish rule over both kingdoms," she finished quickly, stumbling over the last part.

He smirked at her. "When we marry, you mean?"

Zalia's face turned red. "You knew what I meant," she grumbled.

His smile faded, and she could tell he was actually considering what she said. After what seemed like forever, he said, "I'll think about it." That surprised Zalia; she expected more of a fight.

Maybe he's starting to get used to me, Zalia thought to herself. Then she laughed. *Probably not.*

Valen looked at her. "What are you laughing at?" he asked.

Zalia just smiled at him. "Just myself. Come on. We've been gone long enough. There's not going to be any breakfast left, and I'm starving!"

Valen gave her a full smile as they headed out the door and back into the kitchen. Zalia walked in with Valen right behind her. She met Beckam's eyes as she moved towards the table. He lifted an eyebrow and winked at her. Zalia rolled her eyes at him. She moved over to the open chair next to Raven. Raven leaned close and whispered in her ear, "It's okay, I would need Valen time too if I were you." Zalia elbowed her. Zalia started to reach for food to fill her plate, avoiding Mari's knowing glance and smile as she did. When she tried to lift a particularly heavy bowl with her bad arm, she grimaced. Immediately, Valen lifted it out of her arms. He gave her a helping and set it back without a word.

Zalia leaned close to him for a moment. "Thank you," she said quietly. He just nodded and continued the conversation he was having with his brother and Beckam.

After breakfast, Zalia walked with Raven to the training hall. Beckam, Valen, and Reid were right behind them. Raven hooked her arm through Zalia's good arm and asked her, "How are you doing with everything?" Zalia knew her all too well. What she was really asking was, "How are things going with Valen?" Zalia smiled.

"Really good," she whispered to Raven.

Raven leaned even closer. "Has he kissed you yet?"

Zalia smacked her arm. "No," she whispered.

Raven continued quietly, "Well, when he does, I want all the details."

"Stop it," she said. Raven just grinned at her. They got to the training hall and Zalia started out with a nice easy jog. Valen fell into place next to her. She looked up at him as she jogged. "What are you doing?" she asked him.

"I'm training with you," he replied without looking at her.

Zalia frowned and sighed. "I suppose you'll be taking over all my training now, huh?"

"Yes," he answered. Zalia groaned, and he looked down at her with a cocky smile.

Zalia spent some of her time just trying to get back in the swing of things. Valen had her start some light strength training for her bad shoulder. Then she did light work with her sword and dagger.

They broke for lunch, and everybody came in and sat down. Zalia smiled, listening to the conversation flowing around her. As she sat there, her body started stiffening.

She realized after a little bit that her arm was starting to hurt. By the time she was done eating, her shoulder was throbbing. The pain was starting to get to her, but she didn't want to say anything. She was contemplating what to say when Valen stood up. "We have a few things to do, so we won't be joining you for afternoon training," he told the others at the table.

Everybody just nodded. If Zalia had more energy, she would have argued with him; but she was in too much pain to think about it now. Valen put his arm around her waist and gently pulled her up out of her seat. He walked them towards the door and into the hall. As soon as the door closed behind them, he swept her up into his arms. Zalia was too worn out and in pain to argue. She simply put her head on his chest.

He looked down at her and frowned. "You did too much today. I shouldn't have let you do so much."

Zalia said quietly, "I'm fine. I have to start somewhere to get back on track with my training," she said quietly. She didn't say anything more. She was too weary. When they got to her room, Valen opened the door and placed her gently on her bed. She grit her teeth when her shoulder bumped the bed. It was really bothering her now after her training. She knew she had overdone it. She tried to just lay still and let the pain ease in her shoulder. Valen bent over her and touched her cheek gently.

"I'm going to get some healer's brew from Mari. I'll be back in just a few minutes," he said quietly.

Zalia nodded and kept her eyes closed. It wasn't long before Valen was back and helping her drink down her dose of healer's tea. It didn't take long for it to take effect, and she fell asleep.

Chapter Twenty

Zalia awoke some time later, surprisingly rested. She was beginning to think there was something in the tea that kept her nightmares away. She looked over and saw Valen sitting in the chair next to her bed, looking at a map or something in his lap. As soon as she turned her head towards his, he looked up at her and put it away. Zalia looked at him, confused. "What are you doing in here? You have a life; I don't expect you to stay by my side all the time," she finished.

Valen looked intently at her for a moment. Then he stood up. "I am going to help you get packed." He turned around and grabbed the bag she had brought with her from her grandfather's castle.

Zalia sat up, surprised. "What are we packing for?" she asked. Just then, somebody knocked on the door. Valen turned around and opened it, and Beckam strolled in. He was dressed in his warrior clothes, with his daggers tucked around his waistline.

He looked down at her and then to Valen. "The royal guard should be here in about twenty minutes; we need to be ready to move." Valen nodded. Beckam looked at Zalia. "Do you need any help?"

Valen moved in front of Beckam. "I got it." Beckam smirked and headed out the door.

"Wait!" Zalia called out as she stood up. "What's going on? Where are we going?"

Beckam walked back over to Zalia. "We're moving our training back to the castle. The training center's been compromised."

"But I thought you said you killed all the soldiers who made the attack?" Zalia asked in confusion.

Valen supplied, "We did, but we're not taking any chances with your life."

"We will have more security at the castle," Beckam said

Zalia looked at Beckam, then at Valen. "Won't everybody know who I am? Wasn't the whole point in coming here to keep my identity a secret until I was ready to head back to my kingdom?"

Beckam nodded. "Yes, but..."

Valen interrupted him "The plan's changed. Now let's

get you packed."

Zalia put her hands on her hips. "Wait just a minute. I'm not going anywhere until you tell me what's going on. How has the plan changed?" She looked at Beckam and Valen. Neither of them would say anything. "Hello, anybody going to answer me?" she asked.

"Beckam, what is the change of plan?" Beckam opened his mouth but hesitated and looked at Valen.

Valen spoke calmly, "We're going to your grandfather's castle to be bonded and then engaged. Once my ring is on your finger, Beckam and I will lead a contingency of soldiers to Arrosa and take back the power there. Then we will overthrow my father's rule in my kingdom. After that, we will merge the two kingdoms under our combined leadership."

Zalia's head spun. Her mind shut down right after he said bonded and engaged. Then she caught something he had said. "Wait, what about me?"

Beckam started slowly backing up and heading towards the door, but Zalia was not going to have that. "Stop," she called out, looking right at Beckam. She crossed her arms and glared at the two men. She narrowed her eyes at Valen. "You said you would think about me going with."

Valen didn't look the least bit intimidated when he replied. "I thought about it and decided against it. You will stay with your grandfather until I acquire both kingdoms. Then you will join me, and we will be married."

Zalia stared at him. Beckam at least had the decency to squirm. Valen didn't move a muscle, nor did he look away.

Zalia met his eyes. "I am not going to be staying in Cascadia. Those are my people, and that is my kingdom. I have been training for this, and neither you," she looked at Valen, "nor you," she said looking at Beckam, "are going to stand in my way. I will return with you to the castle. When it is time, I will go with you and fight with my people to overthrow your father's rule."

Valene shook his head. "I don't think so."

Zalia looked at him in shock and anger. "Well, you don't get a say."

Valen just narrowed his eyes at her. "Yes, I do."

Zalia stepped right up next to him and tipped her head back to look up at him. She was beyond angry. "You listen to me, Prince Valen," she spit out. "Just because I bear your marks, does not mean you get to tell me what to do. You don't get to order me around. I will return to my kingdom and take back the throne that is rightfully mine. I don't need you. Grandfather told me his men would return with me and fight with me. I will return as the rightful heir of Arrosa, and nobody will stand in my way. That includes you and you," she said looking first at Valen then Beckam.

"Now please leave my room, both of you. I need to pack, and I don't need your help to do it."

Beckam stood there for a moment, looking sorry. Then he turned and walked out. Valen wasn't going to be so easy. "Out, Valen," she said.

"Or what?" he asked calmly.

Zalia just stared up at him. He was making her furious. "Or I'll make you," she said.

He smirked at her. Zalia was so angry. Her emotions were all over the place, and his smirk was the final straw. Zalia stalked towards him, calling up every ounce of training she had been through. She began a series of punches and kicks meant to bring him down. His eyes showed just a hint of surprise at her first hit, but years of training kept him from taking her hit. He deflected each hit she threw at him but didn't fight back. Zalia was angry. She hit harder and moved faster.

"Zalia, stop," he said as he continued to deflect her blows. "You're going to hurt your arm."

Zalia didn't stop. She didn't think about her arm, she didn't think about her pain, she just let her feelings of rage consume her.

"Zalia stop!" Valen ordered. Zalia kept going. "Enough!" he roared at her. Then he took her down hard on the floor. Just as her head would have hit the floor, he put his hand there, cushioning the hit. His full body pressed into hers on the ground, effectively pinning her down. An instant later, he had her good arm pinned above her head with one of his hands and her other arm pinned between their bodies. He leaned his body weight on his other arm, so he didn't crush her. He stared into her eyes. His gray eyes had darkened.

Zalia couldn't move. He had effectively pinned her. This made her even more furious, and she glared at him.

Valen took a deep breath. "You can't come with us into battle," he began.

Zalia opened her mouth to respond in anger but Valen cut her off. "Let me finish, and then you can attack me again," he said calmly. "If you were with me, I wouldn't be able to focus on what I need to do. I would be worried about you the entire time, and I could make a mistake."

Zalia opened her mouth again to argue, but Valen leaned close to her face. "I lost the only woman in the world I ever loved. Please don't ask me to put myself in position to let that happen again," he spoke the words so quietly, Zalia almost didn't hear them.

She looked up at him in shock. *Did he just admit he loves me?* Zalia didn't have a clue how to respond.

Valen continued in his quiet, low voice, "My mother was the light in our very dark world. She made the long days bearable. She loved my brother and me. She sang us to sleep at night; she stood before my father on a regular basis for us, defending us. When she died, I didn't think my world would ever have light in it again. I'd grown so accustomed to the darkness, but you brought light back into my life. You brought hope and joy for the first time in a long time, and I started seeing the world in color again. Zalia, you are my light. I can't lose you. If I lose you, I will be completely overtaken in darkness. I will become my father. You keep me from that. You have to survive. I have to know you're safe. That gives me the power to carry on."

Zalia was completely shocked. She didn't know what to say. Her heart felt such sorrow for this man and all that he had been through. She felt her cheek dampen as a tear slid down her face. Valen let go of her arms and very carefully wiped the tear away with his thumb. He cradled her cheek in his hand. He looked carefully in her eyes as if seeking permission, then slowly lowered his head, giving her plenty of time to pull away.

Zalia closed her eyes as Valen's lips descended on hers. It didn't last nearly long enough, and Zalia was already craving more. She felt him gently kiss her eyelids and then her forehead before he pulled back. Zalia slowly opened her eyes and met his. He was staring at her with such deep emotion that Zalia forgot how to breathe for a moment.

She wasn't used to emotion from Valen. He always seemed so cold. Zalia was just about to open her mouth and probably say something stupid when her door abruptly opened, and Raven stuck her head in.

"Hey Zalia, do you need help..." her words died off suddenly before she said, "Oops, sorry. I'll come back later." She was gone a second later.

Zalia felt her cheeks turn bright red, and she felt more than heard Valen's low chuckle through his chest. Valen rolled off her and stood up fluidly. He reached down and took her hand to help her off the floor. Once she was on her feet, he didn't let go of her hand right away. "Did you hurt your shoulder?" he asked softly.

Zalia rolled her shoulder a bit. It was sore, but not nearly as sore as it had been after training this morning. "It's okay," she told him. She tried to pull her hand away to start packing, but he didn't let go of his hold on it.

"Please promise me that you will stay in your grandfather's castle and under his protection," he asked her with pleading in his voice.

Zalia's heart felt heavy. "Valen, I want to, but I just can't. Those are my people. It's my battle."

Valen pulled her towards him and looked at her with such intensity in his eyes that it almost frightened her. "Then let me fight for you. You're a princess. You shouldn't have to be a warrior too. Let me be your warrior. I've trained my entire life for this. Your life is way too valuable."

Zalia frowned up at him, "Your life is just as valuable, Valen. I don't know why..."

Beckam stuck his head in, "The guard is here. We leave in five. Let's go." He was gone as quick as he came.

Zalia tried to pull away from Valen, but he didn't let her arm go. "Promise me, Zalia."

Zalia looked up at him. She knew when to fight and when to surrender. She knew instinctively this was not a battle she could win, and she didn't want to strain their very tentative relationship. "Fine. I promise. Now please let me go. Beckam's going to kill me."

Valen pulled her close to his body and exhaled. "Thank you," he said against her hair. Then he pulled away and was back to business, "I'll deal with Beckam if we need to. You just pack. Do you have your dagger?"

Zalia nodded as she kept packing. It only took her a few minutes, as she didn't have much to pack. The last thing she packed was her sketchbook and pencils. Valen looked at them in interest but didn't say anything.

"Okay, I'm ready," she said moving towards the door. Valen took her bag from her. With one hand on her back, he hurried them through the door. As they walked down the hallway towards the front of the building, Valen looked down at her.

"I packed your sword for you," Valen told her.

Zalia nodded. "Thank you," she said. They quickly arrived at the front of the training center. Mari stood there, next to the door. She approached Zalia and wrapped her in a hug.

"Zalia, my dear, I'm going to miss you. Don't be a stranger," she said as she stepped back.

Zalia looked at her in confusion. "Aren't you going with us?"

Mari just shook her head. "This is our home. This is where we belong."

Zalia opened her mouth to argue, but Mari continued on. "We will be fine. Don't you worry about us. We will keep this training center in optimal shape so you can come back and train again soon."

Zalia was sad to be leaving her. She had become like a mom to her after losing her own. She was surprised to find tears leaking from her eyes as she hugged Mari. Mari hugged her tightly. "My dear, you've been through so much for someone so young, but you're a fighter. You keep fighting. Don't let life keep you down. Your parents would be so proud of the woman you have become."

Zalia's tears fell in earnest now, and her throat clogged so that she couldn't say anything. She felt Valen move in close behind her. Mari pulled back and looked over Zalia's shoulder to Valen. "You take care of our girl. Protect her but don't crush her spirit."

Zalia didn't know how Valen responded, but then he stepped close and put a hand on her shoulder. She knew that was her cue to keep moving. Zalia said one more goodbye to Mari and turned to head out the door. Before she opened it, Valen stepped in front of her and stopped her. "You okay?" he asked in his quiet, low voice. Zalia still didn't trust her voice, so she just nodded. Valen put a finger under her chin and tipped her face up to meet his eyes. Zalia looked up into his dark eyes. He seemed to approve of whatever he saw, because he nodded. Then he reached down and grabbed her hand, opened the door, and led her out to the waiting group of soldiers.

Zalia took a deep breath as she headed outside. This was the next step of her journey. She had a feeling it was going to get worse before it got better.

Chapter Twenty-One

Once outside, Zalia let Valen lead her over to two horses. Beckam headed their way, angry. "Took you long enough," he said by way of greeting. Valen dropped her hand and turned to step in front of her before Beckam got to them.

"Leave it," Valen said. Beckam looked at him for a moment, then spun away.

"Let's ride," Beckam called out to everybody.

Valen loaded Zalia's bag on her horse, then put both hands on her waist and boosted her up. "Thank you," she said quietly. He quickly moved to the horse next to hers and mounted up. Several riders, warriors from Cascadia, quickly surrounded Zalia. The way they positioned themselves made Valen have to pull his horse behind Zalia.

As they began riding, the solider to her right looked over at her with a smile. "Princess, I'm Edgar. It's an honor to be guarding you."

Zalia turned towards him and gave him a kind smile. "It's nice to meet you, Edgar." She looked at him for just a moment. He appeared tall with blond hair and blue eyes. He was good looking and knew it. He would be a danger to women. Good thing he didn't do anything for her. She was more into the silent, brooding type. As she looked at him, he gave her a rakish smile and waggled his eyes.

Zalia couldn't help it, she laughed out loud. "I bet you're popular with the women," she said with a smile.

"Well, a gentleman wouldn't agree to any such thing," he said with a wink. Zalia relaxed into her ride as Edgar kept her entertained with stories the entire ride. He was telling her an enthralling tale of one of his conquests as the castle came into view.

"Then out of nowhere, we were surrounded. We had to fight our way out of there in the darkness. The smell was terrible. We cut our way through the band of soldiers and found ourselves facing something that none of us ever expected." He paused for a moment for effect.

Zalia looked up at him, "What was it?" she asked out of mild curiosity.

"The serpent of Apep," he said, his eyes twinkling. Zalia knew he had her. She smiled at him.

"That's a pretty great tale. All you're missing is the

beautiful maiden at the end of the story," she laughed.

"Aw, that's where you're wrong, Princess. There *is* a beautiful maiden at the end of this story," he said as he winked. He then flashed her a mischievous smile.

Oh boy; this guy is trouble. Zalia smiled and looked away. She hadn't looked back at Valen and was wondering if he was catching any of this conversation. Zalia cringed and hoped not.

When they arrived in front of the castle, they were instantly surrounded by more of Beckam's warriors. She glanced up and saw more of his warriors on the walls of the castle in the ready position.

Zalia pulled her attention from all the security and looked back in front of her. Everybody had stopped and started dismounting. Edgar was off his horse in a flash and reached up for her. Zalia paused, knowing this probably wasn't going to end well. But knowing she didn't want to make a scene, Zalia allowed him to put his arms around her waist and pull her off her horse. When he put her down, he didn't drop his arms but took a step closer to her with his hands on her waist.

Zalia panicked for a moment. A second later, she heard him. "If you want to keep both hands, I suggest you take them off her," she heard Valen's low, deadly voice.

To her horror, Edgar didn't even flinch but drew her a

step closer. She looked up at him in alarm. He bent down to her ear and asked, "How far do you want to push him?" He pulled back and grinned at her. Zalia couldn't form a reply. Then again, she didn't need to. Valen grabbed him from behind, spun him around and cracked him across his jaw before Edgar even saw it coming. Edgar spun back after his hit with eyes blazing. Zalia saw his intent and moved between the two men before they made something more of this.

"Enough," she said softly so that they could hear her but nobody else around them could. She put a hand on each of their chests. She glanced at Valen and saw his eyes were black. His jaw was locked, and he was mad. She needed to diffuse this situation quickly. Before she said anything, Edgar stepped back and gave her a cocky smile.

"No worries, Princess. I'll back off." He backed away slowly. He started to back away from Zalia and Valen. Zalia took a deep breath of relief, and then he threw out, "Just keep your door unlocked at night," he said with a cocky smile.

"Shoot!" Zalia blurted out and turned in an instant to throw herself against Valen. He was going to kill Edgar! Zalia pushed against Valen with both arms, but he moved her away from him, his eyes locked in fury on Edgar.

Zalia didn't know what to do to stop him, so she did

the only thing she could think of. She stepped up on her tiptoes and threw herself into kissing him. He held himself rigid for a second before he pulled her close to his body as he deepened the kiss. This kiss was much different than their first kiss. This was a claiming kiss. He kissed her with so much passion. Her entire body was on fire. She needed to get closer to him. He must have felt the same thing, because without breaking the kiss, he lifted her closer to him. She straddled his waist with her legs and he cupped her backside. Zalia felt like she was drowning in his kiss. He pulled back and looked into her eyes, breathing hard. Zalia looked up at him in shock and ran her tongue over her swollen lips. He groaned and kissed her again. Zalia was totally lost in her emotions, until she heard a throat clear.

Like a splash of cold water, it brought Zalia to her senses. She looked down and realized she was off the ground in Valen's strong arms. She wiggled and he put her down gently but didn't step away from her. Zalia peeked back and saw that Beckam was standing there with his arms crossed and a big grin on his face. "You done, or do you need me to show you to a room?" he asked slyly. Zalia could feel her face heat up and knew she was a horrible shade of pink.

Zalia couldn't look at Valen. She was mortified at how she had responded to him. She kept her head down as she asked quietly, "Is everybody watching?"

"No. They all took off after you jumped me," he said. Zalia just groaned and put her head on his chest.

Beckam said, "Everybody took off after your showdown with Edgar." At the mention of his name, Valen turned angry again.

He looked down at Zalia and cupped her face in his hand. "Don't ever stand in front of me when a guy is angry and coming at me," he said in protective mode. Then his jaw clenched, and he said, "And keep away from Edgar. He's trouble," he said angrily.

"I will," she said seriously. "And I will lock my door at night."

"You don't need to worry about that," he said darkly.

"Why not?" Zalia asked.

"Because you will be in my room, and I will keep you safe," he said matter of fact.

Zalia sputtered, "I can't stay in your room! We're not married or even engaged!"

Valen just smirked, "I'm a prince. You're a princess. We can do whatever we want."

When Zalia opened her mouth to argue, he interrupted her. "But there's nothing to worry about. Our room is a two-bedroom suite. Now, let's get inside and unpacked." He grabbed their bags and gave the groundskeepers the horses to take away. He put his hand on her back and guided her towards the stairs. Beckam was waiting for them right in the entryway.

"Come on. I'll show you to your room. We have two hours until supper. Valen, my grandfather will want to meet as soon as possible." Valen nodded, and Beckam walked ahead of them.

He showed them to their room and left them. Valen opened the door and ushered Zalia inside where they found a large bed and a small table. Further into the room was a decent size sitting area and another door that led to a smaller bedroom. Zalia took her bag from Valen and took it into the smaller room. She made quick work of unpacking and putting her clothes away. She decided to take a bath to try to get the dust off from their afternoon ride. She started gathering fresh clothes when she felt Valen's presence. She turned to look at him.

He stood in the doorway of her room with his arms crossed, leaning against the doorframe. "How are you feeling?" he asked.

"My shoulder's feeling really good. I think it's almost one hundred percent. That healer's brew works wonders," she said.

He studied her quietly for a moment, and Zalia knew something important was coming. Zalia held herself perfectly still and waited for him to say something. She didn't have to wait long, and she was right. It was huge!

"I want to bond tonight," Valen said calmly.

Zalia stared at him in shock, then she opened her mouth and her thoughts came tumbling out. "Tonight?" she squeaked. "I mean, I know we've talked about it, and it's inevitable. But it's so soon. You don't even know if you like me. What if you want to kill me after we bond? I mean it's not like we get along great. Half the time you just put up with me. We don't even..."

In the blink of an eye, Valen had crossed the distance between them and put his mouth over hers, effectively silencing her. He kissed her long and hard. She responded to his kiss and kissed him back. He pulled back too soon, and Zalia breathlessly looked up at him. Her brain was a little fuzzy at the moment.

He reached up and cradled her face in his hands. "I do like you. I like you a lot. And we are going to bond. We need to bond before I leave. I need to know you're safe. Also, the bond will help ground you if you do any healings while we are separated. I think it may help with your nightmares too. You seem to do better when I am around, so maybe our link will help keep your nightmares away. I have to plan with Beckam and your grandfather, but after that, we are bonding. So, do whatever you need to do to talk yourself into it."

Zalia couldn't think of anything to say, so she just stupidly nodded. He bent down and kissed her lightly on the lips. "I have to go now. I'll be back to take you to dinner. Rest while you can, okay?"

Again, Zalia just nodded. She was going to have a full-blown panic attack, but she would wait until he was gone to do it. He studied her for a moment longer before turning and walking back into his room. He called out before he left, "Lock the door behind me, and keep your dagger on you at all times."

"I will," Zalia called out weakly. She stayed where she was until she heard the door close behind him. Then she walked over to the bed and lay down on her back. *What am I going to do?* She groaned to herself. It wasn't that she didn't like Valen. She liked him a lot. Sometime over the course of the last few months, she had given much of her heart away to him. She just felt so on edge with him. He seemed to be attracted to her, but would he be if she didn't wear his marks? She lay there for a few more minutes before hearing a knock at the door.

She opened the door to her friend. Raven walked in carrying a beautiful black dress. Zalia's interest was piqued. "What's the dress for?"

Raven laid it carefully down on Valen's bed and spun

around to give Zalia a hug. "It's for my best friend to wear for her bonding ceremony."

"And just like that, I can't breathe again," Zalia grumbled. Raven stepped back and looked at her compassionately.

"How are you doing with all this?" she asked Zalia.

Zalia just moaned. "I think I am going to be sick."

Raven walked over to a chair and sat in it. "Are you scared?" she asked quietly.

"Of Valen? No, I know he would never hurt me. I mean, he does scare me sometimes but not that he would ever do anything to harm me. I'm more scared that I am going to lose my heart to somebody that doesn't love me back."

Raven looked up at her. "I think he loves you."

Zalia looked at her in surprise. "Half the time he can hardly stand me."

Raven shook her head. "No, I've been watching the two of you for a long time. I think he loves you but is careful to not show you too much. If you could have seen the look on his face when Edgar was flirting with you, you would know what I'm talking about. That was not the look of a man who can't stand you."

"He hated me for so long that it's hard to get used to anything different," Zalia said.

Raven shook her head again. "No, I don't think he ever

hated you. I think he was attracted to you from the very beginning but couldn't allow himself to be. He dutifully waited for the woman bearing his marks. Then he found out it was you, and he allowed himself to have those feelings. By then, though, you were convinced he hated you. So, it has been a difficult road for both of you."

Zalia was quiet for a moment. "He's never said he loves me," she said quietly to Raven.

Raven sighed. "I'm sorry. Maybe he's waiting for you to say it first. Maybe he needs to know you're okay with all this." She sighed. "What do I know? I'm single. I've never even had a guy interested in me. So maybe I'm way off track, but I really don't think I am."

Zalia thought for a moment. "I do know that Valen is never going to be super expressive in his love. He's going to be more of the protector kind of lover. Maybe you're right. Maybe he's waiting on me, too scared of giving me more than I am ready for."

Raven stood up. "Well, we have a bonding ceremony to get ready for. We need to get to it."

Zalia looked at her. "It's after supper isn't it? I have plenty of time."

Raven frowned at her. "We are going to need those few hours to get you looking your best. You are tying your life to the tall, dark, and handsome Prince. You need to make this memorable. You're skipping dinner to beautify your-self. Beckam told me the ceremony will be right after sup-per. So, we have less than three hours."

Zalia spun around. "I'd better get started on a bath. Where is the ceremony going to be? Do you know?"

Raven was already busy pulling out supplies to make Zalia beautiful. "I think it's going to be outside by the fountain."

Chapter Twenty-Two

The next three hours flew by. Two hours in, Valen knocked on the door because Raven locked it. Raven met him at the door and told him he wasn't allowed to come in. Zalia heard her tell him that she was getting ready for the binding ceremony and wouldn't be attending dinner. Zalia couldn't hear his low response from where she stood in her room, but it was obvious he was not happy. Somehow Raven worked her magic and got him to leave. He told Raven he would be back in forty-five minutes.

Now, it was just a few minutes before that time. Zalia stood in front of the mirror, taking in her appearance. The dress Raven had brought was black, a tribute to Astra. She felt it only right since Zalia was marrying their prince. Zalia had been skeptical at first, but now as she looked at it, she realized Raven made the right choice. The dress had a rounded neckline that came just to the tip of her shoulders, and the back was rounded, leaving her marks on display. It had long sheer sleeves. The top was fitted, forming a V-shape at the waist. The dress was long, and the lower half had a sheer overlay. Tiny crystals embedded in the dress made the dress appear to shimmer as Zalia walked. The dress flowed around her elegantly. Raven piled Zalia's curls on top of her head and left a few down around her face. The effect was elegant and regal, a look befitting a princess. Raven helped redden Zalia's lips with a red stain. The black dress paired well with Zalia's light-colored skin and dark curls. She was pleased with how everything turned out.

As she stood staring into the mirror, she started thinking about what she was going to do. Then the panic started. With working so hard to get ready all afternoon, she hadn't had time to think about it but now all her doubts and fears came flooding in.

I'm going to be tied to him forever. Maybe this is a mistake. Zalia heard a knock at the door. Raven looked to her. "You look exquisite, Zalia. I love you. I am so happy for you," she said and hugged Zalia. She stepped back and looked her in the eye. "You are going to be fine. It will all work out. Now take a deep breath and be the strong, confident princess you are." Raven's words brought calm to her heart.

Raven turned and walked away to let Valen in. She heard Valen's low voice and just like that, the panic came flooding back. She couldn't catch her breath. There was a roaring in her ears that was getting louder by the second. She needed to get away, to run. She turned around and froze. Valen stood there silently taking her in. He was dressed in his royal attire. He looked devastatingly handsome in his black pants and white tunic top. He wore his black robe and had his sword strapped to his back. He looked every inch the Warrior Prince.

He stared at her with his unrelenting dark eyes. He stepped forward slowly until he was standing directly in front of her. He took a deep breath and seemed to be struggling with what to say.

Zalia was crestfallen. "It's the dress, isn't it? Raven told me I should wear black, but that was a bad idea. I can change. It will only take me a moment. I can just..."

"Please don't change," he said. His voice was lower than usual and a little husky. "You look beautiful. Can you turn around?"

Zalia nervously turned around slowly, presenting her back to him. She felt him caress his marks on her back. After a moment, he put his hands on her shoulders and gently turned her around. He stared down into her eyes. "You are the most beautiful woman I have ever seen," he said huskily. Then he bent his head slowly and kissed her. It was brief, but it seemed to settle them both. He pulled back and looked down at her. "Are you ready?"

Zalia was still trying to catch her breath, so she simply nodded. Valen walked toward the door and held it open for her. Once they were in the hall, he held out his arm to her. She placed her hand in the crook of his elbow, and he pulled her close. She felt absolutely regal, walking arm-in-arm with Valen down the hall. They walked outside together and Zalia saw people gathered around the fountain up ahead. She caught her breath. She didn't know people were going to be watching. She thought it was just a private ceremony. She started panicking. She couldn't do this. She started to pull her arm away from Valen's, but he wouldn't let her.

He stopped and turned towards her. "Zalia, everything is going to be okay; I promise. Nothing is going to happen tonight. It's just a bonding ceremony." He paused for a moment. "Can you tell me why you're so scared?" He asked her quietly. Nobody but Zalia could hear him.

Zalia looked up at him. "I'm not scared," she whispered to him.

"Sweetheart, you're shaking like a leaf," he said in concern. "Tell me what's wrong, so I can help fix it."

Zalia looked up at him, suddenly feeling bolder. "Do

you love me? Or are you just doing this because I have your mark?" She held her breath, scared to hear his answer.

He locked eyes with her and looked at her intensely. "I love you, Zalia. I have been unwilling to say it to you because I didn't want to scare you away. I have loved you for a long time but wouldn't act on it because I couldn't. Once I found out you bore my marks, I didn't want to scare you away with the intensity of my feelings. So, I just kept them to myself. I can see now I shouldn't have. The last thing I wanted was for you to doubt my love."

With that, the panic slid away and was replaced by tears. "Oh Valen," she said through her tears. He pulled her tightly to his chest.

He simply held her for a moment. Then he stepped back and looked into her eyes. "Are you ready to do this, my love?"

Zalia smiled up at him and placed her arm back in his. "Yes, my Prince. I am."

Together, they walked to the fountain where a few people were gathered. Her grandfather stood there surrounded by the smiling faces of Reid, Raven, Beckam, and Henrietta, the healer. Several armed guards stood around the perimeter, but they had their backs to them. Zalia smiled at each person gathered there.

Valen walked them over to her grandfather. Zalia released his arm for a moment to reach out and give her grandfather a hug. He looked at her seriously. "Are you okay with this, Zalia?"

Zalia smiled at him. "I am. I really am."

He smiled at her. "Well then let's get this ceremony started. Valen and Zalia, you stand here in front of me and join hands."

Zalia swallowed. It felt like a wedding ceremony after all. She looked up at Valen, and he eyed her with concern. Zalia forced a smile up at him. His eyes narrowed, but he didn't say anything. *He knows me so well*, she thought to herself with a smile.

Seeing her smile for real, Zalia could tell Valen relaxed. He stroked both of his thumbs over the tops of her hands as he held her hands for the ceremony.

The ceremony was a blur to Zalia. She had a hard time focusing with Valen looking so intently at her and rubbing her hands so intimately. Her grandfather talked about the bond between a royal and the one who bears his marks. He talked about what the bond entails and how it would take place. Finally, it was time to get to the actual bonding. Zalia looked away from Valen to focus on her grandfather. He pulled a dagger from his waistband. Zalia took a deep breath, knowing what was coming.

"I need both of you to hold out your right wrist," her grandfather said. Valen and Zalia did. Zalia noticed hers was slightly shaking. Her grandfather looked at her. "Zalia, I'm not sure exactly what will happen to your healing powers when you bond. I've never seen anyone bond with your powers before. We will just deal with it as it happens."

Zalia nodded and glanced at Valen. His jaw was tight. Her grandfather stood beside them and said, "This bond will forever bind the spirit of Zalia, daughter of King Warren of the Kingdom of the Red Rose to Valen, son of King Mylan of the Kingdom of the Dark Moon.

Then he slit each of their wrists quickly. Zalia grit her teeth against the pain. Zalia's instantly started glowing blue and little blues wisps floated up from her cut. She turned to Valen, alarmed. He looked to her grandfather. Her grandfather just motioned them together. Zalia turned her wrist to line up with Valen's. As soon as their wrists touched, a jolt hit them both hard. It was powerful enough that Zalia would have fallen backward if Valen hadn't grabbed her around the waist with his non-injured arm.

After the jolt, the blue sparks seemed to intensify instead of fade. Then they burst a bright blue color and slowly faded away. Zalia stood still. Henrietta came over as soon as they were done and put a healing salve on Zalia's wrist. Zalia reached for Valen's wrist to heal it, but he pulled away. She frowned up at him. He looked down at her and said quietly, "I want the scar." Then he held out his wrist for Henrietta to put salve on it. The moment she was done, he drew Zalia gently into his arms and kissed her. Everybody watching broke into cheers and whistles. Zalia pulled back and blushed.

You're so beautiful when you blush. Zalia froze. She looked up at Valen. He smiled down at her. Zalia continued looking at him while she tried out the connection.

Valen? she called out tentatively in her head.

It's me. What do you think? he asked.

It's amazing. Will we always be able to talk to each other this way or is there a distance where it no longer works? she asked.

It will always work, he said in her head. Then he smiled down at her. *Come on, beautiful, let's head back to our room.*

Valen walked over to thank Zalia's grandfather. Zalia was so happy in that moment. The next moment, everything went disastrously wrong.

There was a loud battle cry as soldiers came up over the wall in an attack. Valen shoved Zalia behind him and drew his sword. The warriors from Cascadia converged from all directions to take on the threat. Zalia withdrew her dagger from under her dress and held it in her hand. It didn't take long for her to be separated from Valen. A soldier came up behind her, but Zalia heard him coming. She spun around and dodged the blade he thrust at her. Zalia kept moving, using her quick feet to keep her out of the way of the blade. Her dagger wasn't going to help her with this. She wouldn't be able to get close for a killing blow because of his sword. Zalia saw her chance a moment later when he was fully extended. She went low and kicked his legs out from under him. He went down hard, and she followed with a killing blow to his heart. There was no time to think. Two soldiers came at her as she stood up. She quickly grabbed the sword from the fallen man and swung it around. It took her only a moment to get used to the different feel of it. It wasn't much heavier than the sword Valen had her practice with. She would have been okay with one soldier, but two was not quite her speed. Zalia knew she was going to be in trouble soon. Just as she was starting to feel desperate, Valen moved in front of her and killed both men. He whirled for a second, "Are you okay?"

"Yes," Zalia said breathlessly. Then they were separated again. Another soldier came towards her and Zalia fought against him. As soon as she killed him, another took his place. She killed him quickly. She was feeling pretty confident in her abilities when all of a sudden, she felt a sharp pain in her side. She looked down and saw an arrow sticking out. Shock held her in place for a moment, then she collapsed to her knees. She couldn't move. She felt herself being dragged away from the fight into the shadows of the castle. She looked up as Raven's face swam before her eyes.

Zalia! What happened? Where are you? Zalia heard Valen's panicked cry in her head. She wanted to answer him but couldn't form the words. She was losing consciousness fast.

I've been hit, she said to him weakly. *I'm by the wall,* she managed to say to him.

I'm coming, he said. She looked up to see him battling his way through soldiers. He was cutting down anyone that stood between them. He was furious. Zalia hoped Beckam's warriors stayed out of his path, or he would kill them too.

Soon he was kneeling next to her. He shook his head, and his eyes cleared a little. He sucked in a sharp breath when he saw her wound. "Zalia," he breathed. He looked into her eyes. "It's going to be okay. Just stay awake for me." Zalia felt herself fading fast. She looked down as he grasped the arrow. He looked up into her eyes. "This is going to hurt. I'm sorry." Then he yanked out the arrow. Zalia screamed in pain. He put his hands over her wound to stop the blood. He looked up in shock at her. Blue light began to show beneath his hands. His panicked eyes met Zalia's. "What do I do?" he asked. Zalia was barely hanging on to consciousness.

"Just hold it there," she said faintly. The pain intensified, then started to fade. Zalia closed her eyes and willed her body to relax. After a few minutes, the pain was gone. Zalia looked up in shock at Valen. She quickly remembered the battle and looked over his shoulder.

"It's over," Valen said darkly. "Let's get you inside," he said.

Chapter Twenty-Three

Valen gently picked her up and carried her inside the castle. If Zalia hadn't watched what played out, she would have never believed it. "I can't believe you healed me!" she said to Valen.

Valen looked down at her and his eyes softened slightly. "How are you feeling?"

"I feel absolutely no pain. It's incredible," Zalia said breathlessly. "I can walk now," she said to Valen.

"I know," Valen simply replied.

"Aren't you going to put me down?" she asked. He shook his head. "Why?"

Valen looked down at her. "Zalia, be patient with me. Just a few minutes ago, I thought I was going to lose you. Give me a few minutes to come back from that."

Zalia shifted herself so she could wrap her arms around

his neck. She felt his strong arms tighten around her in response. She didn't say anything more as he walked them to their room, and he didn't either.

When they got to their room, Valen carefully set her down on his bed. Zalia stood up. "I want to get this dress off and look at the wound." He nodded and stepped out of her way.

"Need help?" he asked her as she walked towards her room.

Zalia shook her head no and closed her bedroom door behind her. Once inside the privacy of her room, she reached around behind her to start unhooking her dress. After five minutes of frustration, Zalia realized it was no use. She couldn't maneuver all the tiny clasps behind her. She walked over and opened the door. "Valen?" she called out quietly.

He walked towards her. "I can't get the dress undone. Will you help me, please?" she asked without looking at him. She knew her cheeks were red again. Valen slipped quietly behind her and began undoing her dress. He moved quickly and methodically. When he was done, she didn't look at him. She just slipped quickly into her room. She stepped out of the ruined dress and into her bathroom and looked down at her side. She stared in wonder at the area where she had been hit. If not for the dried blood, you would never have known she had taken a hit. The area was completely smooth. There wasn't even a scar. Zalia stood staring at it a few more minutes before climbing into the bath and cleaning up quickly. She knew Valen was waiting for her. Once she was washed up, she changed into something more comfortable and walked back out into the sitting area.

Valen stood leaning against the wall. He looked tense and upset. When she walked out, he turned to look at her but didn't say anything.

Zalia walked over to a chair and sat down and curled her legs up next to her. He didn't join her. "So," Zalia began quietly. "I guess my healing powers passed to you during our bonding."

He turned his head towards her. "They did, but it only works on you."

"What?" Zalia asked in confusion.

"I tried healing some of the other wounded men out there, but nothing happened. I guess it only works on you. I don't really know. Maybe my power isn't as strong as yours." He shrugged.

Zalia stood quickly. "The other soldiers. I totally forgot about them! I need to heal them," she began.

Valen cut her off. "Henrietta is seeing to them. There are no life-threatening injuries. Everything will heal with the brewer's tea," he said.

Zalia nodded. Then she thought about what he said. "Maybe it's another aspect of the bond. You're able to heal me, so I can then heal others," she said.

"I leave tomorrow morning," he said abruptly.

"Okay," Zalia said simply.

"No, it's not okay," he said angrily. Zalia could see he was really worked up. His eyes were flashing, and he didn't look very in control of his temper. She needed to tread lightly. She opened her mouth to say something, but he cut her off.

"How am I supposed to leave knowing you could get hurt here? Tonight should have never happened. What is the point of castle guards when they can't even do their jobs? I don't trust anybody to protect you but me, and I'm not going to be here." He moved away from the wall and glared down at her.

Zalia knew he was mad, but she also knew this might be her chance to get him to agree to take her with him. She stood up. "Then let me come with you," she said boldly.

He took a step towards her. "No," he said angrily.

"Valen, you just said you don't want me to stay here without you. So, take me with you. Let me return with you to my kingdom and my people. I can be a help to you. I have my healing magic, and I..."

Valen stepped close to her. "No," he said. again

"But Valen, I can help. I..."

She broke off abruptly as he grabbed her and pressed his mouth down on hers. The kiss was aggressive. He pulled her tight against his body. She returned his kiss with heat of her own. Slowly, he relaxed and toned it back. He pulled away slightly and pressed his forehead to hers. Zalia was glad he was holding her up, or her knees would have given out.

"I can't lose you," he said quietly. "You don't understand my father. He is evil. If he were to get his hands on you..." he shuddered. "He can't ever know you exist, not only because of your healing powers but because of what you mean to me. He would use you to get me to do whatever he wants, and I would. Zalia, I would do horrible things if it meant keeping you safe. He can't ever have that bargaining chip. Promise me, Zalia."

Zalia looked at him in confusion. He continued, "Promise me you will stay here when I leave. I have to know you are here, safe and protected."

Zalia stared up at him for a moment, then said quietly, "I promise." She didn't want to stay, but she understood what he was saying. They couldn't take the chance of his father finding out about their relationship.

"I will double up your security. I will talk with Beckam

tonight and make sure things are as secure as possible. You will have guards on you all the time, even at night." He looked angry again. "Let them stay in the hall, though. Nobody comes in your room, especially Edgar," he spit out.

Zalia bit back a grin. "Okay," she managed straight-faced.

"We will be able to stay in constant contact through our bond. You can reach out to me anytime. If I don't respond, it's probably because I am fighting. I will always respond as soon as I can. Also, you can feel strong emotion through the bond. I won't shut the bond down in case you need me; but if you feel intense anger, know it's not directed at you," Valen said.

"What do you mean shut the bond down? Can you do that?" Zalia asked.

Valen nodded. "If you imagine a wall in your mind, I won't be able to feel your emotions. I may do that at times when I am fighting, but I won't close it off all the way."

Zalia asked, "Can I try it?" He nodded. "Just imagine putting up a wall to keep people out of your thoughts." Zalia did as he said. He frowned at her.

"Yes, that's it; but don't do that. You have no need to hide anything from me," he said.

Zalia held the wall, practicing. "Stop," he practically growled at her. "I don't like not being able to feel you," he said angrily.

Zalia just laughed and dropped the wall. *How's this?* she asked him.

Much better, he said. Though it was still more of a growl. Zalia opened her mind more and let her thoughts of care for him flow towards him. He closed his eyes. When he opened them, he was staring at her with a ferocious intensity. He pulled her into his arms and just held her. Zalia sighed.

I've decided there's no better place in the world than right here in your arms, she said through their bond. He pulled her closer and kissed the top of her forehead. He met her eyes and then pulled her up to meet him in a searing kiss. When neither of them could catch their breath, he slowly released her. His eyes bore into hers.

"As soon as this is over, we're getting married," he said in a husky voice.

Zalia just nodded, too overcome with emotion to speak. "You'd better get some sleep," he said reluctantly. "I have to check on a few details for tomorrow. I'll be back soon. A guard will be posted outside our door. If you need me, just call out to me through the bond. I leave early in the morning, but I'll wake you before I leave."

"Okay," Zalia said. Then she stepped up on tiptoe and kissed him lightly on the cheek. "I'll see you in the morning." Then she walked away quickly to her room, so she wouldn't hold him up anymore. What she really wanted to do was stay in his arms all night where it was safe and not have to ever be separated from him. She was scared for him and what lay ahead. She worried about him getting hurt or something happening to him.

I will be fine, my love, his low soothing voice rolled over her in her mind. *Just try to get some sleep.*

Zalia felt calmer than she had a moment before. She had forgotten he could feel her emotions. She would have to keep her thoughts and emotions in check in the days to come. She quickly got ready for bed, and soon she was staring at the ceiling. Before she could talk herself out of it, she sent to him, *I wish you could just hold me.* She waited a moment and didn't hear anything from him. After several minutes, she figured he was probably planning out tomorrow's details and couldn't talk. She started getting sleepy and started to doze off.

Sometime later, strong arms cradled her to a masculine chest. "Valen?" she asked sleepily.

She felt a light kiss on her forehead. "Go back to sleep, love. I've got you," she heard his low voice say. Zalia instantly relaxed into him and fell right to sleep.

Zalia woke the next morning to Valen shaking her slightly. "Zalia," he called quietly. Zalia opened her eyes and looked sleepily up at him. He sat on the edge of her bed, fully dressed and in battle mode. He had his sword strapped to his back, another sword at his waist. She knew from experience he had several knives and daggers on him. Gone was the gentle, loving Valen. In his place was the Warrior Prince.

Zalia sat up. She didn't know what to say. She had dreaded this day but knew she needed to be strong. "Be safe," she said simply.

He nodded. He leaned forward and kissed her on the mouth. "You too," he said. Then he stood up. "I will keep in touch through our bond." Zalia nodded. And then he was gone.

Zalia sat in her bed quietly for a moment, then got up to start getting ready for the day. She needed a distraction. She decided to find her grandfather and ask what guard he would recommend to train with her. That spurred her on. She was glad to have a purpose. Just a few minutes later, she was dressed in training clothes and headed to her grandfather's quarters.

The guard standing outside his room let her in. Her grandfather was standing over a map when she walked in. He looked up and smiled at her. "Zalia, my dear. How are you feeling today?"

"Perfect," she replied. "I can't believe Valen was able to

heal me," she said.

Her grandfather nodded. "It's pretty extraordinary," he said. Then he scowled. "Of course, he wouldn't have needed to if we hadn't been attacked."

"Did you find out who they were and who sent them?" she asked.

Her grandfather frowned. "No, and that is your fault."

"My fault?" Zalia questioned, not understanding.

"Once your Prince realized you were hurt, he single-handedly destroyed the remaining attackers," he said ruefully.

Zalia grimaced. "Sorry. He tends to be a little protective of me," she said. *That's my Valen,* she thought with a smile.

Her grandfather smiled at her. "Well, I'm glad he is. He will make a wonderful husband for you. Circling back to the attackers, our best guess is that they were from King Mylan's kingdom. Valen didn't recognize any of them, but that doesn't really mean anything. His father is smart. He wouldn't have sent warriors that Valen recognized. I have commanded for extra security measures. We will keep you protected, Zalia," he said earnestly.

"I know," she said with a smile. "You need to be protected, too," she said.

"I am," he said.

"Grandfather, do you have any warriors that you could

recommend to continue with my training?" Zalia asked him.

Her grandfather nodded. "Kell would be perfect to continue training you."

Zalia looked at him in surprise. "I had assumed he went with Valen and Beckam."

"No, he stayed to lead the guards here at the castle," he told her.

"Do you think he would mind training me?" Zalia asked.

"I know he won't, but you can ask him," he said. "I'll call for him." He walked towards the door and opened it. He talked to the guard there a few minutes and then came back. "Kell will be here momentarily. While we're waiting, do you want breakfast?"

"Sure," Zalia said. She didn't feel hungry, but she knew she would need food for fuel to workout. "I'm going to go ask Raven if she wants to join us, if that's okay," Zalia told her grandfather.

He waved her on. "Of course. Kell should be here by the time you return."

Zalia headed to Raven's room. When she knocked on the door, Raven answered immediately. She was dressed and ready for the day. She reached out and gave Zalia a hug. "How are you today?" she asked with concern.

"I feel great," Zalia said. "I guess I shared my healing power with Valen when we bonded."

Raven nodded. "I saw when he healed you," she said.

Zalia looked at her. "Thank you for saving me last night," she said quietly.

Raven smiled at her. "Of course! What are friends for?" Then she shuddered. "You should have seen Valen after he realized you were hurt. That man is scary!"

Zalia grimaced. "I heard."

Raven smiled. "He really loves you," she said.

Zalia smiled and didn't argue with her.

"So, what are we doing today?" Raven asked.

"We're training with Kell. I need something to take my mind off Valen and what's coming," she said. Zalia worried about the standoff between Valen and his dad.

"I totally understand. Come on," she said linking her arm through Zalia's. "Let's go eat breakfast and then destroy Kell."

"Uh, Raven, you do realize he is the captain of the King's Guard, right?" Zalia asked.

Raven nodded. "Yep, and he's not going to know what hit him when we get done with him," she said. Zalia laughed.

They walked arm-in-arm to her grandfather's quarters. Once they got there, a guard opened the door and let them inside. Zalia was surprised to see someone else standing there.

"Ladies," her grandfather called out to them. "Come this way. I have somebody I want to introduce you to."

Zalia and Raven walked over to her grandfather and the newcomer. The newcomer turned around and Zalia caught her breath. He was tall with dark bronzed skin. His head was shaved. He looked like one scary guy. When he turned all the way to look at them, Zalia saw marks covering his entire arm. *He must be one of the royal first-born princes*, she thought to herself.

"Zalia and Raven, meet Prince Adaire of Sol, Kingdom of the Rising Sun," her grandfather said by way of introduction. "Prince Adaire, this is my granddaughter, Princess Zalia of Arrosa, Kingdom of the Red Rose; and this is her friend, Raven."

Raven and Zalia both bowed to him. "It is a pleasure to meet you, Your Highness," Zalia said graciously. Zalia peeked at Raven out of the corner of her eye. She seemed mesmerized.

Prince Adaire stepped forward. "It is a pleasure to meet you, Princess, and you too, Raven." He kissed the back of each of their hands. He spoke with just a slight lingering accent. Zalia watched as he seemed to stare at Raven for a moment longer than necessary. Then he turned back to her grandfather.

Her grandfather looked at Zalia and Raven. "Go ahead and eat breakfast. Prince Adaire and I have much to discuss." Kell came walking in just then. "Ah good, you're here," her grandfather said to Kell. He looked at Zalia. "I'm sorry. I need to speak with Kell for a time. Then he can be free to help you," he said apologetically.

"No problem," Zalia said. She watched as her grandfather led Kell and Prince Adaire from the room.

Once they were gone, Zalia whirled around to look at Raven. "What was that all about?" she asked with a smile.

Raven was still staring at the door where the men had left. Zalia waved in front of her face. "Hello?"

Raven jumped. "Oh, sorry."

Zalia grinned at her. "Are we a little smitten with the Prince from Sol?" she asked teasingly.

Raven just grinned and looked at Zalia. "Can I just say, 'Wow'?" Zalia cracked up.

Zalia looked at her. "I think he thought the same thing about you too," she said.

Raven laughed. "I don't think so, but a girl can dream right?"

Zalia didn't say anything, but she knew she was right. The scary prince had definitely noticed Raven. Zalia and Raven ate their breakfast and talked through a plan for the day. After some time passed, the three men came back out to where the girls were sitting. Zalia noticed Raven immediately straightened in her chair, and Zalia bit back a smile.

"Zalia and Raven," Zalia's grandfather began, "Prince Adaire has agreed to stay here for a few days to discuss kingdom matters. In the meantime, he has agreed to help with your training. There is none better than Prince Adaire with a bow and arrow. Have either of you trained with a bow?"

Raven shook her head no, while Zalia shook her head yes. Her grandfather smiled and said, "Kell and Prince Adaire, you will begin training with these two ladies today."

Zalia and Raven looked at each other in surprise. *Things just got more interesting around here,* Zalia thought with a smile.

Chapter Twenty-Four

Zalia and Raven went back to their rooms to wait for Kell and Prince Adaire. While Zalia waited for them, she spent her time wondering how Valen was doing.

Valen? she reached out to him tentatively. She only waited a moment.

Yes love, he responded.

Zalia smiled. *I'm sorry to bother you. I just wanted to check with you and see how you are doing.*

You're never a bother, he responded. *Everything is good on this front. We're traveling quickly and haven't seen any sign of any other soldiers. That's a good thing. What are you up to?*

Zalia filled him in quickly about Adaire.

Just make sure they both keep their distance from you. Especially Adaire; he's single, he said in typical Valen style.

Zalia responded with a laugh. *I don't think you have any-*

thing to worry about with the Prince and me. He seems quite taken with Raven.

Raven? he responded. *That's interesting. She's from Sol originally, isn't she?*

Yes, Zalia said.

Okay, well keep your distance anyway and be safe training. You tell them if they hurt you, they answer to me, he said.

Zalia smiled. *No reason to threaten them, my handsome prince. I won't keep you but be safe. I,* she paused for a moment, *I love you.*

He was quiet for a moment. Then he said, *I love you too, Zalia. Thank you.*

Zalia knew she had a big grin on her face, but she couldn't help it. She loved that man! Kell and Adaire came in moments later in training mode. Adaire took her aside first to train with her. Raven went to work with Kell.

"Have you ever shot with a bow?" Adaire asked Zalia.

Zalia nodded. "My brother used to sneak me outside and train me. He wanted me to be able to protect myself," Zalia told him.

"Did you train with a bow with Beckam and Valen?" Adaire asked. Zalia shook her head. "Why not?" Adaire asked quizzically.

Zalia shrugged. "Maybe they were going to but never had the chance. Valen was more concerned about teaching me sword fighting, and Beckam loves his daggers," she said.

"Well, that's about to change," Adaire said. "You're going to get better at this than any of your other weapons. The bow and arrow is the best weapon of defense for a girl. You can stay away from the action and do just as much damage. It's much safer than a sword or dagger in battle."

"Well, don't tell Valen that. He believes the best weapon is the sword," she said.

Adaire nodded. "He's the best there is; you're not that good."

"Hey, how do you know that?" Zalia asked offended.

Adaire looked at her. "Because I've been on the other side of the sword against Valen," he said again.

Zalia just laughed. "Of course, you're right. He's the best. I can't even come close."

Adaire picked up a bow and arrow and brought it over to Zalia. "The reason I'm training you on a bow and arrow instead of a crossbow is while the crossbow requires less upper body strength, you can only shoot two bolts per minute. In a battle of life and death, that's too slow. Also, the range is not as far as a bow and arrow. So, we are going to train you on my favorite weapon—the bow and arrow. It's ideal for you because you don't have to get into the heat of the battle to make a difference. I'm sure

Valen will appreciate that. Now, here's the problem with the bow. It takes a lot of upper body strength, something I doubt you have." Zalia frowned at that but didn't argue. Adaire continued. "We are going to put you on a special protein-heavy diet, and I am going to work you really hard on upper body strength. Do you think you will be able to keep up?" he asked her.

Zalia stood tall. "Of course," she said, speaking with a confidence she didn't feel.

"Are you ready to get started?"

"Yes," Zalia said.

"Okay, let's go. Grab Raven, and let's head out," Adaire said as he left the room.

Zalia walked over to where Kell and Raven were working out. "Adaire said to grab you and head outside," Zalia said.

Raven looked at Kell. "That's fine," he said. "I need to do my rounds anyway." He waved them off, and Raven and Zalia reluctantly headed outside.

They found Adaire waiting for them outside the door. He led them to an area in the back of the castle, almost off the castle grounds. He walked over to a large tree. "Okay," he said to Zalia. "Up you go."

Zalia just stood staring at him. "You want me to climb that tree?" she asked incredulously.

He looked at her. "Have you ever climbed a tree before?"

Zalia shook her head reluctantly. He looked down at her with an evil smile. "Well, there's a first time for everything," he said.

Zalia stood there a moment longer before she decided she might as well get on with it. "Come on, Raven. Let's go," she called out.

Adaire shook his head. "Nope, just you."

"Why just me?" Zalia asked.

"Because you're first. Let's go," he said, clapping his hands.

Zalia glared at him. She was starting to not like this guy. She stared up at the tree, then walked forward and reached out for the first limb. Grunting, she tried pulling herself up. She promptly lost her grip and fell on her backside. "Ugh," she said. "This is going to be harder than I thought," she muttered to herself. She stood up and tried again. This time, at least, she kept her grip and pulled herself up into the tree. She reached up to the next limb and climbed again. She kept up the hard work until she finally got far enough that Prince Adaire said she could climb back down.

Zalia stood at the top, frozen for a moment. She slowly began her descent. When she was finally on solid ground,

Prince Adaire said, "Again."

"What?" Zalia blurted out.

"I said 'again'," Adaire said. Zalia just stared at him before turning around to the tree.

"Miserable, conceited princes. They're all the same," she mumbled under her breath.

"What did you say?" Adaire asked with a smirk. Zalia just stuck her tongue out at him, and he laughed.

Zalia began her ascent again. She climbed trees for the rest of the morning. Her only consolation was that Adaire made Raven do the same thing in a different tree. After a short break for lunch, their training the rest of the afternoon was more of the same. Adaire found more trees for them to climb. Then he created a really fun game of lifting heavy rocks and carrying them so many yards and placing them down, then picking them up again and carrying them to where they started. It was great fun. NOT! It was horrible. Zalia's arms were a quivering mess by the time she was done. Finally, Adaire told them they could take a break for dinner. Zalia ate quickly and was ready to head to her room when Adaire told her it was time to train again.

Zalia groaned in her seat. "I can't even move my arms," she complained.

"That's why we're not going to be working with your arms. We're going to be conditioning your stomach muscles. Oh, and only protein for the next few days. Don't eat any breads, jellies, juices, or puddings. We want to add some muscle to your body." With that, he stood up and walked out.

Zalia stared after him. "It's official. I hate him!" she moaned. Raven just laughed at her. Zalia scowled. "Hey, don't think I don't notice he's going easy on you. You only have to do about half of what I have to do each time."

Raven smiled mischievously. "I know. Isn't it marvelous?" Zalia picked up her linen napkin and threw it at her. Raven just laughed harder.

True to his word, Adaire spent time teaching Zalia how to tone up her stomach muscles, so she could get more use out of her arm muscles. They trained until darkness descended. Finally, Adaire clapped his hands. "All right. That's it for today. Be sure to take a hot bath and soak your muscles. We will train again tomorrow."

Zalia was so grateful to take a bath she thought she might cry. She didn't bother to thank Adaire or even talk to him. She barely managed to get back to her room. As soon as she stepped in the door, she saw Valen's bed. Out of sheer exhaustion, she started crying. She knew she was just tired. She had never been pushed that hard in her life. She realized now that Valen and Beckam had been taking it easy on her. Maybe they shouldn't have, because now she was paying the price.

With tears running down her cheeks, she stripped off her clothes and dropped them to the floor as she stepped towards the bathtub. She turned it on and let it run for a few minutes before climbing in. As she sunk down into the warm water, her tears turned into a full-on cry. Between missing Valen and being scared for him and the horrible beating her body had taken today, Zalia's emotional quotient was shot. She put her head back and cried it all out.

Zalia! What's going on? Valen demanded. He was in protective warrior mode. Whenever he got like this, people got in trouble.

Zalia answer me now! What is going on? Are you hurt? Zalia's failure to answer him right away was sending him into full-blown warrior mode.

It's nothing. I'm sorry. I'm just crying in the bathtub. You must have picked up on my emotion. Zalia communicated to him.

Why are you crying? Are you hurt? he asked.

I'm fine, really. It's silly. I'm sorry for bothering you, she said.

He was quiet for a moment. Then he said, *What happened that you're crying in the bathtub?*

Zalia could feel his confusion through the bond. She sighed. She didn't really want to tell him, because then he would get mad. At least he wasn't anywhere near to be able to beat Adaire.

Zalia! I'm trying to be patient.

Zalia hurried into it. *I'm just sad because I miss you. I'm scared something's going to happen to you, and my body hurts ridiculously bad. Adaire had me climbing trees, lifting rocks, and doing other strength-related training all day. But it's okay. I'm in the bath now, and then I'm going to bed. See, nothing to worry about.* Zalia cringed as she waited for his reply.

Valen's voice was calm, too calm. That always meant he was really mad. *Zalia,* he said calmly, *why did Adaire have you climbing trees and lifting heavy rocks all day and whatever other ridiculous things he had you do?*

Zalia put her head back on the edge of the tub and groaned. *He's working on my upper body strength, for shooting the bow and arrow.*

Valen was quiet a moment. *Well, you can just tell Adaire — from me — that in our future, only one of us needs to have upper body strength for what we want to do. That's going to be me, so he can just back off!*

Zalia didn't even think before she blurted out, *What do we want to do that you need upper body strength for?* She paused for a moment, and then it hit her. *Oh!* was all she managed.

She could feel his laugh through the bond. She closed her eyes tight. She was so glad he couldn't see her right now. She was mortified.

He was still chuckling when he started talking to her again. *My little innocent. Seriously though, tell Adaire that he needs to back off, or he will deal with me. Can you tell him that, Zalia?*

Zalia said quietly to herself, "And just like that, we're back in protector mode. *Yes, Valen,* she said.

I'm sorry you're hurt, he said.

I'm fine. Let's talk about you. How are you doing? How was the first day? she asked.

Uneventful, he said. *As boring as that is, it's a good thing. That means we haven't captured my father's attention yet. We have about three more days until we reach Astra, if all goes as planned.* He paused for a moment; then he was back. *Hey love, I have to go deal with something. I will say goodnight now, because you need to get some sleep. Are you still in the tub?* he asked.

Zalia nodded, then remembered he couldn't see that. *Yes,* she said with a yawn.

Go ahead and wash up and get out while I'm talking to you. You sound really tired, and I don't want you falling asleep in the bathtub, he said to her.

Zalia yawned again. *I'm fine,* she said sleepily. It was so nice talking to Valen, and the tub was so warm. She closed her eyes to relax.

Zalia! Zalia snapped her eyes awake. *Get out of the tub now,* he ordered.

Zalia was so sleepy. *Zalia!* She heard again. *Are you out of the tub?*

Zalia shook herself and pulled herself up and out of the tub, even though she didn't want to. *I'm out,* she said to Valen.

Zalia could feel his frustration. *I hate that I'm not there to take care of you.*

Zalia almost cried, she was so tired and miserable. *Me too,* she squeaked out.

It's going to be okay, sweetheart. You just need some rest, he said in his calm voice. *Go ahead and get ready for bed. Let me know when you're done.*

Zalia quickly put on her sleeping clothes and brushed her hair. Then she climbed into bed and under her covers. *Okay, I'm in bed,* she told Valen.

Tomorrow, you're going to be even more sore than today. Tell Adaire that I said to take it easy on you. There's no reason to push you. Tell him if he doesn't treat you with respect, he will answer to me. Do you understand? Zalia?

Zalia was already asleep and didn't hear his soft chuckle or him saying, *Sweet dreams, my love. Dream of me. I know I will be dreaming of you.*

Chapter Twenty-Five

Zalia opened her eyes slowly the next morning and groaned. "I hate Adaire," she said. She sat up on the side of the bed. Every muscle in her body hurt. It took her forever to get dressed and ready for the day. She ate a quick breakfast and walked outside to meet Adaire for training.

He was already outside and waiting for her. "Good morning, Princess. How do you feel this morning?" He asked with a grin.

Zalia glared at him. "You know very well how I'm feeling," she snapped at him. He just laughed. Zalia crossed her arms. "Valen said to tell you, well I can't repeat some of what he said, but he said to back off or he will deal with you when he gets back," Zalia said, smiling smugly at him.

Adaire crossed his arms. "If you think that's going to get you out of training, it's not. Valen's not here, is he?"

Zalia groaned. "Why are all you princes the same?"

Adaire grinned. "Come on, let's go."

Zalia looked around. "Where's Raven?"

Adaire's face instantly closed up. "She's inside training with Kell."

"Why?" Zalia asked him.

"It's better that way," Adaire said. He didn't say any more and Zalia wasn't about to ask. He was intimidating.

They got to work training. They spent more time working on developing arm strength.

For the next three days, they continued in the same fashion. Adaire pushed Zalia all day and late into the night until she fell into bed exhausted each night. Zalia checked in with Valen periodically, but they never had a chance to talk more than a few minutes. Zalia questioned her sanity a multitude of times. Why was she letting Adaire push her so hard? The only answer she came up with was at least it helped pass the time and keep her mind busy until Valen and Beckam returned. She was pretty sure it gave something for Adaire to do too. She had asked him one day why he stayed here, and he answered that he was waiting to hear the report from Beckam and Valen before he returned to his kingdom.

She hadn't heard a lot from Valen. She knew that they made it to Astra but didn't know more than that. He didn't say a lot, and she was exhausted each night when she fell into bed.

On the fifth day, Adaire brought a few bows and lots of arrows to training. Zalia's heart rate picked up. *Finally!*

Adaire walked towards her. "You said you have some training, right?"

Zalia nodded. A pang of grief hit. She took a deep breath and pushed it aside. She would deal with it later.

Adaire nodded. "All right. Well, let's see what you got. I know we need to keep developing your upper body strength, but give it a try. Do you know the proper form?" he asked.

Zalia nodded. He gave her a bracer and a pair of leather gloves. She put the bracer on her arm to protect it and put the gloves on. Zalia took the bow and arrow from him. He pointed at a tree. "Just try to hit the tree," he said.

Zalia nodded. She got in a ready position. Adaire called out, "Ready?"

"Yes," Zalia called out.

"Okay, go ahead and nock it," he said. Zalia put her arrow on the bow and readied herself by using the corner of her mouth as an anchor point as Kael had taught her.

"Draw," Adaire called out. "Release," he gave the order.

Zalia let go and watched as it cleanly hit the tree. She smiled. Adaire looked at her and smiled. "You're better than I thought you would be. Let's move right to target practice." He led her over to an area where he had already set up some targets.

"Okay," he said, stepping back. "Let's see what you've got." He stepped back. Zalia took her time with each shot. When she had shot about six arrows, Adaire stopped her.

"You've got a natural skill, Zalia. You're really good. Was your brother a good archer?"

Zalia thought for a moment. "I guess so. I mean he always hit his mark and taught me how, but I never saw him in a battle or anything?"

Adaire nodded. "He was probably really good because you're trained really well. We just need to build up your arm strength and get you used to shooting for long periods of time. Let's try it again. I just want to correct a few things."

They spent the rest of the day working with her bow and arrow. When she went to bed that night, she was exhausted and sore but content. She felt like this was really something she could master. She fell asleep before she had a chance to reach out to Valen to see how he was doing.

The next day brought more training and honing Zalia's skills at archery. Adaire kept praising her and complimenting her skill. That night when she was ready for bed, she reached out to Valen.

Valen, she called. She lay in bed and waited for a little bit. *Valen, are you there?* She waited a little longer but didn't hear anything from him. *That's odd,* she thought to herself. Zalia didn't concern herself too much. She couldn't imagine what he would be dealing with in Astra. She hated not knowing what was going on, but she trusted him to reach out to her when he could. She had no idea if she would be able to hear from him for several days now. She would have to be patient and wait it out.

Zalia spent every day training with Adaire. She felt herself getting stronger each day, and each day she was growing more confident in her archery skills. Adaire drilled her relentlessly. He found ways to create scenarios where she had to shoot under pressure. She learned how to release an arrow while moving, on top of a horse, in a tree, and more. Zalia fell into bed every night exhausted and worried. During the day, she didn't have time to focus on Valen, but every night she lay in bed wondering where he was and if he was okay. Every night before bed, she tried reaching out to him, but never received a response.

She asked her grandfather repeatedly if he had heard anything, but his answer was always the same. "No news is good news."

So, each night, Zalia went to sleep, praying for the safe return of Beckam and Valen.

One night, two weeks after Beckam and Valen left, Zalia was roused in the middle of the night by someone banging on her door. Zalia sat up quickly, startled. She grabbed a robe and threw it around herself as she walked quickly to the door, rubbing the sleep from her eyes. She opened the door to find Kell standing there.

"Princess, it's Beckam, he's asking for you," he said urgently.

Icy fear flooded Zalia's body as she closed her door and ran behind Kell. Kell threw open the door and ushered Zalia into her grandfather's room. Zalia froze for a moment when she saw Beckam. He was barely alive, but he called out her name when she walked into the room. Zalia ran to his side. "You're... a...live," his voice trailed off as he slipped into unconsciousness.

Quickly taking control of the situation, she told Kell and the others who had gathered around the bed. "Get his shirt off quickly. I have to have access to his wounds." Beckam was completely unconscious, so they were able to move quickly without disturbing him. Zalia stared down at his stomach in horror.

What have they done to you, Beckam, she thought horrified. He had deep lacerations all over his body.

Her grandfather turned his angry eyes to hers. Zalia took a small step back. She had never seen him angry before. "You're our only hope. We tried a healer's brew and it did nothing," he said angrily.

Zalia shook herself. This was not the time to fall apart. She straightened her shoulders. "Okay, let's see what I can do. She stepped forward and found the worst of his injuries and started there. She placed her hands over the first of many deep lacerations. Her hands started to tingle, and the blue light started to appear. Zalia kept her hands over the wound until it was completely healed. She moved on to the next one, and the next. Too soon, Zalia started to see dark spots. She knew she was already starting to fade. She looked at her grandfather in alarm.

"How are you feeling?" her grandfather asked her anxiously.

"It's too soon," she said. She shouldn't be tiring this soon. Not after her bond with Valen, but Zalia knew she wasn't going to be able to finish healing Beckam before the darkness came for her. She did her best to finish as much as she could before the darkness claimed her.

Zalia slowly opened her eyes, feeling like a weight was sitting on her chest. She looked around her and realized she was still in her grandfather's room. She sat up from the couch slowly. Henrietta sat next to her and lifted a teacup to her. "Here, drink this," she said softly.

Zalia drank the healer's brew. "Thank you," she said.

She let it settle for a few moments, then stood up and moved back towards Beckam. "How is he?" she asked her grandfather.

Her grandfather was sitting in a chair next to Beckam. He looked at Beckam for a moment. "He's tough. He's hanging in there," he said. He looked at Zalia. "How are you?"

Zalia shrugged. "I'm okay. I don't understand why I passed out. Since I bonded with Valen, it's been so much better. I didn't even get halfway through the healing before I passed out," she said in confusion.

Her grandfather looked thoughtful but didn't say anything. Zalia bent over Beckam. "I'm going to get back to work," she said to her grandfather. She pulled the blanket back to look at his wounds. She put her hands on his stomach and started the healing process again. It took a few more times before all his wounds were healed.

When Beckam's wounds were all healed, her grandfather hugged her. "Thank you, Zalia," he said, his voice emotional. Zalia hugged him back then sat down to wait until Beckam woke up. His face was starting to develop a little color. They waited several hours before Beckam finally started coming around. He cracked his eyes open and looked around in confusion.

His eyes found Zalia's, and relief showed on his face.

"You're alive," he said hoarsely, like he hadn't used his vocal cords for a little while. "You healed me," he said. Zalia found herself emotional. She just nodded. "Thank you," he said. Again, Zalia nodded.

She stood up and walked over to Beckam and took his hand. "Where's Valen?" she asked quietly.

Beckam's face turned stone cold, and just like that, Zalia's stomach dropped. Icy fear once again flooded her veins. "Is he... Is he..." she choked on the words.

"He's alive, but I don't know for how long," Beckam said gruffly.

Zalia couldn't breathe. She felt like a huge rock was sitting on her chest. Her grandfather came around and looked down at Beckam. "How are you feeling?" he asked quietly.

Beckam pushed himself into a sitting position. "I can't believe Zalia's healing powers. I feel absolutely no pain. I'm weak and hungry and tired, but my body doesn't hurt at all. It's amazing."

"Are you up to telling us what happened, or do you need to eat and rest first?" her grandfather asked him.

Zalia held her breath. She didn't want to pressure him, but she really needed to know where Valen was and if he was okay. *Valen?* she tentatively reached out to him but didn't receive a response.

Beckam looked right at Zalia. "I will tell my story now.

You all need to know what happened." He sounded so defeated. Zalia wasn't sure she wanted to hear this story. She was scared for Valen.

Beckam began, "It took us close to five days to get to Astra. Our plan was to get in quietly and have Valen set up a meeting with his father. Then we would take him out."

He looked down for a moment and then back up in anger. "It was an ambush. King Mylan knew we were coming. He and his army were waiting for us inside the castle walls. We walked right into a trap. The small number of men we took with us was no match for his entire army." He paused for a moment and tried to rein in his anger. They waited silently, giving him time to compose himself.

"He killed all my men, leaving only Valen and myself alive," Beckam said in fierce anger.

Beckam was quiet again. Zalia felt sick to her stomach. *Those poor soldiers.* She knew so many of them personally. Beckam didn't say anything more. She hated to push him, but she had to know.

"What happened to Valen?" she asked softly.

Beckam pinned her with his eyes. Then he looked away. "Beckam what is it? What happened?"

Beckam looked back at her, his jaw rigid with anger. "They took him away," he said in anger.

Zalia felt as if the wind was knocked out of her. "But

how? He's the best sword fighter there is? There's no way they would have been able to take him down," she said, fighting tears.

"He went willingly," Beckam said.

"Why?" Zalia asked quietly. Beckam looked down and wouldn't meet her eyes. "Beckam?" she questioned keeping her voice soft and calm, as she had learned from Valen.

"Valen's father said he had you locked up. He said if Valen went with him willingly, he would let you go," he paused. "His father did something to him, and Valen couldn't feel you anymore. He couldn't contact you, so he had no way of knowing if his father was bluffing or not. Valen wouldn't take the chance," he said quietly.

Beckam looked her in the eye. "I'm sorry. Valen would never let anything happen to you, so he let them take him. They carried him away in shackles. I, I think his father is going to kill him for trying to overthrow his rule."

"NO!" Zalia cried out. This couldn't be happening! She had to do something. "Why would he do that?" she screamed at Beckam.

Beckam looked at her solemnly, "Because he loves you."

Zalia couldn't hold on any longer. She felt her knees weaken and thought her knees might give out on her. Strong arms grabbed her arms and held her upright. She looked up into Kell's eyes. "Are you okay, Princess?" he asked.

No, she thought. *But I will be.* Zalia took a few deep breaths and nodded at Kell. He released his hold on her but didn't step too far away. Zalia took one more deep breath and then looked at Beckam. "You're sure Valen is in Astra now?" she asked.

Beckam looked at her sadly. "Yes." Then he looked at her face and said, "Zalia, whatever you're thinking, just stop. There's a reason King Mylan let me go. He wanted to be sure I came back here and told you about Valen. He *wants* you to come after Valen. Otherwise, he would have killed me."

Zalia didn't say anything. Her mind was racing with a plan. She lifted her head and looked at Beckam. "Valen would come for me," she said.

Beckam nodded, "Yes, but Valen is a trained warrior. He's practically an assassin. You're a..."

Zalia interrupted him. "If you say I'm a girl, I will hurt you," she said angrily.

Beckam smirked. He abruptly hid it when he saw her face. Zalia looked at him and crossed her arms. "I *will* be going after Valen, and you can't stop me. You can either come with me and help me or you can just wait for my return."

"Kell," she called out. "Will you go with me?"

Kell looked at Beckam for a moment, then at the King. Beckam just glared at Zalia, but Zalia's grandfather nodded slightly. Kell turned back to Zalia. "I would be honored to, Princess."

Her grandfather, who had been silent during the exchange walked over to Zalia. "What's your plan, Zalia?" he asked quietly.

Zalia's mind had been racing and planning since the moment she heard what happened to Valen. She had so many thoughts, but the plan locked into place in her mind the moment her grandfather looked at her.

Zalia lifted her head. "I am going to return to Arrosa and take my rightful place as Queen of the Kingdom of the Red Rose. I will raise up my father's army. I'm hoping Kell can take a group of soldiers with us. I am going to ask Adaire to head back to Sol and bring his army to meet me in Astra. Maybe he can even persuade Prince Ryder to join us. Surprise didn't work before, and I have no doubt it won't work again. King Mylan has spies everywhere. We won't go for stealth; we will go with strength and mass. Using our combined armies, we should be able to destroy King Mylan. When we get to Astra, we will attack from all sides. While the soldiers are busy, we will send a small group in to retrieve Valen."

Nobody said anything for a few moments. Kell looked

at Zalia with interest. "How are you going to overthrow King Mylan's rule in your kingdom?"

Zalia thought for a few minutes. "Beckam, how many soldiers did King Mylan leave in charge in my kingdom?"

Beckam was still not happy, but he answered anyway. "From the intel we gathered, it doesn't seem like he left a huge contingency. The people fear King Mylan, so he doesn't need a lot of soldiers to keep the peace."

"Do you know where all my soldiers are?" she questioned.

Beckam answered. "The leaders and all the members of the King's Guard are imprisoned in the chambers under the castle. The rest of the foot soldiers were sent home."

Zalia looked at him questioningly. "Why would they willingly go home?"

"Because King Mylan is sick. The soldiers told us that he demonstrated what would happen to any soldier who didn't step down and follow the soldiers from Astra," he said angrily.

Zalia was scared to hear the answer but needed to. "What did he do?" she asked quietly.

Beckam was silent a moment. "He led a demonstration in the courtyard. Five soldiers and their families were brought out. He bound the soldiers, then killed their families in front of them," Beckam said angrily.

Zalia's heart broke for those soldiers, while her heart grew in hatred for King Mylan. "King Mylan needs to be stopped," she said. The men all agreed on that.

Zalia was quiet a moment. "Kell and I will sneak into the castle. Kael and I used to do it all the time. We will head to where my soldiers are being held. We will free them and take down the guards from Astra.

The King looked at Beckam and Kell. "It's a good plan," he said reluctantly. Kell nodded; Beckam didn't respond. "Beckam," he called gently. "What do you think?"

Beckam looked at Zalia. "Valen will kill me if I take you there."

Zalia just rolled her eyes. "He will not."

Beckam argued with her. "He really will. Zalia, you don't understand how much he loves you, and his protective instincts are a little over the top with you. He literally could kill me for taking you into his father's kingdom."

"Well, I won't let that happen. But Beckam, I am leaving for Astra whether you come or not."

Beckam stared at her with a hard look, but Zalia didn't back down. "Fine," he finally gave in.

Zalia breathed a sigh of relief. She would do it without Beckam, but she had really hoped he would go with. "All right, we will meet tonight to strategize. Then we will leave tomorrow morning at sunrise. Beckam, you rest today. I'm going to find Adaire and talk him into going with us. Kell, you prepare the soldiers that we will be taking with us." With that, she whirled around and headed for the door.

She wasn't quite out the door when she heard Kell laugh and say, "She's going to handle becoming queen quite well."

She heard her grandfather's amused reply, "Indeed."

Just as she was about to close the door, she heard Beckam's grumbled response. "If she doesn't get killed first.

Zalia closed the door and leaned against the wall for a moment. *This is for real. We're really doing this.* She stepped away from the wall and took a deep breath. "Valen, hang on. We're coming for you," she said out loud as she strode down the hall to find Adaire and talk him into her plan.

Chapter Twenty-Six

It didn't take Adaire nearly as long to convince as it had Beckam. He agreed to meet with the team at dinner to discuss the plan. After her talk with Adaire, Zalia headed to her room. She needed extra rest after her healing today. She wanted to be at her best for the days ahead. She went to her bathroom and took a relaxing bath. After she washed her body and her hair, she climbed out, toweled off, and got dressed. She spent a few minutes setting out what she would need. Then she lay down on her bed hoping to be able to sleep for an hour or two, so her body could rejuvenate from healing. She had a hard time shutting her thoughts down. She didn't fall into a deep sleep, but she did rest for two hours.

By the time it was time to meet up, Zalia had packed everything she would need for the next several weeks and set out clothes to put on the next morning. She grabbed Raven from her room and headed to the meeting.

On the way, Raven asked. "How are you doing?"

Zalia responded. "I just want to get moving. Waiting is killing me. Now that I know he's in danger, it's killing me to just stay here."

Raven looked at her. "Do you think Prince Adaire will be able to get Prince Ryder to join us?"

"I'm not sure," Zalia said. She glanced at Raven. "Do you know anything about him?"

"No," Raven said.

Zalia stopped Raven before they went in to meet with everybody. "Listen, are you sure you want to go with us?"

Raven looked at Zalia stoically. "We've come this far. I'm not leaving you now. We're in this together," she said earnestly.

Zalia's eyes teared up. "I don't deserve you, Raven," she said with a smile. She reached out and hugged Raven tightly. "I have no idea how this is all going to turn out," she said when she pulled back.

Raven nodded. "I know. We have to just take it one step at a time. We can do this. We've spent months training for this. Now it's time to prove ourselves," she said.

Zalia agreed. "All right. Let's go."

They walked into the room and saw King Avery, Beckam, Kell, and Adaire all gathered around a map at a small table. They stood up and greeted the girls as they walked in. Zalia walked right over to Beckam and hugged him. "How are you feeling?" she asked. He looked so much better than earlier, now that he had washed up and put on clean clothes.

He smiled down at her. "Great, cousin! I slept all afternoon and feel human again."

Zalia looked up at him and asked quietly so the others couldn't hear, "I know you may be ready to return physically, but what about mentally? I know you went through a lot. Don't think I haven't noticed you haven't told us how you received all those cuts."

Beckam's smile faded as she talked and his face hardened. "I'll be fine. Nothing to worry about." With that, he turned back to the conversation at hand. Zalia knew he was redirecting her, and she let him. But, she was worried about him.

Dinner was a quick affair. Nobody wanted to linger when they had much to plan. After the plates were carried away, their dinner table became their battlefield. They put out the map of the five kingdoms on the table. They spent the next three hours talking battle strategy. Zalia listened and gave input occasionally, but mostly she left it up to the guys. This was their domain.

By the time they all parted ways to get some sleep, it was decided that they would leave at first light. They would travel with fifty of the guards from her grandfather's kingdom. They would ride quickly to reach Arrosa within three to four days. Once they reached Arrosa, Adaire would split and head to his kingdom to rally his army and hopefully convince Prince Ryder to join on the way.

Zalia and her crew would camp out in the woods. At nightfall, Zalia, Raven, Beckam, and Kell would sneak into the castle and find the prisoners in the basement. The remaining guards would stay in the woods and wait for the signal. Once they were able to free her guards, Zalia along with Kell and Beckam would lead them in an attack against King Mylan's guards. The waiting soldiers from Cascadia would help take out the guards on the outer walls and courtyard area.

Once Zalia established rule, she would gather the foot soldiers from their homes and rebuild her army. Then they would march alongside Beckam and his soldiers to Astra, Kingdom of the Dark Moon. There, they would meet up with the rest of the army from Cascadia and join forces with Adaire's army and attack. Once they reached the castle and everyone was distracted with the battle, Beckam, Adaire, Raven, and Zalia would sneak inside to find Valen and take out King Mylan. Kell would lead the army outside.

It was a good plan, but they needed everything to work out perfectly. A lot could happen along the way, but they would just have to deal with it as they went. They wrapped up their meeting, satisfied with the plan. Everybody headed off to get some sleep, as morning would come quickly.

The next morning, Zalia walked outside with Raven and saw a large group of soldiers prepped and ready to go. Her grandfather was talking to Kell. He looked up when he saw her and walked towards her. When he reached her, he wrapped her in a tight hug. "Please stay safe," he said simply. "I love you and am so proud of you." He stepped back and looked her in the eye. "I will see you when you return with Valen."

Zalia nodded. "I love you too, Grandfather," she said as she gave him one more quick hug. Then she turned and walked towards Kell, Beckam, and Raven.

"Are we ready?" she asked.

Beckam nodded. Kell pointed out her horse to her and Zalia attached her bag to the saddle and mounted.

Kell called out, "Mount up." He waited until everyone was ready. Then he called out, "Let's ride."

Zalia pulled her horse next to Raven and lined up somewhere in the middle of the group heading out. She waved and blew a kiss to her grandfather. He returned the gesture; then they were off.

Zalia was grateful to be on a horse this time around making the journey between Cascadia and Arrosa. It was much better than on foot, but it still seemed to take forever. The days seemed to pass slowly. They would ride hard, stopping only for a quick break at noon and supper. They would ride until it was too dark to go any further each night. The pace was grueling, but Zalia was grateful to finally being able to do something besides worry.

Raven and Zalia stayed in the same tent at night. They usually crashed and fell right asleep, rolled out of bed the next morning and kept going. Because of their grueling pace, they were able to get close to Arrosa by the end of the third day. Zalia went to bed grateful they had made it safely but worried about what was to come.

The next day, Adaire prepared to move on to his kingdom. Zalia gave him a hug. "Thank you so much for training me and for being willing to join us in this battle."

Adaire grinned down at her. "You're welcome. I'll see you when we're ready to take down an evil king." With that, he was off. His guards left with him.

They spent the morning talking through plans and contingency plans for if things failed. By afternoon, Zalia was getting antsy. She was tired of waiting. She wanted to get moving. Beckam suggested they rest in their tents because there was no guarantee of sleep tonight. Zalia didn't think she would be able to sleep, but surprisingly she did doze for a little bit.

Finally, it was time to get moving. Dusk had fallen. Beckam pulled everybody together and went over the plan one more time. Then Beckam, Zalia, Kell, Raven, and two of Beckam's warriors left to sneak into the castle. The rest of the soldiers would get into position and wait until they saw Beckam and Zalia emerge with the soldiers from the Kingdom of the Red Rose.

Beckam gave the signal that it was time to head out. Zalia grabbed her quiver of arrows and put it on her shoulder. She carried her bow in her left hand and followed Beckam and Kell silently. Raven walked quietly next to her, and the two warriors followed behind them. When they got close to the castle walls, Zalia stepped in front of Beckam, taking the lead. As she walked, she took in everything around her. So far, everything was quiet. Once they got to the outer wall, Zalia guided them to a small area that was crumbling. There was a bush covering the opening, but she knew from years of sneaking in and out that it was there.

She pushed aside the bush and crawled through the small opening. She hoped the big guys following her could fit. Moments later, all six of them were through the opening. Zalia quietly stepped forward in front of the guys again. They started moving quietly until Beckam suddenly grabbed her arm and pulled her low.

Zalia caught her breath and tried not to move as she assessed the threat. She heard voices and footsteps coming. Panicking, she thought quickly. They were still too far away from the castle to get in. They would have to go back. Beckam must have been thinking the same thing, because he pulled her backwards. The two warriors went through ahead of them, then Raven and Kell. Beckam practically shoved Zalia through. He followed, just as a group of soldiers came into view.

It was obvious they were not on duty, or maybe they were but didn't care. Zalia silently hoped all the soldiers were like this. It would make them a lot easier to take down. The soldiers stayed in the courtyard for a while. Zalia watched, completely dismayed when they sat down and started playing cards. They were loud and boisterous; it was obvious they had been drinking.

Beckam silently beckoned them to sit down. They all leaned against the castle wall and waited silently. Zalia was so frustrated. She had no idea how long they would have to sit here.

Zalia wasn't sure how much time had passed. It felt like hours. Finally, the men finished their game and left. Then it was quiet once more. They waited another fifteen minutes or so before Beckam pointed at Kell. Kell quietly moved to the entrance area they had used. Kell disappeared through the opening. Zalia held her breath and didn't move. A few minutes later, Kell returned and motioned for them to follow him.

Once again, they moved towards the castle wall, being careful to stay in the shadows and low to the ground. They were able to get to the wall of the castle with no further mishap. Zalia stepped in front of everyone once again and began to lead them around towards the back of the castle. When they got to the corner, she felt a hand on her shoulder. She stopped moving and pulled back a little from the corner as Kell came up and stood in front of her. He carefully peeked around the corner. He turned back to look at the two soldiers with them. He made hand motions and all three of them quickly disappeared. Zalia heard only the slightest noise. A few moments later, they were back and Kell motioned them to move forward again.

It was an agonizingly slow process. Every time they came to a corner, Kell would repeat the same process. Soon, they reached the secret entrance. It was a large vent that connected to the kitchen. Zalia quietly removed the grate, thinking as she did how many times she and Kael had done this very thing. It took a few moments to get everybody in and moving. Zalia climbed in last and carefully and quietly replaced the grate.

She let Beckam lead them. She had explained in great detail how to navigate them to their next location. They crawled quietly for a few minutes. Finally, Beckham quietly removed the grate and climbed out. After checking quickly, he motioned them all to climb out. Once they were out of the vent, Zalia took the lead once more to lead them to the chambers under the castle.

Lucky for them, the grate dumped them out not far from the entrance that would take them below the castle. They only ran into two soldiers on the way, and Beckam and Kell made quick and quiet work of them. They hid the bodies the best they could but didn't take too much time to worry about it. It was time to free the guards. They had a battle to get to.

Chapter Twenty-Seven

Zalia once again stepped into the lead and led them quietly to the door that led to the underground chambers of the castle. Beckam helped her pull open the massive door. They all stepped in and down the first two steps, pausing for a moment to let their eyes adjust to the darker area. Zalia wrinkled her nose at the smell; musty with body odor and sweat mixed together. Zalia moved to step forward, but a hand on her arm stopped her. Kell motioned for her to follow him. Zalia was all too happy to let him lead. She had only been down here once and never wanted to return. They walked silently down the steep stairs. A few crude torches lit the way. When they finally reached the bottom step, Kell held up his hand to stop them. He silently disappeared. After only a few minutes, he was back and motioning for them to follow him.

Zalia thought it was funny that they hadn't run into any guards until she saw two dead guards on the way. That explained it. Kell had killed them. They walked further into the underground chamber. Ahead of them, she started seeing cells with iron bars. They moved silently through the corridor, edging closer to the first of many cells.

It was late, and they planned on most of the prisoners being asleep. They didn't want to cause any commotion and risk guards coming to check on the noise. They reached the first cell, and Zalia looked in. Beckam and Kell looked at her and waited. Zalia shook her head, and they kept moving. After the third or fourth cell, Zalia started questioning the wisdom of her plan. She thought she would be able to recognize her soldiers, but now she wasn't so sure. These men were all wearing clothes that were dirty and worn. She knew her soldiers wouldn't be wearing their trademark tunics with the red rose, but she had hoped there would be something that would distinguish them.

Beckam and his warriors led her past each cell. Zalia peered into each one looking for anybody that she knew or anything that would distinguish her father's men. Cell after cell passed, and Zalia started to panic. What was she going to do if she didn't recognize them? They needed to keep moving. They had already lost so much time waiting for the stupid card game to finish.

She was starting to lose hope when suddenly she saw him. "Silas?" She couldn't believe he was alive. She had seen him lying on the ground covered in blood. He must have survived. "Silas!" she called out quietly. Beckam, Kell, and the other warriors had drawn close behind her, their weapons drawn. There was movement within the cell as a few men started stirring. Silas lay on the ground near the back of the cell. A man close to the cell door stood up and came to the cell door and leered at Zalia. She felt Beckam step up beside her, using his massive form as intimidation.

The soldier looked up at him for only a second. "What do you want?" he barked out. Zalia felt a moment's panic. Soldiers were starting to stir. They really didn't want to cause an uproar. More soldiers were waking up not only in this cell but in the cells around them. A guy from another cell yelled out, "Hey, keep it down. I'm trying to sleep." Muttered curses and yells followed his outburst.

Beckam moved closer to Zalia. "We need to do something quickly," he muttered. Zalia's mind was whirling now as she tried to figure out what to do to get them out of this mess. If they didn't get the situation under control quickly, guards would be coming down the stairs.

Zalia did the only thing she could think of. She stepped back a step and lowered the hood of her cloak. "I am Princess Zalia, second descendant of King Warren of Arrosa, the Kingdom of the Red Rose. I have come to take my rightful place as Queen." She finished and held her breath, awaiting their reactions.

The silence was deafening. All Zalia could hear was the beating of her own heart. "Princess Zalia!" Silas called out as he made his way to the cell door.

Zalia could have wept when he stepped forward. She locked her emotions down because she needed to be strong in this moment. "Silas, it's so good to see you. I thought you were dead," she said, and her voice cracked momentarily on the words.

Silas grinned. "You can't kill me that easily." By this time, most of the men were on their feet mumbling and talking amongst themselves. An intimidating guy from the back stepped forward. Zalia watched as other soldiers stepped out of his way. He walked close to the cell door, and Zalia fought the urge to step back. She held her ground as he stared her down.

Silas looked from Zalia to the huge soldier. "Princess, this is Ulric. He served as second to the Captain of the King's Guard." Silas looked uneasily from Ulric to Zalia. Zalia stared up at him. One particularly nasty scar ran across his face, giving him a dangerous vibe. Zalia swallowed as she looked up at him. As she did, she realized it had grown quiet.

Lifting her head high, she said in her most authoritative voice. "I realize this comes as a shock. My parents hid my existence all these years. During the attack, I was hidden away in the north tower. Through some help, I was able to escape. I escaped to Cascadia where King Avery and Prince Beckam," she pointed to Beckam, "helped hide me and train me until I was able to return to take my rightful place as heir to the throne. I know you don't know me, but I hope to earn your trust. I need you, all of you," she said, looking around. "King Mylan killed my father, my mother, and my brother—Your King, Queen, and Prince. He has taken what doesn't belong to him. His days are numbered. I will avenge the deaths of my family, and I will overthrow his rule here in our kingdom. I need your help to do this."

Nobody said anything, so Zalia continued on. "Prince Beckam of Cascadia brought soldiers to fight alongside us. Prince Adaire of Sol is returning to his kingdom even now to amass his army and meet us in Astra." Zalia stepped back and looked at the soldiers all around her. "I know you all have been through so much, but I need you now. We need to return our beloved kingdom back to its original glory." Zalia finally stopped, not knowing what else to say.

It was absolutely silent. The huge soldier in front of her hadn't made a single expression the entire time she spoke. She couldn't get a read on him even now. Zalia was completely shocked when he growled out, "You have the looks of your mother, but the spirit of your father. I would recognize you anywhere." She bit back a gasp of surprise when he took a knee. "Princess Zalia of the Kingdom of the Red Rose, heir to the throne, I pledge my allegiance to you. I will fight for you and help to overthrow King Mylan and the Kingdom of the Dark Moon."

Zalia watched in amazement as the soldiers all around Ulric began taking a knee, one by one. Zalia's eyes began to tear up, but she pushed back the tears. "We will fight. Together we will avenge our King, Queen, and Prince, and we will take back the Kingdom of the Red Rose!" she yelled. The men yelled and cheered their agreement.

Moments later, they heard the cry of guards. Beckam, Kell, and the warriors made short work of the three guards that came running to check on the noise. Ulric grabbed Zalia's hand through the gate. "We need to move quickly before they send more guards. What's the plan?"

Zalia said, "First, where are the keys for this door?"

"They will be on whoever was lead guard tonight. Tonight, it should have been Ronan. He's a big ugly blond," he said. Zalia knew exactly who he was talking about. He was one of the first two guards they had taken down. She quickly sent one of the warriors to get the keys from his body. She took the next few minutes to explain the plan to

Ulric.

As she explained, Beckam came back with a key and began trying keys until he found the right one. He finally got it, and the men began rushing out of the cell. One of the soldiers took the keys from Beckam and moved to the other cells to start freeing the other soldiers.

Zalia quickly finished relaying the plan to Ulric, being careful to leave Valen completely out of the plan. They would explain his involvement at a later point. Ulrich nodded. "It's a good plan. We need weapons. I know where to get them, but we will need to borrow some until we can get there."

Zalia looked at Beckam. He removed an extra dagger from his hip and a knife from each boot. His warriors did the same. Ulric took them and handed them out to a few guys.

"Okay, listen up," Ulric called out. His authoritative voice carried in the underground cavern. "Here's the plan. We need to get to the armory for weapons. If you find clothes on the way, grab them. Any guards you see on the way, kill them—but quietly. We need to try and stay as quiet as possible for a surprise attack on the guards." The men nodded, moving around restlessly.

Then Ulric started giving orders. "Leo, you take twenty-five soldiers and head for the barracks. Kill every guard sleeping in there. Plan your attack so you can enter quietly and kill them in their sleep." A soldier nodded and began walking away, calling out soldiers to follow him.

"Dain, you take a crew of twelve men and cover the eastern portion of the castle inside. Kill all the guards. Charles, you take twelve and cover the western portion." Two soldiers headed off and began forming their teams.

"Gregory and Peter, you each take ten men and head into town. Begin gathering our footmen from their homes and lead them back to the castle grounds. Be prepared to fight when you get here," he ordered. Two more men began forming teams.

Ulric gave time for those teams to head out. "The rest of us will take down the guards outside the castle. Prince Beckam," he called. "You have soldiers waiting outside?" he questioned.

Beckam nodded. "I have fifty men waiting for our attack to start, and they will join in."

Ulric nodded. "Okay, I'll take ten men with me and head to the front of the castle and join Prince Beckam's men. Silas, you lead the remaining soldiers out the back. Leave no man alive. Once our mission is accomplished, we will reconvene and make a plan to attack the Kingdom of the Dark Moon."

With that, Ulric lifted his fist into the air. "For Arrosa," he yelled. The soldiers repeated his cry.

Zalia felt tears well up in her eyes. She placed her hand on Ulric's arm. "Thank you," she said softly.

He looked down at her solemnly. "Thank you for coming back and freeing us," he said. He looked away for a moment and then back at her. "My men... they were starting to lose hope. We've been away from our wives and our children for too long. Without knowing if they are okay..." he stopped and shook his head.

Zalia put her hand on his arm. "I'm sorry to have to ask you to stay away longer. If there were any other way..."

He interrupted. "Princess, the only way to protect our families is to take out the threat. Then we can sleep peacefully at night. To kill a snake, you have to take off its head."

Zalia nodded her agreement. Ulric looked away from her to his soldiers. "Let's go. Princess, you stay away from the battle. I will have several of my soldiers take you to a safe room."

"Actually, I will be going with you. I've trained for this. This is my battle, too. I will stand beside my men and fight."

Ulric looked like he was about to argue, but Beckam shook his head. "You're not going to win that argument," he told Ulric.

Ulric nodded and turned back to his men. "Stay by me,"

he threw out to Zalia over his shoulder. "Gavin and Asher, flank the Princess," he called out.

Beckam walked with Ulric as they headed for the exit. Zalia followed the two of them, flanked by her new buddies. "Thank you," she told each of them. They looked down at her and smiled. She glanced over her shoulder to make sure Raven was following. When she met her eyes, Raven said, "Good speech," with a grin. Zalia just laughed.

All conversation ceased when they reached the stairs. Once they reached the top, Ulric sent a few soldiers to clear the way to the armory. Zalia knew the armory wasn't far from the door. A few minutes later, they began moving again. They headed to the armory and every soldier loaded up with weapons.

At Ulric's command, the two groups split. Zalia's group headed for the front of the castle where the most guards would be. The other group headed to the rear of the castle. When they got nearly to the front, Ulric stopped everyone for a moment. He divided his group in half. He instructed half to go after the soldiers on the walls. The other half was to take out the soldiers on the ground. He spoke quietly. "We're going out blind. We don't know their formation for guarding the castle, but we know ours. So, we are going to just plan on it being similar. Whatever you do, keep moving. They may have guards hidden we can't see. Let's go."

Zalia pulled out her bow and grabbed an arrow, ready to head out into the midst. Raven stood next to her with her dagger out and ready. Zalia reached out and put her hand on Raven's arm. "Be careful out there," she said.

Raven nodded. "You too."

Before they opened the doors, Ulric turned back one more time. "Protect the Princess at all cost," he said. Then they heaved open the doors. Zalia took a deep breath and charged behind them into the battle.

Chapter Twenty-Eight

The chaos was instant. In the blink of an eye, the battle had begun. Zalia let her eyes adjust just for a moment, then she joined in. She stayed close to the doors, in the shadows with her bow ready. She took aim at one of the soldiers on top of the wall. She let the arrow fly and felt a moment of satisfaction as she watched him fall from the wall. The hit boosted her confidence. She nocked the next arrow and hit the next soldier on the wall. She systematically worked her way around the wall, and in less than a minute or so, she had taken down the guards on the immediate wall surrounding them. She stepped from the shadows and moved out into the inner courtyard. Her eyes immediately found another patch of shadows she could work from. She headed quickly for it. Before she could get there, a guard stepped into her path with sword raised. Without thought,

Zalia let her arrow fly. He fell with a grunt, and Zalia kept moving.

She made it safely to the area she chose to cloak herself in. She looked up at the wall and set to work eliminating the guards still on the walls. Within minutes, the battle died down. Ulric looked around and called out to his soldiers. "Gather up our wounded and let's move to the rear."

Zalia looked around and was thankful to see it was mostly guards from Astra littering the ground. A few of her soldiers were down, but none of them appeared dead. She started to follow Ulric and stopped beside one of her soldiers who had a nasty gash on his chest.

She dropped down on her knees next to him. "Here, let me help you," she said soothingly. He watched her apprehensively. She reached out and touched his wound through the hole in his shirt. He flinched back in pain. "It's okay," she murmured. "I'm going to heal it."

She placed both of her hands gently over the wound and grit her teeth as the familiar tingling and pain began to travel up her arms. In a few moments, the wound was completely closed. Zalia lifted her arms and let the blue whisps fade away. She looked into the soldier's eyes. He was staring at her in shock. Zalia noticed suddenly that the courtyard had gone completely still. She glanced over her shoulder and saw Ulric and the other men staring at her in awe.

Zalia stood up slowly, unsure of what to say. Ulric approached her slowly. "You're a magical healer," he breathed. "There hasn't been one in over a century," he said in a voice full of reverence.

Zalia nodded. "I think that might be why my parents hid my existence," she said quietly.

Ulric simply nodded once. "All right, well, it's good to know you're on our side," he said. He turned and addressed his soldiers. "This stays with us until we figure it all out. And the Princess needs our protection more than ever," he said fiercely. The soldiers nodded and Ulric led them inside.

The teams from inside the building met up with them and reported to Ulric that they had killed all the guards indoors. Ulric sent a large team to go aide the team taking on the soldiers in the barracks. Ulric sent soldiers to the kitchen to ask for food and for any healers available.

Zalia stood against the wall resting a moment, and Raven joined her there. Zalia hugged her. "You okay?" she asked.

Raven smiled. "Never better," she said. "How about you? I saw you take out most of the guards on the walls," she said. Zalia smiled at her.

Beckam came and stood by them. "You both okay?" he

asked. Raven and Zalia nodded.

Zalia smiled at him. "First step accomplished," she said.

Beckam looked at her in pride. "Nice work with the guards on the wall," he said with a smirk.

Zalia beamed under his praise. A moment later they were joined by Kell. "Prince and Princess, are you both okay?" he asked, looking over them in concern.

Beckam smiled and clapped him on the shoulder. "Never better. How did you fare?"

"Good. We made short work of those guards," he said with a smile.

"I'm going to make my rounds and see who needs to be healed," Zalia said. Beckam looked at her in concern.

"Will you be okay? Grandfather said you haven't been as strong since... Well, since Valen left," he said.

Zalia shrugged. "I'll be careful. If I get weary, I'll stop and take a break," she said. She hated talking about Valen; it made her sick to her stomach, wondering if he was okay. Pushing thoughts of him aside, she walked over to the wounded soldiers.

She spent the next two hours healing soldiers with wounds. None of them were horribly severe. A few she had to take a break and come back to, but she was able to help the soldiers who were the worst off.

Beckam found her when she was finishing healing a

knife wound on a young soldier. "Zalia," he said, "You need to get some rest. We will be heading out first thing tomorrow morning."

Zalia nodded. "Let me just finish up these last two and check in with the kitchen staff. Then I'll take a break," she said. At his skeptical look, she followed up with, "I promise." He left her alone then.

True to her word, Zalia finished healing the last two soldiers and headed to the kitchen to greet and thank the staff.

As soon as Zalia stepped into the kitchen area, all conversation stopped. Zalia froze as all the servants in the kitchen turned to stare at her. Zalia didn't know what to say for a moment. She hadn't thought this through. Suddenly, a woman with a familiar face stepped forward.

"Princess, it is so very good to see you again," she said with tears in her eyes. Totally breaking protocol, Zalia stepped forward and gave her a hug. Tears sprang to her eyes as it felt like being hugged by her mom. "Thank you for coming back for all of us," she whispered. Zalia stepped back and saw the tears in the woman's eyes.

"Forgive me for having to ask, but what is your name?" Zalia asked embarrassed.

The woman smiled graciously. "My name is Alice," she said. Zalia smiled at her.

Zalia stepped back and looked around the room at all the individuals. Some she recognized; some she did not. "First of all, I want to say thank you for your service to Arrosa and to my family," her voice broke slightly over those words. Many of the staff and servants looked down. Some had tears in their eyes.

"When I return, I will take my rightful place as heir to the throne. At that time, any of you who no longer wish to serve here are free to return home. I know many of you were taken from your homes. I am sorry for that. While I can't change your past, I can help with your future. Any of you who wish to stay and serve can do so, but I will establish wages for you. You will be paid for your services, and you may choose to live here in the castle or in a home in town." Zalia looked around at the looks of astonishment on their faces. "I only ask that you stay here until this battle is waged, and King Mylan is killed. That is the only way I can guarantee your safety." Heads nodded all around. "Now, if you wouldn't mind, I need some help. We have a lot of soldiers who haven't eaten properly in months. I need lots of food." Zalia paused. "Do we have lots of food?" Zalia asked uncertainly.

Smiles appeared all around her. "That we do," Alice said. "We will see to it."

"Thank you. Thank you, all of you! We will speak again

soon!" Zalia blew them all a kiss and headed out of the kitchen back to where the soldiers gathered. She wondered briefly what Valen would have thought of her tonight. She smiled briefly, thinking of him. That was quickly chased away by a sense of fear and foreboding. She needed to get to him soon.

She located Beckam and headed towards him. "What's the plan?" she asked.

"We leave tomorrow at first light," he said. "But first, we have some business to attend to." Zalia looked at him questioningly. Then she saw Ulric walking towards her with her mother's crown and royal red robe in his hands.

Zalia's breath caught in her lungs. She just stared at Ulric as he walked towards her. Zalia watched as her soldiers spread out around her until she was surrounded on all sides. Behind them, she saw the kitchen staff come out from the kitchen and quietly line the walls surrounding the great hall, where they stood.

Ulric stepped towards Zalia and stopped. "Princess, would you please kneel?" Zalia just stared at him. He smiled slightly. Then motioned her down with his head. Zalia sank to her knees.

Ulric turned serious and looked around the room. "Today, we witness history as we crown our first Queen, Queen Zalia of the Kingdom of the Red Rose. Zalia, do you pledge to serve this kingdom as a fair and just queen, to always uphold the law with justice and mercy?"

Zalia took deep slow breaths as she listened to him. When he paused and waited for her, Zalia nodded and said, "I swear it."

Ulric looked around the room at all those gathered there and said, "Ladies and Gentlemen, I present to you Queen Zalia, your rightful Queen and heir to the throne." Ulric gently placed the crown on her head and placed the robe around her shoulders. All around her, cheers and clapping broke out. Zalia stayed on her knees for a moment until Ulric put his hand out to help her up. Zalia turned in a full circle, taking in the faces of her people. She knew she looked nothing like a queen, standing there in fighting clothes, but it was time for a change. Her kingdom needed to be brought into modern times.

Zalia waited for the clapping to slow down, then she opened her mouth to say what was in her heart. "Tonight, we have taken back control of our castle," she said. Cheers and clapping spontaneously broke out. Zalia smiled and waited a moment before continuing. "Our soldiers are going to head into town and wipe out the rest of the threat. Then our army will unite with Prince Beckam's army from Cascadia and Prince Adaire's army from Sol to march to Astra. We will kill King Mylan and his Royal Guard. We will avenge the deaths of our King, Queen, and Prince." More cheers rose around her. "We have much to look forward to in the days ahead, but right now we need to stay focused on this war. Tonight is just the first battle. I make this promise to you. I will return."

"Ulric, will you please explain the next steps?" she asked.

Ulric nodded. His booming voice took over. "Our soldiers will head home to be with their families. The foot soldiers should be arriving soon from their homes. Prince Beckam's soldiers will stay and protect the castle."

Zalia moved around the room talking to her people, accepting their congratulations, and answering their questions. After her third or fourth yawn, Beckam appeared at her side. "Come on. We've done all we can do for now. Let's get some rest."

"Where's Raven?" Zalia asked.

"I just sent her to find a room," Beckam said.

"Oh," Zalia said. She was too weary to say anything else. Her adrenaline was starting to exit her body, leaving her exhausted. "You can tell your soldiers to sleep wherever they find a room." Then she headed towards the front of the castle, towards the staircase that led to the sleeping quarters. She trusted her kitchen staff to take care of feeding all the soldiers.

Zalia pulled her weary body up the stairs. It was mid-morning. She needed to sleep for a few hours. When she reached the top of the stairs, she paused for a moment. She debated on which room to sleep in. She decided to head to her room. She didn't think she could handle anything else tonight. She walked slowly into her room. It felt like a lifetime ago she had lived in this room. She felt so removed from that life, from the girl she used to be.

She quickly shut down her emotions. She couldn't handle it today. She needed to get some sleep. She closed the door and quickly changed out of her battle clothes. She was too tired to take a bath, so she settled for washing her hands and face. She put on a chemise from her drawer and climbed into her bed. Her bed felt amazingly soft. Zalia felt her whole body relax as she drifted off to sleep.

Chapter Twenty-Nine

Hours later, Zalia lay in bed trying to sleep. It had been a long, emotional day. She was nervous for the coming battle, and she had a hard time shutting her mind down. Finally, it was time to get up and moving for the day. Zalia dressed quickly in her battle clothes—her black leather pants, a tunic top, and her leather boots. She packed her bag with what she would need for the days ahead. She planned on heading to the armory to get more arrows. She grabbed her bag, her bow, and her quiver and headed downstairs.

Downstairs there were hundreds of soldiers inside and outside the castle. The footmen had arrived, and the soldiers from yesterday's battle had all returned. The servants must have worked all night to prepare enough food for this army. Zalia headed right to the kitchen to thank them. She ate a quick bowl of pottage and some brown bread. When she finished, she went looking for Beckam or Kell or Ulric.

Zalia ignored the stares she was receiving from the men. The foot soldiers arriving were seeing her for the first time. Zalia had too much on her mind to be worried about it. She finally found a familiar face. "Kell," she said.

"Good morning, Princess," he said kindly.

"Is everything on schedule?" she asked.

He nodded. "It is. We will be loading up and heading out in waves. The first wave leaves soon. You and Raven will be with Beckam and myself. We will be with the first group heading out," he said.

Zalia nodded. "Sounds good. Do you know where Raven is?" she asked.

Kell shook his head. "I'm not sure."

"Okay, thanks. I'm going to see if I can find her," Zalia said as she headed off to the kitchen. Zalia found Raven laughing with the kitchen staff. Zalia didn't say anything but just watched her for a moment. When Raven saw her, she came over to talk to Zalia.

"Raven, I want you to stay here," Zalia wasted no time saying. Raven looked at her in shock.

"Why?" Raven asked.

"I need someone I trust to stay behind and help run things here. I'm going to ask Kell what soldiers we should leave behind to protect the castle and our people while we are gone, but I need to know someone is here overseeing things. You know this castle, you know the staff, and you are familiar with the way things run. Would you stay here for me until this battle is over?" Zalia pleaded with her. She knew if somebody were asking her to stay away from the battle she would not be pleased. But she really needed someone she could trust to stay behind, and she believed Raven was the right person for the job.

"Okay," Raven said suddenly, startling Zalia. Zalia looked at her in surprise.

"Really?" Zalia couldn't help herself; she smiled and launched herself in Raven's arms. "Thank you. I can't say how much I appreciate this, Raven," Zalia spoke sincerely. She stepped back and looked in Raven's eyes. "After this, we will find your family. I promise."

Raven smiled. "I'm counting on that," Raven said simply. Raven looked at her solemnly. "Be careful out there," she said. "Don't take any unnecessary risks. We need you; Arrosa needs its queen." They hugged one more time, then split ways.

Within the hour, Zalia and the first wave of soldiers left the castle. Zalia found herself in the middle of the group. Beckam rode on one side, and Kell rode on the other. The ride to Astra took two days. The two days passed without incident. When they got within a half-day's journey of the castle, they pitched camp. They needed to wait for the rest of the soldiers to arrive.

The next two days were the longest of Zalia's life. It took two days to get all the soldiers there and to wait for Prince Adaire and his army. Finally, they were ready. They had gone over the plan a thousand times. Now, they just needed to execute it.

Unlike before with Valen's group, this time they weren't going for stealth. They wanted to attack in broad daylight. Sheer numbers would ensure their victory. Once the fight was underway, Beckham, Kell, Adaire, and Zalia would sneak inside to find Valen and hopefully take out King Mylan on the way.

Zalia waited nervously astride her horse. They had traveled the remaining distance this morning. Now they were armed and ready for attack. They could see the outline of the castle in the distance. Surely by now, King Mylan knew he was under attack, but they hadn't seen any soldiers from his kingdom yet. That would soon change.

They waited for word back from the scouts they sent ahead. It seemed to take forever. Zalia's nerves were stretched thin. She jumped suddenly when she heard the bellow of some kind of horn. It echoed all around them, loud and long. Zalia sat in silence until it was done. Then she looked at Beckam and Uric.

"What was that?" she asked apprehensively.

Beckam and Ulric's faces were set and their eyes trained in the distance. "*That* was a call for war," Beckam said tensely. "He's sending out his army to meet us."

Zalia's eyes swept over the hundreds of soldiers lining the battlefield. The soldiers from Cascadia waited in place behind Beckam. The soldiers from her kingdom amassed across the field. On the far end, stood Adaire's soldiers. Adaire sat astride his horse in front of them.

After the bellow, Adaire and Ulric began riding towards Zalia and Beckam. Beckam rode towards them and Zalia followed with Kell right beside her. They stopped in the middle. The men kept their eyes trained on where their enemy would be appearing. Zalia reached her arm out and placed it on Adaire's arm. "Thank you for fighting in our war with us," she said sincerely.

He looked at her briefly and nodded. "It is our honor to stand with you. I'm sorry I couldn't bring more soldiers. My father does not agree with this war. He believes we can stay neutral. I have tried to convince him otherwise," he said in frustration.

"I'm sorry," Zalia said.

Zalia looked back towards the castle in the distance and knew they wouldn't have long before the battle began.

"Do you mind if I address the soldiers?" she asked nervously. The men nodded and moved out of her way. Zalia rode closer to the soldiers. She looked out over the field of soldiers from three different kingdoms, the majority being from her kingdom. She took a deep breath and tried to squelch her nerves and find her courage. She threw her shoulders back.

Zalia pulled her red hood back from her hair, so the soldiers could clearly see her. She felt the breeze blow her hair and stroke her face. She yelled as loudly as she could, hoping the hills would carry her voice to the farthest soldiers. "My name is Princess Zalia of Arrosa, the Kingdom of the Red Rose. King Mylan invaded my kingdom, killed my father, mother, and brother. I am now the sole heir to the throne. Our soldiers have overthrown his rule in our kingdom, but now it's time to take off the head of the snake. King Mylan is evil and corrupt. He has to be stopped. I have heard of his plans to try to invade Verdia next," Zalia paused and let her words have the desired effect. The soldiers were very responsive now. "If we don't stop him, he will take over one kingdom at a time until he is too strong to be overthrown. We have to stop him before he does that. Today, you stand with the Kingdom of the Red Rose and fight with us in our battle, but make no doubt... this is each of our kingdom's war. We are fighting for each of our kingdoms. You are fighting for the freedom of your wives, your sons, your daughters, your brothers, and sisters. We must stand united or be destroyed individually. Thank you each of you for your bravery and courage to fight this war. Victory will be ours today, and King Mylan will be killed, his kingdom overthrown. Years from now, we will look back on today and recognize it as the beginning of the change, the beginning of the walls coming down between our kingdoms."

Zalia turned around when she heard shouts from the men behind her. She faced the rider coming towards them. Instantly, soldiers all around her trained their weapons on the rider. When he came into view with his hands turned up in a universal sign of surrender, Zalia gasped. "Lower your weapons," she called out quickly. She turned around and ordered everyone's weapons down. "He's on our side," she shouted. Beckam and Adaire motioned to their warriors to lower their weapons. Zalia turned back to face the rider.

She jumped down from her horse and ran towards him. He jumped down from his horse. "Reid!" she called out and gave him a huge hug. "You're safe," she breathed out. Reid returned her hug and then quickly stepped back.

"Princess Zalia, I came to fight with you. My father's army heads this way," he said in anger. Beckam came over and gave him a handshake. Adaire just nodded at him.

Zalia and Reid both climbed back up on their horses and turned to face the battlefield. Even now, Zalia could finally see movement in the distance. She glanced quickly at Reid. Zalia's insides tightened. "Is Valen a-alive?" she asked. She almost didn't want to hear Reid's answer. He nodded once but didn't look at her. Zalia wanted to ask more, but she heard Uric start commanding orders.

Kell yelled to Zalia, Beckam, and Adaire. "Remember, our objective is to go straight through the front door. We will have to fight our way through. Keep moving and try to get there as quickly as possible." Zalia and the Princes nodded.

Beckam and Adaire went into battle mode, and Zalia shook her head. It never amazed her how kind these princes could be in one moment and how deadly they were in the next. That made her think of her own prince, and she straightened her shoulders. She was ready for a fight.

Zalia saw the dust begin to billow before them in the distance. She heard Adaire and Beckam yelling orders at their soldiers. Beckam came riding over to Zalia. "Back of the soldiers," he said as he pointed with his chin towards the rear.

Zalia shook her head. "I'm staying here and fighting with my soldiers," she said emphatically.

"Zalia!" he ground out.

"Save it!" she shouted. It was getting loud now. The army from Astra was now within eye distance. Ulric, Beckam, Adaire, and Zalia all sat facing the oncoming enemy. Zalia readied her bow and arrow and tried to take a calming breath.

"Ready your weapons!" Ulric bellowed. "Standby for my order!"

As Zalia waited for the command, she opened herself up to the bond once again and called out to Valen. *Valen?* She waited a few moments but heard nothing in return. Anxiety started to plague her. She shut down her thoughts quickly. She needed to focus on the mission that lay ahead of her. She watched for a moment as Reid lined up with the soldiers from her kingdom.

With a war cry, Ulric lifted his sword and charged forward. Beckam, Adaire, Kell, Ulric, and Zalia were instantly at his side. As her horse thundered towards the battle, she could feel the ground trembling from not only the army surrounding her, but King Mylan's army moving towards them. A war cry surrounded all around her and Zalia took courage and strength from them and added her own cry to their midst. It was time to end this!

Chapter Thirty

In moments, the battle was upon them. Zalia had already started shooting arrows the moment she could distinguish bodies. Adaire rode next to her, shooting arrows faster than Zalia thought possible. They charged forward and were soon surrounded by soldiers. Zalia didn't slow down. Their goal was to make it through the battlefield and into the castle. More than once, she had a close call. They cut their way through soldiers on all sides, never once slowing down. When they were well on their way, Kell and Ulric fell back to lead the soldiers outside. Beckam, Adaire, and Zalia continued their race for the castle walls. Vaguely, Zalia became aware that another rider had joined them, but she didn't take her attention away from the battle in front of her to see who it was.

When they finally neared the castle walls, Zalia's heart

sank. They had hoped to pull most of the guards away from the building, but it looked like dozens of guards still held their positions on the castle walls. Zalia and Adaire immediately began taking them down from a distance, but Zalia knew it would be near impossible to get past all of them and into the castle. Suddenly, she saw the rider who had joined them pull off to the side and motion for them to follow him. Zalia glanced over quickly and realized it was Reid. She automatically turned her horse, spurring him in the direction Reid was leading them. Adaire and Beckam quickly did the same. They continued picking guards off the walls. Zalia realized gratefully that some of their soldiers had broken through and were now giving them cover as they sped towards the castle. The guards had to focus on the new threat and couldn't continue following their rogue group.

They charged around the side of the castle, still following Reid. Soon, Reid jumped from his horse and ran towards the wall. Zalia quickly dismounted and followed him, with Beckam and Adaire right on her heels. He led them to a small opening in the wall. They followed Reid as he led them around the side of the castle and up a steep set of stairs. From there, he led them towards an open window. He motioned them to stay low as they walked. When they stepped inside, he held his finger to his lips. They followed him silently. He led them quickly through a myriad of hallways and finally into a room. He closed and locked the door behind him. "We can speak freely in here, but we need to make it fast," he said.

Zalia couldn't wait any longer. "Reid, is he alive?" she asked.

Reid looked at Zalia compassionately. "He is, but I don't know if he is the same guy you knew, Zalia," he said sadly.

Zalia felt her knees weaken. "Wh-what do you mean?"

He looked at her for a moment, like he was trying to gauge how much to tell her.

"Just tell me," she said impatiently.

"My father destroyed your bond," he said. Zalia had been prepared for a lot of things, but not for this.

"What?" she questioned dumbly. Beckam ran his hand through his hair in an angry fashion. Adaire muttered something unkind under his breath.

"How did he do that?" Beckam asked angrily.

Reid looked at the two of them. "I don't really know. All I know is my dad works with some of the worst kinds of people. Somehow, he found somebody who could undo the blood bond," he said angrily.

Zalia just stared in confusion. It was too much to take in. "I don't understand..."

Reid sighed, then said in a low voice, "I think he was a

warlock or something. He is ancient and evil. I don't know how my father found him. Anyway, after Valen came out of the spell, my father told him he had killed you. Valen believed him. He said he couldn't feel you anymore. He," Reid looked away for a moment. "He went off the deep end." Tears welled up in his eyes. "He started turning into my father. He was angry and... a monster. Father used him to do horrible things, but it wasn't his fault." Reid tried to plead for Zalia to understand.

Zalia's eyes flooded with tears. *Oh Valen, what has he done to you?*

Beckam blew out a frustrated breath. He looked at Adaire. "We need to find and kill Mylan and free Valen. We will decide what to do with him after that," he said in an angry voice. Adaire nodded.

Zalia wiped away her tears and said, "Okay. I'm ready."

Beckam turned to look at her. "Not you," he said. "You're staying here."

Zalia stared at him in shock. "Why?" she demanded.

"This changes everything," Beckam said. "The emotional blow is too much for you, and Valen is a loose thread. We don't know what we will be dealing with. We may have to take him down, and I will not have you there for that," he said with pain in his eyes.

Zalia sucked in a harsh breath. Then she stepped right

up to Beckam. "I am going, and I will deal with Valen when we get there. Valen would never hurt me," she said angrily.

"You don't know that," Beckam said. "You don't have any idea what he's been through."

Reid looked at Zalia sadly. "He's not the same man you remember. He's changed," he said quietly.

"I don't care. I'm going. If you stop me, I'll just go on my own. Then you won't be able to protect me," she said angrily.

Adaire just grinned. Beckam snarled at him. "What are you grinning at?"

"You know she's right. If we leave her, she will just sneak out. Besides, she may be the only one who can help Valen. He might indeed try to kill us, but she might be the only person who is safe."

Zalia could have hugged Adaire in that moment. She could see Beckam was considering it. She wanted to get moving before he decided against it. "Come on," she said. "We've wasted too much time already. We need to move!"

Beckam finally nodded.

"Follow me. I can get you to where he's being held. One more thing," Reid said. He looked at Zalia. "He's taken a lot of beatings." Reid didn't say anymore, and Zalia knew what he was trying to communicate. They didn't know what kind of shape they would find Valen in. With her heart hammering, Zalia followed the three guys.

Reid led them again through a maze of hallways and down a few flights of stairs. Finally, they ended up in an underground area. Reid held his finger up to his lips. When they had walked a distance, he put his hand up to stop them. He left them for a minute. When he came back, he held up three fingers. Beckam and Adaire nodded. Zalia was guessing that meant there were three guards on Valen. She quietly pulled her bow out and slid an arrow into the ready position.

Her heart was slamming against her chest now. She couldn't believe she was so close to seeing Valen. Reid led them around the corner to a large open area. Three guards instantly came towards them. Reid, Beckam, and Adaire took them down quickly. Zalia didn't stop moving. She saw Valen, and her feet moved forward without her permission. As she got closer, she wasn't sure if he was conscious. He sat on the ground with his arms chained to the wall behind him, and his head slumped down on his chest.

Dried blood coated what was left of his clothes. He was covered from head to toe in filth and deep bruises. Cuts marred every inch of his body. Zalia wanted to weep for him. She approached him slowly. "Valen," she called out softly. "It's me, Zalia. I've come to take you home." No response. "Valen?" she called again. Still no response.

She was close enough to touch him now. She knelt down in front of him. She heard Beckam's intake of breath and his deep voice, "Zalia." At that, Valen's eyes flew open, startling Zalia. She fell on her backside in front of him. Valen instantly tried to break out of his chains. He was growling like a crazy person at Beckam. Beckam moved closer to Zalia.

"Zalia, get away from him," he yelled at her. He stepped forward, and Valen more fiercely pulled at his chains.

Zalia got onto her knees and started crawling slowly towards Valen. Beckam yelled at her again, but she ignored him. "Valen," she said softly in a soothing, low voice. "It's me, Zalia. I'm here to help you." He looked at her and Zalia froze. His eyes were the darkest black she had ever seen. He didn't move or make a sound; he just watched her. "I'm here to take you home, Valen. Everything is going to be okay." She kept talking to him in soothing tones. She was close enough now to touch him, but she didn't.

"Zalia," Beckam warned again. At that, Valen jerked in his chains again, growling at Beckam.

Zalia called out softly. "Valen, focus on me. Don't focus on anybody else. Just me." She began crawling closer to him. She finally sat right next to him on her knees. She didn't touch him yet. She just waited. When he didn't look away, she reached out and gently touched his arm. He jerked momentarily, but then he held still. "I'm going to get you out of here, okay? Everything is going to be okay. Reid," she called out quietly without ever taking her eyes from Valen's. "Do you know where the key is?" Reid disappeared a moment later.

Zalia continued to look into Valen's eyes. When he didn't look away, she reached up ever so gently and palmed his cheek. He shuddered when she did that and closed his eyes for the first time. Zalia sighed a breath of relief. Her relief was short-lived.

"How touching is this?" an evil voice called out and suddenly they were surrounded by guards. Valen and Zalia both jerked. She didn't have to turn to know it was King Mylan.

All of a sudden, Zalia felt herself being moved as Valen used his legs to try to position her as close to him as possible. She held herself straight, being conscious not to lean against him because of all his wounds. Zalia's eyes teared up because she knew he was still her Valen, no matter what he had been through. He was still trying to protect her.

Zalia slowly turned her face around and was surprised to not see the evil king anywhere. Slowly she scanned the room. She finally located him on a platform high off the ground. She saw Beckam and Adaire standing to the side in warrior mode.

"Princess Zalia, you are a hard person to track down. I had heard such lovely things about you, but then you led this army straight to my door. I must say, I am extremely disappointed," Mylan said.

Zalia felt a rumble roll through Valen. She reached out and gently touched his shoulder. As she did, Zalia eyed her bow. It had fallen to the side when Valen slid her around. While watching King Mylan, she reached out her foot and dragged it towards her.

"Prince Beckam and Prince Adaire, it's so nice of you to join us. I wish it wasn't under these circumstances. Oh, and please drop your weapons. If you do not, I will be forced to punish Valen again. Or maybe this time, the Princess can take his place," he said with an evil laugh. Valen struggled now, pulling against the chains and growling. King Mylan just laughed.

Zalia stroked Valen's arm. "It's okay," she said softly.

Beckam and Adaire both tossed their weapons to the ground. Zalia knew for a fact they both had knives in their boots, but she didn't know if they would do any good at this distance. What they needed was for Adaire to take him down with his bow. There was nobody better. Right now, however, that wasn't an option. Zalia glanced down quickly at her bow again. She realized that King Mylan must not have been able to see it at this angle. Either that, or he didn't think she was a threat. *That will be his mistake.*

Zalia waited a few more moments, listening to him drone on with threats of retaliation against each of the kingdoms and more. Zalia knew she would need to take a chance and soon. She saw movement out of the corner of her eye and saw Kell and Ulric had joined them and were standing next to Reid.

They needed to move fast. If more guards got in here, they would all be in trouble. Zalia fingered her bow and pulled it up flush against Valen's leg. She needed to figure out how to reach behind her to get an arrow. She was trying to figure it out when she felt an arrow placed in her hand. *Thanks, Valen!* Zalia started sweating, and her heart was hammering profusely. She was waiting for the perfect opportunity. Her opportunity came a moment later when King Mylan leaned his arms against the wall surrounding the platform. She knew this was it. She turned off her thoughts and relied solely on her hours of training. She grabbed her bow, nocked the arrow, stood fluidly, and released it. As soon as she released it, she dropped and rolled. She had no idea if she hit her mark or not. Chaos ensued as Adaire and Beckam took on the soldiers near them, and Kell, Reid, and Ulric took on the guards further away. Zalia stayed on the ground on one knee. She released three more arrows, each one finding their mark. Then she looked towards the platform where King Mylan had stood. She needed to make sure he was dead. Seeing as everybody else was busy, she knew it needed to be her. She slipped away from Valen and into the shadows. She quickly made her way to the stairs of the platform. She drew out an arrow and readied it. With a deep breath, she began to climb.

She reached the top and suddenly she was grabbed from behind. Zalia's scream was cut off when a hand slapped across her mouth. She fought to free herself, but the hold on her was too tight. "Not so fearless now, are you?" King Mylan whispered in her ear. "You have taken everything from me! Now I'm going to make you pay."

Zalia stilled her movements when she felt the blade of the knife he held against her throat. She resisted the urge to panic. She silently thanked Beckam for the countless hours of defensive training he had given her. In a move Beckam made her practice hundreds of times, Zalia raised her right hand in a form of surrender and then used her left arm to push the arm holding the knife up and away from her. She dropped and rolled and did a sweeping kick to take his feet out from under him. He grabbed her ankle before she could get away from him. Before she could react, he sliced the back of her ankle.

Zalia cried out in pain and fell to the floor. He was on her a moment later. She dodged a blow from his knife. She fought against him. She put everything in her punch to his nose and was rewarded with a horrible crunching sound. She pushed him off of her and got up to run away, but her foot gave out on her and she crashed to the ground. He was on her a second later and this time, she didn't move fast enough to avoid him. A stabbing pain shot through her chest, precariously close to her heart. Zalia cried out in pain. "First, I will kill you. Then I will finish off that worthless son of mine," Mylan said with hatred blazing in his eyes.

Zalia felt time slow down as her body stopped respond-ing to her commands. She watched as he raised his knife again. She fought against him. He stabbed her this time in the other arm. Zalia's body screamed out in pain. She knew she needed to keep fighting him, but it was as if her body was just giving up. Fire erupted in her leg as he stabbed her there next. Zalia could barely hang on to her consciousness.

"Say hello to your mom and dad and brother for me, Zalia," Mylan said with evil hatred in his eyes. Zalia watched as if in slow motion as he raised his hand above her heart. She braced herself. Thinking of Valen one last time, she closed her eyes and waited for the killing blow to come.

It never came. She heard a bellow of rage, then the

weight lifted off her. She watched as Valen plunged his sword into his father's heart with a cry of rage. Zalia lifted her eyes to Valen's as he dropped to her side. "It's finally over," she whispered to him. "I love you," she whispered.

"Don't you dare leave me," Valen's gruff voice commanded her. Zalia tried to respond, but her body failed her. She sank into oblivion.

When she came to, it was quiet. Zalia slowly sat up and looked around her. They were still in the underground area. *I must not have been out for very long,* she thought to herself. She slowly stood up and looked around, looking for Valen. She spotted him the same time he saw her.

Their eyes locked. Zalia moved towards him as he weakly stood up. Reid put his arm around him to hold him up, but Valen shook him off. He hadn't looked away from Zalia yet. Zalia walked over to him and gently put her arms around him. His strong arms shook as he held her. Zalia felt her tears fall as she hugged him. He tightened his arms around her, and Zalia knew that she had never felt anything better in her entire life.

"Is it over?" she asked him.

He pulled her tighter to him. "It's over," he said in a low voice.

Zalia pulled away slightly and looked at him. "Valen, I need you to lie down, so I can heal you." He shook his head angrily. Zalia frowned at him. "Listen, you healed me. Now it's my turn to heal you."

He stared down in her in anger. "You're not healing me," he ground out in anger.

"Yes, I am!" she said just as stubbornly. She softened her voice. "Valen, I need you at full capacity. We have no idea what is ahead of us. I need you. Please let me heal you. If I need a break, I'll take one," she pleaded with him. He stared down at her before finally nodding. She carefully helped him to the ground. Then she gently helped take his shirt off. She found the worst of his wounds and began there. Tears welled up in her eyes as she surveyed his body. She swallowed and pushed them away. Now was not the time.

Zalia wasn't sure how much time passed while she healed Valen. The more Zalia healed Valen, the more color returned to his face; but his eyes stayed the same. His eyes followed her every move, never leaving her face. Zalia lovingly healed broken bones, bruises, and cuts all over his body. It was a lengthy healing. She was beginning to tire, but she pushed on relentlessly. Several times, Valen tried to stop her but she just glared at him. The next time Valen tried to push her away, Beckam stepped in. "We need you completely healed so we can finish this battle and put your kingdom back together. All right?" Valen just glared at him, but he must have gotten the message because he didn't push Zalia away anymore.

Zalia could feel herself on the brink of giving out. She was so close to being finished. She wanted to hang on just a little longer, but she couldn't. She slipped into oblivion, knowing Valen would be there to catch her ... always.

Chapter Thirty-One

Zalia opened her eyes slowly. She felt slow coming completely awake. When she finally did, she looked around quickly as her surroundings came into view. She was in a room she'd never been in before. She sat up quickly as her breathing started coming swiftly. In almost a full-fledged panic now, she moved towards the door. She opened it and two guards turned to look at her in surprise. "Silas," she said, breathing a sigh of relief. "Where am I? What's happening? How long have I been out? And where's Valen?" she rushed through her questions quickly, still feeling panicky.

Silas laughed and held up a hand. "One question at a time, Princess. The battle is over. King Mylan's soldiers have surrendered, and King Mylan is dead. Prince Valen has taken over control of the kingdom. He left you here in his room because you passed out." Silas looked at her questioningly at that. "He left us here to guard and protect you and left orders to send word as soon as you were awake. As for how long you were out, it's been two days." He looked at the soldier next to him. "Find Prince Valen and tell him the Princess is awake," he ordered. The soldier nodded and left.

Zalia breathed out a deep breath. "Two days?" she asked and groaned. "But it's over?" she asked. She couldn't believe it was finally over.

"It's over, Princess." He looked at her silently for a few moments. "I can't believe you're alive, Princess," he said emotionally. "How are you doing?"

Zalia paused. There was so much in that question. "I'm really doing okay, Silas. It was difficult, and I have nightmares often. I miss my family so much, but I'm moving forward. I put my emotions into training hard. Valen takes good care of me," she said with a smile.

"Do you love him, Princess?" he asked solemnly.

Zalia looked up at the man who had guarded her for so many years, becoming more like a grandfather to her than a guard. "I do," she said confidently.

He nodded. "I'm glad. I have worried about you over the years. And how is your health?" he asked.

Zalia smiled broadly. "Well, apparently I'm a magical

healer. My powers manifested once I turned eighteen. They started to become too strong, until I bonded with Valen. After bonding, my power has been much more stable. Well, until the bond broke..." her voice trailed off. "We're working on that," she finished simply. Zalia cocked her head. "You don't seem surprised," she said.

Silas was quiet for a moment. "I've always known there was something special and unique about you, Princess. I just didn't know what it was. It doesn't surprise me in the least," he said.

Zalia didn't get a chance to respond. Valen came striding down the hall, his dark eyes locked on hers. Zalia took a deep breath. Gone was the weak, hurt Prince. In his place was the dark, powerful Prince. Silas backed away slowly as Valen walked right up to Zalia. He grabbed her hand and pulled her into the bedroom and shut the door. Once the door was closed, he turned towards her. Zalia felt her heartbeat pick up as he stared down at her. He gently framed her face with his hands.

"Are you okay?" he asked in a low voice. Zalia couldn't find her voice, so she just nodded. "You're not still hurt anywhere? You just passed out because of the healing?" he asked intensely.

Valia put her hands over his. "I'm okay, Valen."

He stared at her. "I can't believe you're alive," he whispered painfully.

She closed her eyes as he slowly lowered his head to hers and captured her lips in a kiss. The kiss turned passionate quickly. He kissed her with the hunger and desperation of a man who thought he had lost her. When he finally pulled up, they were both gasping for air. Valen crushed her to him. Zalia wrapped her arms around his waist and just clung to him as her tears began to fall. Tears for him for all he had been through. Tears for the boy who had to live with a wicked father. Tears for the family she had lost. She couldn't hold back the torrent of grief that swept through her. Soon she was sobbing into his shirt. He gently unhooked her arms from around his waist and swept her into his arms. Carrying her to his bed, he sat down with her in his lap and held her. He didn't say anything. He just stroked her back. When Zalia felt like she couldn't cry anymore, she finally stopped. She sat there and tried to get control back. When she finally felt more in control, she pulled back and looked up into his eyes. "Are you okay, Valen?" she asked softly.

"You're alive and in my arms. Nothing else matters," was all he said. Zalia let it go for now. Eventually, they would need to talk. Valen would need to talk, so he could heal. But for now, it was enough.

"What happens next?" she asked him.

He sighed. "I need to get this kingdom back in order and establish my rule. We need to do the same with your kingdom. We need to figure all that out. But first," he looked down at her with a dark look. "First, we need to head back to your grandfather's kingdom and get married."

Zalia stared at him in shock. "That is so not what I thought you were going to say," she said.

Valen stared down at her. "I will never allow the bond to be broken again. The man I became when I thought you were gone..." he shuddered. "I can't live like that ever again. We need to fully complete the bond. A completed bond can never be broken; a blood bond can be."

Zalia looked up at him. "A full bond takes place when we..." she didn't finish, and she felt her face turn red.

"When we consummate our marriage," he said, matter of fact. Zalia swallowed. Then she looked up at him and gave herself a mental pep talk. *This is Valen. I love him. He will always take care of me. There's nothing to fear.*

"All right," she said. "When do we leave?" she asked.

"You're not going to argue with me on this?" he asked, surprised.

"I can be reasonable sometimes," she said defensively. He just looked at her skeptically.

"I need to spend the rest of today getting my men set in place. We leave first thing tomorrow morning," he said.

Just then a knock sounded on the door. Valen stood up and placed Zalia gently on her feet. He walked to the door and opened it. Beckam strode into the room and hugged Zalia. "How are you doing, cousin?" he asked with concern.

Zalia smiled at him. "I'm good. Is it really all over?" she asked him.

Beckam blew out a breath. "It is. It's finally over. Life can get back to normal now. Though I guess with you, life will never be normal," he said with a grin.

"Hey!" Zalia said as she smacked him. Zalia looked up to see Adaire come walking into the room. "Adaire!" she said. She walked over and gave him a big hug. She heard a low rumbling from Valen, which she ignored. She stepped back from Adaire and looked him in the eye. "Thank you so much for everything. Thank you for the hours of training me and for bringing your army. We couldn't have done it without you."

"It was my honor, Princess," he said. He smiled mischievously at her and said to Valen, "Hey if you decide not to keep this one, let me know." He winked at Zalia.

Zalia watched Valen move in on Adaire faster than her eyes could track. He punched him square on the nose. Zalia heard a horrible cracking sound. "Valen!" she shouted and ran towards him. She put her hands on his arms, afraid he'd do something more. Valen looked over her head at Adaire. "That's for the comment *and* for making my girl cry in the bathtub," he said in a low tone.

"Oh. My. Word." Zalia ground out. She was mortified and could feel her face blush a deep red. Zalia dropped her hold on Valen and moved towards Adaire to help him and was shocked to see him laughing. "Are you all right?" she asked in concern.

"I'm good. I think my nose is broken, but I deserved it," he said. Zalia couldn't believe he was laughing. Beckam handed him a towel to wipe the blood up.

Zalia turned to Valen. "Now I have to heal him," she reprimanded him. Before Valen could tell her no, she reached up with both hands and quickly healed his nose. She cringed when she heard it pop. She felt Valen right behind her, but he didn't try to stop her.

Once Adaire was all cleaned up, he said, "All right. It's time for me to leave. I need to get my army home. It's been a pleasure fighting with you all. Let's do it again sometime soon. Zalia, you ever need me, you send for me." Valen made a sound in the back of his throat, and Zalia looked at him sharply.

"Adaire, stop baiting him!" she said sternly.

Adaire grinned, "I can't help it. It's too easy," he said. "Seriously, though, if any of you need me, I'll be there. Our kingdom will stand with any of yours."

Beckam walked over and clapped him on the back. "Same here, Adaire."

Zalia looked pointedly at Valen. Valen just crossed his arms and glared at Adaire. Adaire laughed once more, then left. Zalia smacked Valen on the arm. "Good work on diplomacy," she muttered to him.

"I don't like him," he rumbled deep in his chest. Zalia stepped into his arms and he wrapped his arms around her.

Beckam looked at the two of them and smiled. "Valen, I need to head back. What's your plan here?"

Without letting go of Zalia, Valen spoke to Beckam. "I need to finish getting my men in place today. Zalia and I will head to your kingdom first thing tomorrow."

Beckam looked surprised. "I figured you would stay here."

"Zalia and I need to get married as soon as possible and complete the bond. I figured she would want to do that in her grandfather's kingdom, so he can officiate. Then we will figure out what to do with our kingdoms," Valen said.

Beckam looked at Zalia. "You okay with this plan?" he questioned.

Zalia smiled at him. "Yes," she said.

Beckam nodded. "All right. Then you can both head

back with us. It will be safer that way. We will leave at first light," he said. Valen nodded and Beckam left the room.

Zalia felt so good being in Valen's arms, she didn't want him to ever let go. "You probably need to get going," she said unhappily as she looked up at him.

He wrapped his finger around one of her curls. "I do. I have a lot to set in order today. Will you come with me?" he asked.

"Of course!" Zalia agreed quickly.

"Okay, let's get going," Valen said.

Zalia was practically joined at the hip with Valen the rest of the day. Late into the evening, Valen was still working and Zalia felt herself growing really tired. Valen finally led her up to his room. "You can sleep in here tonight. I'll take the floor; you can have the bed. I've got a few more loose ends to tie up. I'll be back as soon as I can. I'll have two guards posted outside your door. Get some sleep." He bent down and gave her a quick kiss on the cheek. With that, he was gone.

Zalia wasn't sure where her bag had gone in the midst of everything, and she was too tired to spare the energy to find out. Rummaging through Valen's drawer, she found a black tunic to throw on. It hung down mid-thigh on her. Zalia crawled into Valen's massive bed and fell quickly asleep.

Zalia awoke to somebody shaking her gently. "Zalia," a low voice rumbled near her ear. She opened her eyes and saw Valen looming over her. "It's time to get up and get ready to leave," he said quietly. Zalia nodded sleepily. She closed her eyes one more time, for just a moment.

Valen chuckled and pulled her hand, pulling her into a sitting position. "Come on sleepyhead. We have a huge day ahead of us," he said. Zalia scowled at him.

"Fine," she muttered. She rolled out of bed and stood up, yawning and stretching. When she opened her eyes to look at Valen, he was staring at her with dark eyes. Zalia glanced down. She forgot she was only wearing his shirt. She shrugged her shoulders. "I needed a shirt to wear," she said. She took a step towards the bathroom but didn't get very far. Valen grabbed her and pulled her against his hard body.

His eyes were dark and intense. "I like you in my shirt," he said in a low voice. "I'm gonna like you even better not in my shirt," he rumbled low in his chest. Zalia couldn't catch her breath. Then Valen pulled her tighter and kissed her hard. Zalia lost herself in the passion of the kiss. Too soon, he pulled back. Taking a rough breath, he whispered, "I need to leave," he said. An instant later, he was gone.

Zalia sank onto his bed, touching her lips. Then she smiled. *I got to Valen,* she thought with a smirk. With that, she headed to the bathroom to take a quick bath and get dressed. After she washed her body and her hair, she got out and wrapped herself in a towel. She walked out of the bathroom and saw her bag on Valen's bed. Valen had found her bag for her. She got dressed in her standard black leather pants and a tunic top. She quickly braided her hair, finished packing her bag, and made Valen's bed. She grabbed her bag, her bow and quiver, and opened the door.

Outside in the hallway, she found two guards. She didn't recognize either of them and couldn't tell which kingdom they were from. "Good morning," she said to them.

"Good morning, Princess," they responded respectfully. The one soldier stepped forward, "Can we carry your things for you?"

"Sure," Zalia returned with a smile. They took her bag, her bow, and her quiver. Then one soldier stepped in front and another stepped behind her. They led her through a long hallway and down a set of steps. After two more turns, they led her into a great hall where a huge table sat, covered in food. There were soldiers everywhere. Just as she stepped inside, she remembered that she left her dagger on the table next to Valen's bed. It was the one Beckam had given her. She turned to her guards. "I forgot my dagger next to my bed. I'm going to return quickly and grab it," she said loudly to be heard over all the noise.

"I can grab it, Your Highness," the one guard said.

Zalia place her hand on his arm. "You stay and eat. I will grab it. It will only take a second," she said. Leaving her guards there was her biggest mistake.

Chapter Thirty-Two

She turned back to return to Valen's room. She couldn't
believe she almost left it. *This is why I don't own valuable
possessions,* she thought to herself. She quickly followed
the path back to Valen's room. A few minutes later, she
stopped. She was turned around. She should have been at
Valen's room by now. She stood looking down a long hallway, debating which way to turn when she heard voices
behind her.

"Well, what do we have here?" a voice said behind
Zalia.

Zalia spun around and took in three soldiers towering
over her. They did not look to be of the friendly sort. Zalia
pegged them for soldiers from the Kingdom of the Dark
Moon.

Holding her head high, Zalia said, "Good morning,

gentleman. I forgot something in my room and was just returning to grab it. I will be on my way now," she finished and took a step to back away from them.

One soldier reached out and grabbed her arm. "Not yet. We haven't even gotten to know each other yet," he said with a sneer.

Zalia tried to pull her arm out of his grasp, but he wouldn't let go. She realized one of them had gone behind her, boxing her in. It was then that Zalia realized she was in trouble. She was so angry at herself for leaving her dagger in Valen's room.

Zalia straightened her shoulders and used her most authoritative voice. "You will unhand me now."

The soldiers laughed at her. One got in her face. "You think you're so high and mighty. You won't be when we get through with you," he said. He looked down at her and licked his lips. "I think you might be tasty, especially with all that attitude."

Zalia's heart was slamming in her chest now, but she was trying to keep calm and figure out a way out of this. "I will be reporting you to your prince. I don't think he is going to take lightly to you messing with me."

The soldier grabbing her arm jerked her forward. "He's not our prince," he ground out. He turned his head and spit. "He's a traitor," he said angrily. He jerked Zalia closer to him.

Zalia did the only thing she could think to do. She let him pull her close, then she kneed him right where it hurt. He dropped his hold on her arm and bent over in pain. Whirling around, Zalia took out the guard behind her with a sweeping kick, but before she could turn around, the third guy grabbed her from behind.

"You need to be taught some manners," he said angrily. He spun her around and grabbed her arms. His hold was so hard, Zalia knew she was going to have bruises. This was getting out of control fast. She opened her mouth and screamed for Valen. She didn't even get his name all the way out before the soldier smacked her across the face. Her head jerked back, and she saw stars. Then she was grabbed from behind and one of the soldiers kicked her in the stomach. Zalia bent in half. The guy she had kneed grabbed her braid and tugged her head back with it. Her eyes began to tear up in pain. "Not so tough *now*. Are you, Princess?" While he pulled her hair with one hand, he wrapped his other hand around her throat. "We will so enjoy breaking you down," he said as he leered at her.

Zalia was in full panic now. These men were evil, and she knew what they intended to do with her. She opened her mouth to scream again, but the horrible man threw his mouth over hers. He kissed her roughly, then bit her lip.

Zalia flailed her body, but that just pulled her hair more. She tasted blood in her mouth. She tried to knee him again, but he felt it coming and threw her down to the floor. He straddled her, the weight of his body holding hers down. She bucked her hips and thrashed around on the floor. Then to her horror, the other two soldiers joined in. One held down her legs and the other held down her hands. The guy on top of her just laughed at her pain and fear.

"This is so much better," he said. Zalia screamed in horror and tried to move to fight him, but there was nothing she could do. The three of them more than overpowered her. Terror rushed through her veins.

Suddenly, she heard a roar of rage. The weight from her chest was suddenly gone. Zalia sucked in air. She couldn't open her eyes. She was on the verge of full-blown panic. She felt gentle hands probe her face, and she screamed. She started fighting with everything in her. She sat up and scrambled backwards until she hit a wall and couldn't go anywhere. She put her head between her knees and tried to breathe. She heard somebody talking, but she couldn't discern what it was. Then it was gone.

Zalia took herself to another place. She thought of her mother's voice and her wonderful hugs. She wasn't sure how long she stayed in that safe place. Finally, Zalia registered something familiar. "Zalia," she heard a low, soothing voice. "Zalia," the voice called again. Zalia slowly opened her eyes and saw Valen sitting in front of her. "It's okay, sweetheart. It's all over." He reached for her gently. Zalia didn't mean to, but she flinched away from his touch. She couldn't help it. She saw anger flare in his eyes for just a moment and his jaw harden; then it was gone. He took a deep breath and exhaled. "I'm not going to hurt you; I just want to make sure you're not hurt." He continued to speak in low, soothing tones. He reached out slowly and touched her face. The contact was all it took for Zalia to break out of her trance. Then she was reaching for him and crying. He swept her into his arms and carried her. Zalia didn't know where they were going. She only knew that she was safe now.

Valen carried her to his room and closed the door. Without saying a word, he set her down and pulled her torn shirt up and over her head. He quickly replaced it with one of his. He helped her slide out of her pants. Then he picked her up and carried her over to his bed. He pulled back the covers on his bed, and gently placed her inside. He moved to step away from her, and Zalia reached out to him in fear. "Shh," he said. "I'm not leaving."

She heard low voices talking, but she didn't open her eyes. She couldn't bear to see anybody right now. She thought she heard Beckam's angry voice, but she wasn't sure. Soon, Valen slid in next to her and pulled her into his arms. Zalia stopped fighting her body and fell into a deep sleep.

Zalia had never felt more protected than when she woke up in Valen's arms. She opened her eyes and met his. He was watching her carefully. When he saw she was awake, he pulled her closer to him. "How do you feel, sweetheart?" he asked softly.

Zalia took an assessment of her body. Surprisingly, she didn't feel any pain. Then it dawned on her. "You healed me," she said quietly. He just nodded.

His eyes filled anger. "Zalia, I'm so sorry..."

Zalia cut him off with a hand over his mouth. "Valen, it's not your fault. Those men were evil, but they're gone now." She looked up at him quickly. "They are gone now, right?"

Valen's eyes hardened. "They will never bother you again," he said.

Zalia didn't question him further. She wanted to remove the episode as far from her mind as possible. "Did Beckam leave without us?" she questioned.

"No, he said they would wait until tomorrow. Do you think you will be up to traveling tomorrow? I hate to push you, but we really need to get back to your grandfather's castle." His eyes darkened. "We need to get our bond back in place. If we had our bond intact, this morning would have never happened," he said angrily.

Zalia rubbed his arm soothingly. "It's all right. I am fine to travel. Do you want to get going today?" She saw him hesitate and knew she had her answer. "Let's get going. We can still get a few hours in today."

Valen was silent for a moment. "All right, but only if you're sure you are up to it." Zalia nodded. Valen rolled over and climbed off the bed, then held out his hand to help Zalia up. He walked to the door and told the guard on duty to go tell Beckam to prepare to leave.

He walked back over to Zalia and looked at her intensely. "You stay with me at all times," he ordered.

Zalia scowled up at him. "Yes, Master," she said sarcastically.

"Zalia," he warned.

Zalia just rolled her eyes. "Do you know where all my stuff is?" she asked.

He pointed over in the corner. Zalia walked over and picked up her bag and walked into the bathroom to get dressed. When she finished, she packed her remaining items in her bag and grabbed her bow and quiver. Valen took her bag from her and slung it over his shoulder. Zalia walked over to the table and grabbed her dagger. *All that trouble for this,* she thought as she looked at it. She walked over to Valen and opened her bag. She pulled out her sheath and strapped it to her leg. Valen watched her quietly.

"I just don't want to be left without protection again," she said.

Valen growled. "You won't be. You're not leaving my side until our bond is back in place, and probably even after that."

Zalia groaned. Then she hurried to follow Valen out of the room. Zalia followed Valen around for the next hour as he got everything in place to be able to leave.

Finally, they went outside where Beckam and his soldiers were getting ready to depart. Beckam walked over to Zalia and pulled her into a stiff hug. He pulled back and she could see the anger in his eyes. "You okay?" he ground out.

Zalia nodded. "I'm okay," she said softly.

She looked around at the horses. "Which one's mine?" she asked Beckam.

Valen strode over to her. "You're with me," he said.

Zalia just laughed at him. "I'm not riding with you for three days. Where's my horse?" she asked again.

Valen stepped close and towered over her. "You're riding with me," he said emphasizing each word.

Zalia crossed her arms. "No, I'm not," she said.

Valen growled at her. "Don't push me right now. I am hanging on to my control by a hair, Zalia!"

Zalia glanced at Beckam looking for support. He usually grinned and made a wisecrack, but not this time. He met her gaze and pointed his chin in Valen's direction.

"Fine," Zalia said, exasperated. She crossed her arms and waited. Valen walked over to a horse and secured their bags. He brought the horse over to where Zalia stood. Putting both hands on either side of her waist, he hoisted her up on top of the horse. Then he swung up behind her. His strong arms wrapped around her, enclosing her against his chest.

"Shouldn't I be in the back," she asked. "So, you can lead the horse?"

"No," he said. "I don't want you falling off the back if you fall asleep. This way if you fall asleep, I still have a hold on you. Besides, I can see over your head to lead the horse, so don't worry," he said.

Zalia tried to sit tall, so Valen didn't have to hold her weight. "Just relax," he mumbled in her ear. Zalia ignored him. She watched as soldiers fell into place all around them. Beckam rode next to them. Zalia looked for Ulric. He was off to their right a little bit. She waved at him, and he nodded. Then she saw Silas next to him. She waved at him too, and he waved back.

Valen's voice rumbled in her ear. "Do you have to be so friendly with other men?" he asked. Zalia smiled. She loved getting him riled up. They rode in silence for a while. Then Beckam started talking to Valen about his plans going forward for his kingdom. Zalia listened for a while, before tuning them out. She found herself getting sleepy with nothing to do and no one to talk to.

Valen put his arm around her stomach and pulled her closer to him. Zalia resisted at first but then gave in. She relaxed against Valen. Her head rested on his shoulder. Eventually, she dozed off.

The three days of traveling passed slowly for Zalia, but at least she got to spend every moment with Valen. At night, she would sleep in her tent, and he would sleep on the ground outside, right in front of the entrance.

The first night was embarrassing for Zalia as she didn't realize where Valen was sleeping. Early in the morning, she decided to get up and get dressed. She needed to go to the bathroom and couldn't hold it any longer. She carefully unzipped her bag and stepped out right onto Valen. She fell right over the top of him. He caught her in his arms before she could hit the ground.

"Good morning," he said in a voice, gravelly from sleep. "Did you miss me?" he asked, sounding amused.

Zalia quickly pulled away and got back on her feet.

"Sorry, I didn't see you down there."

"Sure you didn't," he said with a roguish grin. Zalia just rolled her eyes and walked away. Valen of course followed, keeping an eye on her from a distance, while she did her business.

After that, Zalia knew to watch out for Valen outside her tent. Finally, they returned to Cascadia. Zalia's grandfather was waiting for them outside when they got there. Valen climbed off their horse first, then reached up for Zalia and lowered her to the ground. She turned and was immediately consumed in a hug from her grandfather.

"How are you, my dear?" he asked gently. Zalia could feel Valen close behind her. She stepped back slightly and she felt his arm slip around her waist, pulling her to his chest. She smiled and put her hand on his arm. "We found Valen," she said with another smile.

Her grandfather smiled at her. "I can see that," he said. He patted her arm. Then he shook Valen's hand. "It's good to see you, son," he said. "Come inside, get some fresh clothes and food; then we can talk."

Before her grandfather turned away, Valen said, "Before we do anything, we need to redo our blood bond. My father destroyed it," he said angrily.

Her grandfather looked angry for a moment, but quickly concealed it. "I figured that must have been why Zalia was so weak healing Beckam," he said.

Valen scowled darkly. Zalia reached out and put her hand in his and squeezed. They followed her grandfather as he led them to his room. There, he once again led them through the bonding ceremony. As soon as it was done, Valen seemed to relax a little.

Much better, Zalia heard Valen say through the bond. Zalia smiled up at him.

Valen turned towards her grandfather and said, "Thank you for renewing the bond for us."

"My pleasure," her grandfather said with a twinkle in his eye. "Now you two get some sleep. I can't imagine how exhausted you must be," he said. "How long will you be staying here?" he asked them questioningly.

"We will be staying here until we are married," Valen said in a commanding voice. "We will never go through that again."

Her grandfather looked at Valen. "I think we can wait a little bit until..."

"No. We're not waiting," Valen said with authority. Then he grabbed Zalia's hand and pulled her with him. Zalia tripped over her feet, trying to keep up with him. He led them to the room they had stayed in before. He closed the door, then pulled Zalia into his arms. "We're getting married and nobody will stand in our way. Nobody will keep you from me. You don't understand who I am without you. You are my light. Without you, all I see is darkness. I become my father. I can't go back to who I was without you. I know you deserve more than me, but I will do everything in my power to protect you and make you happy. I know it's going to take time to grow our relationship, but I am committed to making our marriage work. I love you with everything in me. Do you understand?"

Zalia wiped the tears from her eyes. "Valen, I love you," she said simply. She reached up and wrapped her hands around the back of his neck and pulled him down for a kiss. He complied. He kissed her for a moment, then pulled back. His eyes darkened.

"Tomorrow," he said.

Zalia was still a little light-headed from his kiss. "Tomorrow what?" she murmured.

"We get married," he said,

Zalia choked. "What? Tomorrow? There's no way. I need a dress, we need rings, we need guests, we need food, we need... I don't know what else we need, but there is no way we can do it tomorrow," Zalia said desperately. "Please, Valen."

She could see the "please" softened him up minutely. "You have three days. That's it. I won't give any more than that."

Zalia knew she had to take his compromise before he changed his mind again. "Okay," she agreed. "Three days." Her mind started whirling with all she would need to do in the next few days. *I am so in over my head,* Zalia grimaced.

Chapter Thirty-Three

The next two days flew by. Despite Valen's desire to keep Zalia locked to his side, they spent a lot of time apart. He spent hours with Beckam and her grandfather. They talked strategy and plans, succession, and more. Zalia was too busy to be involved in any of it, but she knew they were trying to establish the political scene for the five kingdoms moving forward.

The second day of wedding preparation brought a surprise for Zalia. She was busy working outside when she heard a familiar voice. "Were you really going to have a wedding without your best friend?"

Zalia spun around to see Raven standing there with a smile on her face. Zalia squealed and ran towards her. They hugged each other tightly. Zalia pulled back with tears in her eyes. "How did you get here?" she asked.

Raven smiled. "Beckam had Silas bring me," she said.

Zalia gasped. "Silas is here too?"

"I am, Princess. I wouldn't have missed it for the world," Silas said from where he stood. Zalia's tears were falling in earnest now. She quickly ran toward Silas and gave him a hug.

Zalia, what's wrong? Are you okay? Zalia heard Valen through their bond.

I'm wonderful. Silas and Raven are here! Beckam made sure they got here for the wedding. Isn't that wonderful? she asked him.

Zalia heard silence for a moment, and then Valen asked, *"Who is Silas?"*

Zalia laughed out loud. *Silas was my guard for my entire life. He was one of the guards who traveled with us. He's like a grandfather to me. You have nothing to worry about. I will only ever love you.*

And I will only ever love you, Zalia, Valen said.

Zalia and Raven spent every moment together planning a quick but perfect wedding. They met with a seamstress for Zalia's dress, the gardener for flowers, the head cook for a meal, a baker for a cake, and so much more. It was going to take a miracle—and her grandfather's entire staff—to pull this wedding off. On the evening before the wedding, Raven and Zalia were working with about twenty staff members to turn the outside courtyard area into a seating area for the ceremony. It had been dark for a while; but Zalia continued working, using lanterns for light. She wanted everything to be perfect for tomorrow. She had just finished talking to the head gardener for the last time when strong arms came around her middle. Zalia jumped for a moment and then relaxed into his arms.

"You need to get sleep before tomorrow," Valen said in a low voice in her ear.

"I still have so much to do," she said.

"Leave it," he said. "You are more important to me than the decorations. You need to get sleep. I'm sure it will be beautiful tomorrow."

Zalia shrugged out of arms. "I just have a few more things to do," she said. She started walking away from him. "Go on in. I'll be there soon," she said as she got right back to work.

One moment Zalia was working on a project, the next she was picked up like a sack of potatoes and thrown over Valen's shoulder. "You're going to bed *now*," he said. With that, he started walking away.

Zalia looked up and saw the staff members staring at them. Some of them were laughing; some were in shock. Raven just laughed and waved. Zalia scowled at her. "Just wait until it's your turn!" she yelled out to Raven. Then they were inside the castle.

"You can put me down now," Zalia said in an irritated voice.

Valen didn't say anything. Zalia was exhausted, and her nerves were shot worrying about getting married tomorrow. That's the only reason she had as to why she started pounding on his back with her fists. She knew it was childish, but she didn't care. She couldn't believe he carried her out of there in front of all those people.

"Stop it," he growled in a low tone. That just made Zalia even more angry, and she hit him harder.

Then to her shock, he smacked her across her backside. Zalia froze. "Did you just spank me?" she cried in outrage.

Valen responded, "You were acting like a child."

Zalia's eyes narrowed at that. Now, she was angry. "How dare you!" she all but yelled at him. "You are the most conceited, selfish, egotistical, tyrannical..."

During her yelling, they arrived at their door. Valen walked in and threw her on the bed. Zalia sputtered as she caught herself and tried to climb off the bed. Valen closed the door before Zalia launched herself at him. She started to punch him, but he deflected it. She tried again, but he stopped her again. This time he grabbed her hand and held on when she tried to punch him. He spun her effortlessly until she was trapped against the wall. He kept his hold on her arm and placed his other arm on the wall, effectively boxing her in.

"Zalia, please. I'm not trying to hurt you. I just need you to get sleep for tomorrow. It's our wedding day. Is it so much to ask for?" he growled at her.

"You can't just pick me up and carry me off when you want me to do something. You need to talk to me and not act like a caveman," she grumbled at him.

"I did; you didn't listen," he said, exasperated.

Zalia paused for a moment. "Okay, I'll concede on that point. Fine, I will try better to do what you are asking, but you need to work at it too. No more forcing me to do what you want me to do," she said warily.

"Fine. I won't force you unless it's for your own safety," he said calmly.

Zalia scowled. "That's not the right answer," she ground out to him.

"Zalia, I'm not compromising on your safety. Ever. We can fight forever about this; I am not going to back down. When it comes to keeping you safe, I will do anything I need to. I *will* pick you up and carry you if you don't listen," he said.

Zalia blew out a frustrated breath. This was not a battle she was going to win. Then again, there were worse things in life. "Fine," she said. "Can you let go of me now?" She was still pinned against the wall.

"No," he said in a low voice.

"Why not? I agreed," Zalia said, confused.

"Because of this," he said simply. Then he lowered his head to hers and kissed her. Zalia stayed still for only a moment before she melted into him. He dropped his hold on her hand and pulled her close to him. When he had kissed her so long, her mind turned to mush, he pulled back. He kept his arms around her. Zalia was grateful for that, or she would have ended up on the floor.

He looked down at her. "Truce?" he asked softly. Zalia just nodded. "All right then, let's get you to bed. Do you need a bath tonight?" he asked.

"No, I will take one in the morning," she said.

He nodded. Then he looked at her for a moment. "Are you nervous for tomorrow?" he asked.

"Yes," Zalia said breathlessly. She was still reeling from their kiss.

"You have nothing to be nervous about. I will be by your side the entire time," he said confidently.

Zalia looked up at him questioningly. "What about afterwards?" she asked.

"When we complete the bond, you mean?" Valen asked.

Zalia felt herself blush, and she stumbled over her words. "No, not that. I just meant what are we going to do... I mean how are we going to..." she felt a deep blush covering her face and neck.

Valen was smirking now. "Do you want me to explain it to you?" he asked.

"NO!" Zalia almost shouted at him, mortified.

Valen chuckled and then tried to stop smiling. "Okay, what is it you're trying to ask?"

Zalia took a deep breath. "Are we going to be coming back to this room after we get married?" she finally spit out. She didn't look into his eyes.

Valen gently tipped her chin up. "Zalia, please don't be embarrassed in front of me. We won't be coming back to this room. Beckam has a place he is going to let us borrow. It's closer than going back to my kingdom or yours," he said.

Zalia nodded. "Okay, do I need to pack before the wedding, or will we have time afterwards?" she asked.

"Go ahead and pack beforehand, so we can leave right from the great hall when we are done," he said. "But Zalia," he said and paused.

"Hmm?" she questioned.

"You don't need to pack a lot of clothes. You won't be needing them," he said with a mischievous grin.

Zalia did not know how to respond to that, so she just squeaked out, "Okay, I don't know how to respond to that so, goodnight. I'm going to bed now." She walked away from him in a daze.

"Uh, Zalia, you forgot something," Valen called out before she got too far.

Zalia turned back around. "What?" she asked questioningly.

"A good night kiss," he said. He strode toward her quickly and pulled her against his hard body. He didn't keep her long but kissed her deeply. "Now you can go to bed," he said huskily.

Zalia didn't look at him again but headed for her room. When she closed her door, she collapsed on her bed with a smile on her face. She lay there for a few minutes, then dragged herself up to get ready for bed.

The next morning when Zalia awoke, it took her only a moment to remember what day it was. She sat up quickly. "I can't believe I'm getting married today," she said out loud. She thought about her parents and brother and sighed. She crawled to the edge and knelt under her bed and pulled out her sketchbook. When she had it in hand, she sat back down on her bed and flipped through the pages until she came to each one of their portraits. She ran her hands lovingly over her brother's face, her father's face, and finally her mother's face. She stayed on that portrait the longest. "I wish you could be here today," she said softly. She missed her family dearly. She turned another page in her book and found Valen's portrait. She ran her hands over his face, and a peace settled deep in her heart. She knew she would be happy, and he would always take care of her.

She heard a knock at her door and quickly wiped away the tears that had fallen. "It's just me," she heard Raven say behind the closed door.

Zalia smiled. "Come in," she called out. Raven opened the door and came in with a huge smile on her face.

"It's your wedding day!" she squealed before tackling Zalia in a huge hug. Zalia laughed. "It's time to turn you into a bride," she said as she clapped her hands. "First up, a bath. While you are in the bath, the staff is going to bring your dress in and everything you need for today," she said, effectively taking charge.

Zalia started towards the bathroom with a smile on her face and butterflies in her stomach. This was going to be a life-changing day.

Hours later, Zalia stared at herself in the mirror and almost didn't recognize herself. All the hours of being worked on had paid off. Zalia's skin practically glowed. Her hair was an intricate design of braids with small flowers woven in on the top of her head, and in the back, her curls hung freely. The dress she wore was exquisite. Zalia couldn't help but stare at it. It had a rounded neckline that was covered in tiny crystals. The front boasted a corset design with pale pink ribbons. The sleeves were sheer and hung free at Zalia's elbows. The bottom of the dress was made of layer upon layer of silk chiffon. Tiny crystals were sewn into the chiffon making the bottom half of her dress billow and shimmer all around her when she moved. Her eyes shimmered, and her lips were a soft pink to match the ribbons in her dress. Soft white leather shoes adorned her feet. Zalia felt that she truly looked like a queen today.

She looked up in the mirror and saw Raven staring at her. "You look so beautiful, Zalia," she said softly. They both froze when they heard a knock at the door. Raven left to go answer the door. Zalia turned towards the door when she heard her grandfather's voice. She walked over towards him and stopped.

Her grandfather's eyes twinkled at her. "Zalia, you look absolutely beautiful," he said with a smile. He walked towards her. "Are you ready for this?" he asked.

Zalia took a deep breath and nodded. "As ready as I will ever be," she said.

"I'm going to go, so I can get a seat," Raven said. With a smile and a blown kiss, she left the room.

Zalia preceded her grandfather into the hall. She noticed several guards lining the wall. Her grandfather came out of her room and offered her his arm. They began walking slowly towards the rear of the castle. Some of the guards walked in front of them; others walked behind them.

"You know, you look just like your mother did on her wedding day," her grandfather said with a smile.

Zalia looked up at him. "Really?" she asked.

He nodded. "She had her hair down much like yours is. Her black curls hung down her back. She looked beautiful, just like you do today," he said.

Zalia was quiet for a moment. "I wish she could be here today," she said softly.

Her grandfather sighed. "I wish that for you too, Zalia. She would be so proud of the woman you have become. Your father and brother would be too. They are with you today. They're looking down at you and celebrating with you, and they're with you here," he pointed to Zalia's heart. "You carry a piece of each one of them. That's who you are. It's made you into the beautiful queen standing before me today."

Zalia blinked rapidly so her tears wouldn't fall and ruin her face and dress. "Thank you," she said simply. Her grandfather patted her hand.

As they got close to the door that would lead them outdoors to the wedding ceremony, Zalia started breathing faster. Her nerves started taking over, and she felt like she might get sick to her stomach. Her grandfather stopped a few steps before the door and turned to look at her. "You're not having second thoughts, are you?" he questioned teasingly, but Zalia could see an ounce of sincerity in his question. "Valen's a good man, but you don't have to do this if you're not ready," he said quietly.

Zalia took deep breaths in and out. *Maybe I'm rushing things. What if Valen decides he doesn't really love me. After all, he doesn't really know me all that well.* Zalia tried to catch her breath but felt like she couldn't. She started hearing a roaring in her ears. It was all too much. She couldn't do this. She started to back away, when suddenly the door in front of her opened.

She locked eyes with Valen. She was in too much of a panic to think clearly and realize he shouldn't be here right now. She just stared at him as he walked towards her and stopped in front of her. She still couldn't catch her breath and felt like she was gasping for air.

"Sweetheart," he murmured quietly before gently taking her in his arms, being careful with her dress. Zalia laid her head on his chest and listened to his steady heartbeat. He gently rubbed circles on her back with his hands, soothing her. The strong beat helped steady her and after a few moments, she felt like she could finally breathe again.

Valen pulled back gently and looked into her eyes. "We

don't have to do this today, if you're not ready. I'm sorry I pushed you. We can wait until you are ready to get married," he said soothingly.

"But what about all the people in there and the decorations and the food and... everything?" she asked helplessly.

Valen responded. "None of that matters. You are the most important person to me. If we need to cancel it, we do. Is that what you want?" he asked, watching her carefully.

Zalia stood before him frozen. *Is that what I really want?* Then as if a book opened up before her eyes, Zalia recalled the first time she saw Valen. The fierce warrior who carried her to safety away from the attack on her kingdom. She saw him training her for hours on end, always demanding her best. She saw his eyes blazing when Beckam hurt her in training. She saw him getting ice for her when she got hurt. She saw him smiling down at her as they danced. She saw him glaring at other men as she got food from the buffet table. She saw him battling his way towards her when they were attacked at the party. She saw him sitting by her beside time after time after her healings. She saw the first time he kissed her, so tenderly. She saw when he carried her after she was attacked in the training center. She saw when he held her after her nightmares. She saw *him*. Valen. He had always been there, loving her and protecting her, since she met him. She knew in that moment that this was the right thing. She loved him, and he loved her. He would always be there for her. He would always stand beside her. He would fight life's battles with her, and he would be the father to their children.

Zalia's eyes brimmed with tears at the overwhelming love flowing out of her heart for Valen. She looked up at him. He gently wiped her eyes. "It's okay, Zalia," he said gently. "I will take care of everything. You just return to our room; I will come to you as soon as I can," he said. Zalia realized he mistook her tears.

She laughed gently and shook her head. "No, Valen. I'm not returning to our room. I'm marrying you. I'm sorry I panicked. I just needed to see you again before heading in there," she said. "I'm sorry for doubting. I love you, and I know you love me," she said softly.

Valen crushed her to his chest and breathed deeply. Then he pulled away and grasped her arms gently. "Are you sure?" he asked, searching her eyes.

"Absolutely!" Zalia said with a huge smile.

"So, if I leave and go back out there, you will come, right?" he asked.

Zalia laughed again. "I promise," she said with a smile. She reached up on her tiptoes and lightly kissed him on the lips.

He stared down at her a moment more. "If you're sure you're okay now, I am going to head out there again to my place," he said.

"I'll be right behind you," Zalia said. He leaned down and kissed her once more, a little more intensely than the kiss Zalia had given him. When he pulled back, his eyes were darker. "By the way," he said in a low voice, "There are no words to describe how beautiful you look. You look like a queen," he said quietly. Without another word, he turned and walked away.

Zalia turned to her grandfather who had been standing patiently and quietly, taking everything in. She smiled sheepishly at him. "I'm ready now. I'm sorry; I just panicked," she said.

Her grandfather took her arm in his and smiled down at her. "It's okay. I think we both benefited from Valen's appearance," he said. They walked slowly towards the doors again. The guards stepped to the side, waiting on her grandfather's command to open the door.

He looked down at her once more. "You ready?" he asked.

Zalia nodded. She knew she was ready. She didn't know what the future held or how everything would work out. She only knew that with Valen at her side, she could face anything. Theirs was a love that would only grow stronger as it was tested by the strands and seasons of time.

Her grandfather nodded and the doors were pulled open. Zalia locked eyes with the handsome prince who had stolen her heart and moved towards her future.

After

Zalia startled awake. She sat up quickly in bed. Valen was already out of bed and moving to put pants on. "What is it?" she asked fearfully.

"I'm not sure. I'm going to go see. Stay here," he said. Then he was gone. Zalia sat still for a moment, trying to calm her racing heart. She looked around the room where she and Valen had spent more time this last week than any other room in the house. The house was a beautiful cottage Beckam owned and let them borrow for the week. She and Valen had had such an amazing time together. Never in her wildest imagination could she have imagined what it would be like to be so thoroughly loved and ravished. She was pulled from her thoughts as Valen came back in.

Zalia took one look at his face in the early morning light and instantly knew something was wrong. "What is it?"

she asked.

He stared at her for a moment. Then he spoke, "There's been an attack," he said in a low angry voice. "Your grandfather was killed," he said.

Zalia felt her heart stop beating. *Not again. I can't do this again.* She felt strong arms come around her as Valen pulled her onto his lap.

"Zalia," he said placing his hands on her face. "I'm right here. I'm not going anywhere. We will get through this together," he said. "You're not alone this time," he added.

With that, Zalia broke. She started sobbing into Valen's chest. Tears for the grandfather she was just getting to know, tears for the family she lost. Valen didn't say anything. He just stroked her back gently.

When Zalia could control her tears enough to at least talk, she asked, "How's Beckam?"

Valen was quiet for a moment too long. Zalia looked up at him. "Valen, what is it?"

He looked away for a moment and then back at Zalia. "Beckam saw who killed your grandfather, but..." Again, he paused. "She got away," he said.

"She?" she asked in shock.

Valen nodded. Then he looked down at her and delivered the clincher. "Apparently she has his markings," he said softly.

Acknowledgments

Thank you to my editor, Caryn for countless hours editing this book. You are the best!

Thanks to my amazing cover designer, Les. Your work is always amazing!

Thank you to my kids for being patient and allowing me "mommy time" to be able to write.

Thank you to my husband, Matthew for hours of formatting. Thank you for always believing in me, even when I didn't believe in myself. Thanks for loving me and inspiring me. I couldn't have done this without you!

About the Author

Amanda lives outside of Philadelphia with her husband and four kids. She and her husband started Greater Philly Church in 2011. Some of her favorite things to do include reading, family days, being a pastor's wife, and watching football on Sunday afternoons with her family.

Connecting with Amanda:
If you enjoyed this book, would you consider leaving me a review on Amazon? I would greatly appreciate it!

I would love to connect with you! You can find me on Facebook and Instagram at A. J. Manney Books. Follow me to stay updated for new book releases!

 facebook.com/ajmanneybooks

 @ajmanneybooks

Don't miss Book Two of the True Marks Series!
Follow me on Facebook and Instagram at AJManney-
Books to catch release dates, book trailers, teasers, and
more.